D0204195

VITTORIO,
THE VAMPIRE

VITTORIO, THE VAMPIRE

NEW TALES OF THE VAMPIRES

ANNE RICE

ALFRED A. KNOPF

NEW YORK · TORONTO

1999

THIS IS A BORZOI BOOK
PUBLISHED BY ALFRED A. KNOPF, INC.,
AND ALFRED A. KNOPF CANADA

Copyright © 1999 by Anne O'Brien Rice

All rights reserved under International and Pan-American Copyright
Conventions. Published in the United States by Alfred A. Knopf, Inc.,
New York, and distributed by Random House, Inc., New York.
Published simultaneously in Canada by Alfred A. Knopf Canada, a
division of Random House of Canada Limited, Toronto, and
distributed by Random House of Canada Limited, Toronto.

www.randomhouse.com

Knopf, Borzoi Books, and the colophon are registered
trademarks of Random House, Inc.

Library of Congress Cataloging-in-Publication Data
Rice, Anne, [date]
Vittorio, the vampire / by Anne Rice. — 1st ed.
p.   cm.
ISBN 0-375-40160-1
Includes bibliographical references (p.).
I. Title.
PS3568.I265V58   1999
813'.54—dc21   98-14209
CIP

Canadian Cataloging-in-Publication Data
Rice, Anne, [date]
Vittorio, the vampire : new tales of the vampires
ISBN 0-676-97186-5
I. Title.
PS3568.I22V36 1999   813'.54   C98-932412-5

A signed first edition of this book has been privately printed by The
Franklin Library. A limited signed edition of this book has been
published by B. E. Trice Publishing, New Orleans.

Manufactured in the United States of America
First Trade Edition

FRONTISPIECE: *Farewell of Saint John the Baptist from His
Parents* by Fra Filippo Lippi. Duomo, Prato, Italy.
Scala/Art Resource, New York.

DEDICATION BY ANNE RICE

This novel is dedicated to
Stan, Christopher, Michele and Howard;
to Rosario and Patrice;
to Pamela and Elaine;
and to Niccolo.

This novel is

dedicated

by

Vittorio

to the people of

Florence, Italy.

VITTORIO,
THE VAMPIRE

I

WHO I AM, WHY I WRITE,
WHAT IS TO COME

HEN I was a small boy I had a terrible dream. I dreamt I held in my arms the severed heads of my younger brother and sister. They were quick still, and mute, with big fluttering eyes, and reddened cheeks, and so horrified was I that I could make no more of a sound than they could.

The dream came true.

But no one will weep for me or for them. They have been buried, nameless, beneath five centuries of time.

I am a vampire.

My name is Vittorio, and I write this now in the tallest tower of the ruined mountaintop castle in which I was born, in the northernmost part of Tuscany, that most beautiful of lands in the very center of Italy.

By anyone's standards, I am a remarkable vampire, most powerful, having lived five hundred years from the great days of Cosimo de' Medici, and even the angels will attest to my powers, if you

3

can get them to speak to you. Be cautious on that point.

I have, however, nothing whatsoever to do with the "Coven of the Articulate," that band of strange romantic vampires in and from the Southern New World city of New Orleans who have regaled you already with so many chronicles and tales.

I know nothing of those heroes of macabre fact masquerading as fiction. I know nothing of their enticing paradise in the swamplands of Louisiana. You will find no new knowledge of them in these pages, not even, hereafter, a mention.

I have been challenged by them, nevertheless, to write the story of my own beginnings—the fable of my making—and to cast this fragment of my life in book form into the wide world, so to speak, where it may come into some random or destined contact with their well-published volumes.

I have spent my centuries of vampiric existence in clever, observant roaming and study, never provoking the slightest danger from my own kind, and never arousing their knowledge or suspicions.

But this is not to be the unfolding of my adventures.

It is, as I have said, to be the tale of my beginnings. For I believe I have revelations within me which will be wholly original to you. Perhaps when my book is finished and gone from my hands, I may take steps to become somehow a character in that grand *roman-fleuve* begun by other vampires in San Francisco or New Orleans. For now, I cannot know or care about it.

As I spend my tranquil nights, here, among the overgrown stones of the place where I was so happy as a child, our walls now broken and misshapen among the thorny blackberry vines and fragrant smothering forests of oak and chestnut trees, I am compelled to record what befell me, for it seems that I may have suffered a fate very unlike that of any other vampire.

I do not always hang about this place.

On the contrary, I spend most of my time in that city which for me is the queen of all cities—Florence—which I loved from the very first moment I saw it with a child's eyes in the years when Cosimo the Elder ran his powerful Medici bank with his own hand, even though he was the richest man in Europe.

In the house of Cosimo de' Medici lived the great sculptor Donatello making sculptures of marble and bronze, as well as painters and poets galore, writers on magic and makers of music. The great Brunelleschi, who had made the very dome of Florence's greatest church, was building yet another Cathedral for Cosimo in those days, and Michelozzo was rebuilding not only the monastery of San Marco but commencing the palazzo for Cosimo which would one day be known to all the world as the Palazzo Vecchio. For Cosimo, men went all over Europe seeking in dusty libraries long forgotten the classics of Greek and Rome, which Cosimo's scholars would translate into our native Italian, the language which Dante had boldly chosen many years before for his *Divine Comedy*.

And it was under Cosimo's roof that I saw, as a mortal boy of destiny and promise—yes, I myself saw—the great guests of the Council of Trent who had come from far Byzantium to heal the breach between the Eastern and Western church: Pope Eugenius IV of Rome, the Patriarch of Constantinople and the Emperor of the East himself, John VIII Paleologus. These great men I saw enter the city in a terrible storm of bitter rain, but nevertheless with indescribable glory, and these men I saw eat from Cosimo's table.

Enough, you might say. I agree with you. This is no history of the Medici. But let me only say that anyone who tells you that they were scoundrels, these great men, is a perfect idiot. It was the descendants of Cosimo who took care of Leonardo da Vinci, Michelangelo and artists without count. And it was all because a banker, a moneylender if you will, thought it splendid and good to give beauty and magnificence to the city of Florence.

I'll come back to Cosimo at the right point, and only for a few brief words, though I must confess I am having trouble being brief here on any score, but for now let me say that Cosimo belongs to the living.

I have been in bed with the dead since 1450.

Now to tell how it began, but allow me one more preface.

Don't look here, please, for antique language. You will not find a rigid fabricated English meant to conjure castle walls by stilted diction and constricted vocabulary.

I shall tell my tale naturally and effectively, wallowing in words, for I love them. And, being an immortal, I have devoured over four centuries of English, from the plays of Christopher Marlowe and Ben Jonson to the abrupt and harshly evocative words of a Sylvester Stallone movie.

You'll find me flexible, daring, and now and then a shock. But what can I do but draw upon the fullest descriptive power I can command, and mark that English now is no more the language of one land, or even two or three or four, but has become the language of all the modern world from the backwoods of Tennessee to the most remote Celtic isles and down under to the teeming cities of Australia and New Zealand.

I am Renaissance-born. Therefore I delve in all, and blend without prejudice, and that some higher good pertains to what I do, I cannot doubt.

As for my native Italian, hear it softly when you say my name, Vittorio, and breathe it like perfume from the other names which are sprinkled throughout this text. It is, beneath all, a language so sweet as to make of the English word "stone" three syllables: *pi-ea-tra*. There has never been a gentler language on earth. I speak all other tongues with the Italian accent you'll hear in the streets of Florence today.

And that my English-speaking victims find my blandishments so pretty, accented as they are, and yield to my soft lustrous Italian pronunciations, is a constant source of bliss for me.

But I am not happy.

Don't think so.

I wouldn't write a book to tell you that a vampire was happy.

I have a brain as well as a heart, and there hovers about me an etheric visage of myself, created most definitely by some Higher Power, and entangled completely within the intangible weave of that etheric visage is what men call a soul. I have such. No amount of blood can drown away its life and leave me but a thriving revenant.

Okay. No problem. Yes, yes. Thank you!—as everybody in the entire world can say in English. We're ready to begin.

Except I want to give you a quote from an obscure but wonderful writer, Sheridan Le Fanu, a paragraph spoken in extreme angst by a haunted character in one of his many exquisitely written ghost stories. This author, a native of Dublin, died in 1873, but mark how fresh is this language, and how horrifying the expression of the character Captain Barton in the story called "The Familiar":

> Whatever may be my uncertainty as to the authenticity of what we are taught to call revelation, of one fact I am deeply and horribly convinced, that there does exist beyond this a spiritual world—a system whose workings are generally in mercy hidden from us—a system which may be, and which is sometimes, partially and terribly revealed. I am sure—I *know* . . . that there is a God—a dreadful God—and that retribution follows guilt, in ways the most mys-

terious and stupendous—by agencies the most inexplicable and terrific;—there is a spiritual system—great God, how I have been convinced!—a system malignant, and implacable, and omnipotent, under whose persecutions I am, and have been, suffering the torments of the damned!

What do you think of that?

I am myself rather mortally struck by it. I don't think I am prepared to speak of our God as "dreadful" or our system as "malignant," but there seems an eerie inescapable ring of truth to these words, written in fiction but obviously with much emotion.

It matters to me because I suffer under a terrible curse, quite unique to me, I think, as a vampire. That is, the others don't share it. But I think we all—human, vampire, all of us who are sentient and can weep—we all suffer under a curse, the curse that we know more than we can endure, and there is nothing, absolutely nothing, we can do about the force and the lure of this knowledge.

At the end, we can take this up again. See what you make of my story.

It's early evening here. The brave remnant of my father's highest tower still rises boldly enough against the sweetly star-filled heavens for me to see from the window the moonlighted hills and valleys of Tuscany, aye, even as far as the twinkling sea below the mines of Carrara. I smell the flowering green of the steep undiscovered country round where the irises of Tuscany still break out in violent red or white in sunny beds, to be found by me in the silky night.

And so embraced and protected, I write, ready for the moment when the full yet ever obscure moon leaves me for the hideaway of clouds, to light the candles that stand ready, some six, ensconced within the thick ruggedly worked silver of the candelabra which once stood on my father's desk, in those days when he was the old-style feudal lord of this mountain and all its villages, and the firm ally in peace and war of the great city of Florence and its unofficial ruler, when we were rich, fearless, curious and wondrously contented.

Let me speak now of what has vanished.

2

MY SMALL MORTAL LIFE, THE BEAUTY OF FLORENCE, THE GLORY OF OUR SMALL COURT— WHAT IS VANISHED

WAS sixteen years old when I died. I have good height, thick brown hair down to the shoulders, hazel eyes that are far too vulnerable to behold, giving me the appearance of an androgyne in a way, and a desirable narrow nose with unremarkable nostrils, and a medium-sized mouth which is neither voluptuous nor stingy. A beautiful boy for the time. I wouldn't be alive now if I hadn't been.

That's the case with most vampires, no matter who says otherwise. Beauty carries us to our doom. Or, to put it more accurately, we are made immortal by those who cannot sever themselves from our charms.

I don't have a childish face, but I have an almost angelic one. My eyebrows are strong, dark, high enough over my eyes to allow them entirely too much luster. My forehead would be a little too high if it wasn't so straight, and if I didn't have so much thick brown hair, making as it does a curly, wavy frame for the whole picture. My chin is slightly too strong, too squared off for the rest. I have a dimple in it.

My body is overmuscular, strong, broad-chested, my arms powerful, giving an impression of manly power. This rather rescues my obdurate-looking jaw and allows to me to pass for a full-fledged man, at least from a distance.

This well-developed physique I owe to tremendous practice with a heavy battle sword in the last years of my life, and ferocious hunting with my falcons in the mountains, up and down which I ran often on foot, though I had already four horses of my own by that age, including one of that special majestic breed made to support my weight when I wore my full suit of armor.

My armor is still buried beneath this tower. I never used it in battle. Italy was seething with war in my time, but all of the battles of the Florentines were being fought by mercenaries.

All my father had to do was declare his absolute loyalty to Cosimo, and let no one representing the Holy Roman Empire, the Duke of Milan or the Pope in Rome move troops through our mountain passes or stop in our villages.

We were out of the way. It was no problem. Enterprising ancestors had built our castle three hundred years before. We went back to the time of the Lombards, or those barbarians who had come down from the North into Italy, and I think we had their blood in us. But who knows? Since the Fall of ancient Rome, so many tribes had invaded Italy.

We had interesting pagan relics lying about; alien tombstones most ancient were sometimes found in the fields, and funny little stone goddesses which the peasants still cherished if we didn't confiscate them. Beneath our towers were vaults that some said went back to the days even before the Birth of Christ, and I know now that is true. These places belonged to the people known to history as the Etruscans.

Our household, being of the old feudal style, scorning trade and requiring of its men that they be bold and brave, was full of treasure acquired through wars without count or record—that is, old silver and gold candelabra and sconces, heavy chests of wood with Byzantine designs encrusted on them, the usual Flemish tapestries, and tons of lace, and bed hangings hand-trimmed with gilt and gems, and all of the most desirable finery.

My father, admiring the Medici as he did, bought up all kinds of luxury items on his trips to Florence. There was little bare stone in any important room, because flowered wool carpets covered all, and every hallway or alcove had its own towering armoire filled with rattling, rusting battle dress of heroes whose names nobody even remembered.

We were incalculably rich: this I had more or less overheard as a child, and there was some hint that it had to do as much with valor in war as with secret pagan treasure.

There had been centuries of course when our

family had warred with other hill towns and forts, when castle besieged castle and walls were ripped down as soon as they were built, and out of the city of Florence had gone the ever quarreling and murderous Guelfs and Ghibellines.

The old Commune of Florence had sent armies to tear down castles like ours and reduce any threatening Lord to nothingness.

But that time was long over.

We had survived due to cleverness and good choices, and also because we were much off to ourselves, in high craggy uninviting country, crowning a true mountain, as this is where the Alps come down into Tuscany, and those castles most near to us were abandoned ruins.

Our nearest neighbor did rule his own mountain enclave of villages in loyalty to the Duke of Milan.

But he didn't bother with us or we him. It was a remote political matter.

Our walls were thirty feet high, immensely thick, older than the castle and keeps, old indeed beyond anyone's most romantic tales and constantly being thickened and repaired, and inside the compound there existed three little villages busy with good vineyards that yielded marvelous red wine; prosperous beehives; blackberries; and wheat and the like; with plenty of chickens and cows; and enormous stables for our horses.

I never knew how many people labored in our little world. The house was full of clerks who took care of such things, and very seldom did my father sit in judgment on any sort of case himself or was there cause to go to the courts of Florence.

Our church was the designated church for all the country round, so that those few who lived in less protected little hamlets down the mountain—and there were plenty—came to us for their baptisms, and marriages, and such, and we had for long periods of time within our walls a Dominican priest who said Mass for us every morning.

In olden times, the forest had been severely cut down on our mountain so that no invading enemy could make his way up the slopes, but by my time no such protection was necessary.

The woods had grown back full and sweet in some gullies and over old paths, even as wild as it is now, and almost up to the walls. One could make out clearly from our towers a dozen or so small towns descending to the valleys, with their little quilts of tilled fields, orchards of olive trees and vineyards. They were all under our governance and loyal to us. If there had been any war they would have come running to our gates as their ancestors had done, and rightly so.

There were market days, village festivals, saints' days, and a little alchemy now and then, and occasionally even a local miracle. It was a good land, ours.

Visiting clerics always stayed a long time. It wasn't uncommon to have two or three priests in various towers of the castle or in the lower, newer, more modern stone buildings.

I had been taken to Florence to be educated

when I was very small, living in deluxe and invigo-rating style in the palazzo of my mother's uncle, who died before I was thirteen, and it was then—when the house was closed—that I was brought home, with two elderly aunts, and after that only visited Florence on occasion.

My father was still at heart an old-fashioned man, instinctively an indomitable Lord, though he was content to keep his distance from the power struggles of the capital, to have huge accounts in the Medici banks and to live an old-style courtly life in his own domain, visiting Cosimo de' Medici himself when he did journey into Florence on business.

But when it came to his son, my father wanted that I should be reared as a prince, a padrone, a knight, and I had to learn all the skills and values of a knight, and at thirteen, I could ride in full battle dress, my helmeted head bowed, at full speed with my spear thrust towards the straw-filled target. I had no difficulty with it. It was as much fun as hunting, or swimming in mountain streams, or having horse races with the village boys. I took to it without rebellion.

I was, however, a divided being. The mental part of me had been nourished in Florence by excellent teachers of Latin, Greek, philosophy and theology, and I had been deep into the boys' pageants and plays of the city, often taking the leading parts in the dramas presented by my own Confraternity in my uncle's house, and I knew how to solemnly portray the Biblical Isaac about to be sacrificed by the obedient Abraham, as well as the charming Angel Gabriel discovered by a suspicious St. Joseph with his Virgin Mary.

I pined for all that now and then, the books, the lectures in the Cathedrals to which I'd listened with precocious interest, and the lovely nights in my uncle's Florentine house when I'd fallen asleep to the sounds of spectacular opera extravaganzas, my mind brim full of the dazzle of miraculous figures swooping down on wires, lutes and drums playing wildly, dancers frolicking almost like acrobats and voices soaring beautifully in unison.

It had been an easy childhood. And in the boys' Confraternity to which I belonged, I'd met the poorer children of Florence, the sons of the merchants, orphans and boys from the monasteries and schools, because that is the way it was in my time for a landed Lord. You had to mix with the people.

I think I crept out of the house a lot as a small child, easily as much as I slipped out of the castle later. I remember too much of the festivals and saints' days and processions of Florence for a disciplined child to have seen. I was too often slipping in and out of the crowd, looking at the spectacularly decorated floats in honor of the saints, and marveling at the solemnity of those in silent ranks who carried candles and walked very slowly as if they were in a trance of devotion.

Yes, I must have been a scamp. I know I was. I went out by the kitchen. I bribed the servants. I had too many friends who were out-and-out routies or beasties. I got into mayhem and then ran home. We played ball games and had battles in the piazzas, and the priests ran us off with switches and threats. I was good and bad, but not ever really wicked.

When I died to this world, at the age of sixteen, I never looked on a daylighted street again, not in Florence or anywhere. Well, I saw the best of it, that I can say. I can envisage with no difficulty the spectacle of the Feast of St. John, when every single solitary shop in Florence had to put out front all of its costly wares, and monks and friars sang the sweetest hymns on their way to the Cathedral to give thanks to God for the blessed prosperity of the city.

I could go on. There is no end to the praise one can heap upon the Florence of those times, for she was a city of men who worked at trades and business yet made the greatest art, of sharp politicians and true raving saints, of deep-souled poets and the most audacious scoundrels. I think Florence knew many things by that time that would only much later be learnt in France and England, and which are not known in some countries to this day. Two things were true. Cosimo was the most powerful man in all the world. And the people, and only the people, ruled Florence then and forever.

But back to the castle. I kept up my reading and studies at home, switching from knight to scholar in a twinkling. If there was any shadow on my life, it was that at sixteen I was old enough to go to a real university, and I knew it, and I sort of wanted to do it, but then again, I was raising new hawks, training them myself and hunting with them, and the country round was irresistible.

By this age of sixteen, I was considered bookish by the clan of elder kinsmen who gathered at the table every night, my parents' uncles mostly, and all very much of a former time when "bankers had not run the world," who had marvelous tales to tell of the Crusades, to which they had gone when they were young, and of what they had seen at the fierce battle of Acre, or fighting on the island of Cyprus or Rhodes, and what life had been like at sea, and in many exotic ports where they had been the terror of the taverns and the women.

My mother was spirited and beautiful, with brown hair and very green eyes, and she adored country life, but she'd never known Florence except from the inside of a convent. She thought there was something seriously wrong with me that I wanted to read Dante's poetry and write so much of my own.

She lived for nothing but receiving guests in gracious style, seeing to it that the floors were strewn with lavender and sweet-smelling herbs, and that the wine was properly spiced, and she led the dance herself with a great-uncle who was very good at it, because my father would have nothing to do with dancing.

All this to me, after Florence, was rather tame and slow. Bring on the war stories.

She must have been very young when she was married off to my father, because she was with child on the night she died. And the child died with her. I'll come to that quickly. Well, as quickly as I can. I'm not so good at being quick.

My brother, Matteo, was four years younger than me, and an excellent student, though he had not been sent off anywhere as yet (would that he had), and my sister, Bartola, was born less than a year after me, so close in fact that I think my father was rather ashamed of it.

I thought them both—Matteo and Bartola— the most lovely and interesting people in the world. We had country fun and country freedom, running in the woods, picking blackberries, sitting at the feet of gypsy storytellers before they got caught and sent away. We loved one another. Matteo worshipped me too much because I could outtalk our father. He didn't see our father's quiet strength, or well-fashioned old manners. I was Matteo's real teacher in all things, I suppose. As for Bartola, she was far too wild for my mother, who was in an eternal state of shock over the state of Bartola's long hair, the hair being all full of twigs and petals and leaves and dirt from the woods where we'd been running.

Bartola was forced into plenty of embroidering, however; she knew her songs, her poetry and prayers. She was too exquisite and too rich to be rushed into anything she didn't want. My father adored her, and more than once in very few words assured himself that I kept constant watch over her in all our woodland wanderings. I did. I would have killed anyone who touched her!

Ah. This is too much for me! I didn't know how hard this was going to be! Bartola. Kill anyone who touched her! And now nightmares descend, as if they were winged spirits themselves, and threaten to shut out the tiny silent and ever drifting lights of Heaven.

Let me return to my train of thought.

My mother I never really understood, and probably misjudged, because everything seemed a matter of style and manners with her, and my father I found to be hysterically self-satirical and always funny.

He was, beneath all his jokes and snide stories, actually rather cynical, but at the same time kind; he saw through the pomp of others, and even his own pretensions. He looked upon the human situation as hopeless. War was comic to him, devoid of heroes and full of buffoons, and he would burst out laughing in the middle of his uncles' harangues, or even in the middle of my poems when I went on too long, and I don't think he ever deliberately spoke a civil word to my mother.

He was a big man, clean shaven and long-haired, and he had beautiful long tapering fingers, very unusual for his size, because all his elders had thicker hands. I have the same hands myself. All the beautiful rings he wore had belonged to his mother.

He dressed more sumptuously than he would have dared to do in Florence, in regal velvet stitched with pearls, and wore massive cloaks lined in ermine. His gloves were true gauntlets trimmed in fox, and he had large grave eyes, more deep-set than mine, and full of mockery, disbelief and sarcasm.

He was never mean, however, to anyone.

His only modern affectation was that he liked to drink from fine goblets of glass, rather than old cups of hardwood or gold or silver. And we had plenty of sparkling glass always on our long supper table.

My mother always smiled when she said such things to him as "My Lord, please get your feet off the table," or "I'll thank you not to touch me until you've washed your greasy hands," or "Are you really coming into the house like that?" But beneath her charming exterior, I think she hated him.

The one time I ever heard her raise her voice in anger, it was to declare in no uncertain terms that half the children in our villages round had been sired by him, and that she herself had buried some eight tiny infants who had never lived to see the light, because he couldn't restrain himself any better than a rampant stallion.

He was so amazed at this outburst—it was behind closed doors—that he emerged from the bedchamber looking pale and shocked, and said to me, "You know, Vittorio, your mother is nothing as stupid as I always thought. No, not at all. As a matter of fact, she's just boring."

He would never under normal circumstances have said anything so unkind about her. He was trembling.

As for her, when I tried to go in to her, she threw a silver pitcher at me. I said, "But Mother, it's Vittorio!" and she threw herself into my arms. She cried bitterly for fifteen minutes.

We said nothing during this time. We sat together in her small stone bedroom, rather high up in the oldest tower of our house, with many pieces of gilded furniture, both ancient and new, and then she wiped her eyes and said, "He takes care of everyone, you know. He takes care of my aunts and my uncles, you know. And where would they be if it weren't for him? And he's never denied me anything."

She went rambling on in her smooth convent-modulated voice. "Look at this house. It's filled with elders whose wisdom has been so good for you children, and all this on account of your father, who is rich enough to have gone anywhere, I suppose, but he is too kind. Only, Vittorio! Vittorio, don't . . . I mean . . . with the girls in the village."

I almost said, in a spasm of desire to comfort her, that I had only fathered one bastard to my knowledge, and he was just fine, when I realized this would have been a perfect disaster. I said nothing.

That might have been the only conversation I ever had with my mother. But it's not really a conversation because I didn't say anything.

She was right, however. Three of her aunts and two of her uncles lived with us in our great high-walled compound, and these old people lived well, always sumptuously dressed in the latest fabrics from the city, and enjoying the purest courtly life imaginable. I couldn't help but benefit from listening to them all the time, which I did, and they knew plenty of all the world.

It was the same with my father's uncles, but of course it was their land, this, their family's, and so they felt more entitled, I assume, as they had done most of the heroic fighting in the Holy Land, or so it seemed, and they quarreled with my father over anything and everything, from the taste of the meat tarts served at supper to the distractingly modern style of the painters he hired from Florence to decorate our little chapel.

That was another sort of modern thing he did, the matter of the painters, maybe the only modern thing other than liking things made of glass.

Our little chapel had for centuries been bare. It was, like the four towers of our castle and all the walls around, built of a blond stone which is common in Northern Tuscany. This is not the dark stone you see so much in Florence, which is gray and looks perpetually unclean. This northern stone is almost the color of the palest pink roses.

But my father had brought pupils up from Florence when I was very young, good painters who had studied with Piero della Francesca and other such, to cover these chapel walls with murals taken from the lovely stories of saints and Biblical giants in the books known as *The Golden Legend*.

Not being himself a terribly imaginative man, my father followed what he had seen in the churches of Florence in his design and instructed these men to tell the tales of John the Baptist, patron saint of the city and cousin of Our Lord, and so it was that during the last years of my life on earth, our chapel was enfolded with representations of St. Elizabeth, St. John, St. Anne, the Blessed Mother, Zachary and angels galore, all dressed—as was the way of the time—in their Florentine finest.

It was to this "modern" painting, so unlike the stiffer work of Giotto or Cimabue, that my elderly uncles and aunts objected. As for the villagers, I don't think they exactly understood it all either, except they were so overawed in the main by the chapel at a wedding or baptism that it didn't matter.

I myself of course was terrifically happy to see these paintings made, and to spend time with the artists, who were all gone by the time that my life was brought to a halt by demonic slaughter.

I'd seen plenty of the greatest painting in Florence and had a weakness for drifting about, looking at splendid visions of angels and saints in the rich dedicated chapels of the Cathedrals, and had even—on one of my trips to Florence with my father—in Cosimo's house, glimpsed the tempestuous painter Filippo Lippi, who was at that time actually under lock and key there to make him finish a painting.

I was much taken with the plain yet compelling man, the way that he argued and schemed and did everything but throw a tantrum to get permission to leave the palazzo while lean, solemn and low-voiced Cosimo just smiled and talked him down more or less out of his hysteria, telling him to get back to work and that he would be happy when he was finished.

Filippo Lippi was a monk, but he was mad for women and everybody knew it. You could say that he was a favorite bad guy. It was for women that he wanted out of the palazzo, and it was even suggested later at the supper table of our hosts in Florence on that visit that Cosimo ought to lock a few women in the room with Filippo, and that maybe that would keep Filippo happy. I don't think Cosimo did any such thing. If he had, his enemies would have made it the grand news of Florence.

Let me make note, for it is very important. I never forgot that glimpse of the genius Filippo, for that is what he was—and is—to me.

"So what did you so like about him?" my father asked me.

"He's bad and good," I said, "not just one or the other. I see a war going on inside of him! And I saw some of his work once, work he did with Fra Giovanni"—this was the man later called Fra Angelico by all the world—"and I tell you, I think he is brilliant. Why else would Cosimo put up with such a scene? Did you hear him!"

"And Fra Giovanni is a saint?" asked my father.

"Hmmmmm, yes. And that's fine, you know, but did you see the torment in Fra Filippo? Hmmm, I liked it."

My father raised his eyebrows.

On our next and very last trip to Florence, he took me to see all of Filippo's paintings. I was amazed that he had remembered my interest in this man. We went from house to house to look at the loveliest works, and then to Filippo's workshop.

26

There an altarpiece commissioned by Francesco Maringhi for a Florentine church—*The Coronation of the Virgin*—was well under way, and when I saw this work, I nearly fainted dead from shock and love of it.

I couldn't leave it alone. I sighed and wept.

I had never seen anything as beautiful as this painting, with its immense crowd of still attentive faces, its splendid collection of angels and saints, its lithe and graceful feline women and willowy celestial men. I went crazy for it.

My father took me to see two more of his works, which were both paintings of the Annunciation.

Now, I have mentioned that as a child, I had played the Angel Gabriel coming to the Virgin to announce the Conception of Christ in her womb, and the way we played, he was supposed to be a pretty beguiling and virile angel, and Joseph would come in and, lo, find this overwhelming male with his pure ward, the Blessed Mary.

We were a worldly bunch, but you know, we gave the play a little spice. I mean we cooked it up a bit. I don't think it says anything in scripture about St. Joseph happening on a tryst.

But that had been my favorite role, and I had particularly enjoyed paintings of the Annunciation.

Well, this last one I saw before I left Florence, done by Filippo sometime in the 1440s, was beyond anything I had beheld before.

The angel was truly unearthly yet physically perfect. Its wings were made of peacock feathers.

I was sick with devotion and covetousness. I

wished we could buy this thing and take it back home. That wasn't possible. No works of Filippo were on the market then. So my father finally dragged me away from this painting, and off we went home the next day or so.

Only later did I realize how quietly he listened to what I said as I ranted on and on about Fra Filippo:

"It's delicate, it's original, and yet it is commendable according to everybody's rules, that's the genius of it, to change, but not so much, to be inimitable, yet not beyond the common grasp, and that's what he's done, Father, I tell you."

I was unstoppable.

"This is what I think about that man," I said. "The carnality in him, the passion for women, the near beastly refusal to keep his vows is at war always with the priest, for look, he wears his robes, he is Fra Filippo. And out of that war, there comes into the faces he paints a look of utter surrender."

My father listened.

"That's it," I said. "Those characters reflect his own continued compromise with the forces he cannot reconcile, and they are sad, and wise, and never innocent, and always soft, reflective of mute torment."

On the way back home, as we were riding together through the forest, up a rather steep road, very casually my father asked me if the painters who had done our chapel were good.

"Father, you're joking," I said. "They were excellent."

He smiled. "I didn't know, you know," he said. "I just hired the best." He shrugged.

I smiled.

Then he laughed with good nature. I never asked him when and if I could leave home again to study. I think I figured I could make both of us happy.

We must have made twenty-five stops on that last journey home from Florence. We were wined and dined at one castle after another, and wandered in and out of the new villas, lavish and full of light, and given over to their abundant gardens. I clung to nothing in particular because I thought it was my life, all those arbors covered with purple wisteria, and the vineyards on the green slopes, and the sweet-cheeked girls beckoning to me in the loggias.

Florence was actually at war the year we made this journey. She had sided with the great and famous Francesco Sforza, to take over the city of Milan. The cities of Naples and Venice were on the side of Milan. It was a terrible war. But it didn't touch us.

It was fought in other places and by hired men, and the rancor caused by it was heard in city streets, not on our mountain.

What I recall from it were two remarkable characters involved in the fray. The first of these was the Duke of Milan, Filippo Maria Visconti, a man who had been our enemy whether we liked it or not because he was the enemy of Florence.

But listen to what this man was like: he was

hideously fat, it was said, and very dirty by nature, and sometimes would take off all his clothes and roll around naked in the dirt of his garden! He was terrified of the sight of a sword and would scream if he saw it unsheathed, and he was terrified too to have his portrait painted because he thought he was so ugly, which he was. But that was not all. This man's weak little legs wouldn't carry him, so his pages had to heft him about. Yet he had a sense of humor. To scare people, he would suddenly draw a snake out of his sleeve! Lovely, don't you think?

Yet he ruled the Duchy of Milan for thirty-five years somehow, this man, and it was against Milan that his own mercenary, Francesco Sforza, turned in this war.

And that man I want to describe only briefly because he was colorful in an entirely different way, being the handsome strong brave son of a peasant—a peasant who, kidnapped as a child, had managed to become the commander of his band of kidnappers—and this Francesco became commander of the troop only when the peasant hero drowned in a stream trying to save a page boy. Such valor. Such purity! Such gifts.

I never laid eyes on Francesco Sforza until I was already dead to the world and a prowling vampire, but he was true to his descriptions, a man of heroic proportions and style, and believe it or not, it was to this bastard of a peasant and natural soldier that the weak-legged crazy Duke of Milan gave his own daughter in marriage, and this daughter, by the way, was not by the Duke's wife, poor thing, for she was locked up, but by his mistress.

It was this marriage which led eventually to the war. First Francesco was fighting bravely for Duke Filippo Maria, and then when the weird unpredictable little Duke finally croaked, naturally his son-in-law, handsome Francesco, who had charmed everybody in Italy from the Pope to Cosimo, wanted to become the Duke of Milan!

It's all true. Don't you think it's interesting? Look it up. I left out that the Duke Filippo Maria was also so scared of thunder that he was supposed to have built a soundproof room in his palace.

And there is more to it than that. Sforza more or less had to save Milan from other people who wanted to take it over, and Cosimo had to back him, or France would have come down on us, or worse.

It was all rather amusing, and as I have said, I was well prepared already at a young age to go into war or to court if it was ever required of me, but these wars and these two characters existed for me in dinner table talk, and every time someone railed about the crazy Duke Filippo Maria, and one of his insane tricks with a snake out of his sleeve, my father would wink at me and whisper in my ear, "Nothing like pure lordly blood, my son." And then laugh.

As for the romantic and brave Francesco Sforza, my father had wisely nothing to say as long as the man was fighting for our enemy, the Duke, but once we had all turned together against Milan, then my father commended the bold self-made Francesco and his courageous peasant father.

There had been another great lunatic running around Italy during earlier times, a freebooter and ruffian named Sir John Hawkwood, who would lead his mercenaries against anybody, including the Florentines.

But he had ended up loyal to Florence, even became a citizen, and when he departed this earth, they gave him a splendid monument in the Cathedral! Ah, such an age!

I think it was a really good time to be a soldier, you know, to sort of pick and choose where you would fight, and get as carried away with it all as you wanted to.

But it was also a very good time for reading poetry, and for looking at paintings and for living in utter comfort and security behind ancestral walls, or wandering the thriving streets of prosperous cities. If you had any education at all, you could choose what you wanted to do.

And it was also a time to be very careful. Lords such as my father did go down to destruction in these wars. Mountainous regions that had been free and pretty much left alone could be invaded and destroyed. It happened now and then that someone who had pretty much stayed out of things got himself worked up against Florence and in came the clattering and clanking mercenaries to level everything.

By the way, Sforza won the war with Milan, and part of the reason was that Cosimo lent him the required money. What happened after that was absolute mayhem.

Well, I could go on describing this wonderland of Tuscany forever.

It is chilling and saddening for me to try to imagine what might have become of my family had evil not befallen us. I cannot see my father old, or imagine myself struggling as an elderly man, or envision my sister married, as I hoped, to a city aristocrat rather than a country baron.

It is a horror and a joy to me that there are villages and hamlets in these very mountains which have from that time never died out—never—surviving through the worst of even modern war, to thrive still with tiny cobbled market streets and pots of red geraniums in their windows. There are castles which survive everywhere, enlivened by generation after generation.

Here there is darkness.

Here is Vittorio writing by the light of the stars.

Brambles and wild scratching things inhabit the chapel below, where the paintings are still visible to no one and the sacred relics of the consecrated altar stone are beneath heaps of dust.

Ah, but those thorns protect what remains of my home. I have let them grow. I have allowed the roads to vanish in the forest or broken them myself. I must have something of what there was! I must.

But I accuse myself again of going on and on, and I do, there is no doubt.

This chapter ought to be over.

But it's very like the little plays we used to do in my uncle's house, or those I saw before the Duomo in Cosimo's Florence. There must be painted backdrops, props of fine detail, wires rigged for flight and costumes cut out and sewn before I can put my players on the boards and tell the fable of my making.

I can't help it. Let me close my essay on the glories of the 1400s by saying what the great alchemist Ficino would say of it some years later on: It was "an age of gold."

I go now to the tragic moment.

3

HE beginning of the end came the
following spring. I had passed my six-
teenth birthday, which had fallen that
year on the very Tuesday before Lent,
when we and all the villages were celebrating Car-
nival. It had come rather early that year, so it was a
bit cold, but it was a gay time.

It was on that night before Ash Wednesday that
I had the terrible dream in which I saw myself
holding the severed heads of my brother and my
sister. I woke up in a sweat, horrified by this dream.
I wrote it down in my book of dreams. And then
actually I forgot about it. That was common with
me, only it had been truly the most horrid night-
mare I'd ever had. But when I mentioned my occasional nightmares to my mother or father or
anyone else, they always said:

"Vittorio, it's your own fault for reading the
books you read. You bring it on yourself."

To repeat, the dream was forgotten.

The country was by Easter in great flower, and

the first warnings of horror to come, though I knew them not to be, were that the lower hamlets on our mountain were quite suddenly abandoned.

My father and I and two of the huntsmen and a gamekeeper and a soldier rode down to see for ourselves that the peasants in those parts had departed, some time before in fact, and taken the livestock with them.

It was eerie to see those deserted towns, small as they were and as insignificant.

We rode back up the mountain as a warm embracing darkness surrounded us, yet we found all the other villages we passed battened down with hardly a seam of light showing through the chinks of a shutter, or a tiny stem of reddened smoke rising from a chimney.

Of course my father's old clerk went into a rant that the vassals should be found, beaten, made to work the land.

My father, benevolent as always and completely calm, sat at his desk in the candlelight, leaning on his elbow, and said that these had all been free men; they were not bound to him, if they did not choose to live on his mountain. This was the way of the modern world, only he wished he knew what was afoot in our land.

Quite suddenly, he took notice of me standing and observing him, as if he hadn't seen me before, and he broke off the conference, dismissing the whole affair.

I thought nothing much about it.

But in the days that followed, some of the villagers from the lower slopes came up to live within the walls. There were conferences in my father's chambers. I heard arguments behind closed doors, and one night, at supper, all sat entirely too somber for our family, and finally my father rose from his massive chair, the Lord in the center of the table as always, and declared, as if he'd been silently accused:

"I will not persecute some old women because they have stuck pins in wax dolls and burnt incense and read foolish incantations that mean nothing. These old witches have been on our mountain forever."

My mother looked truly alarmed, and then gathering us all up—I was most unwilling—she took us away, Bartola, Matteo and me, and told us to go to bed early.

"Don't stay up reading, Vittorio!" she said.

"But what did Father mean?" asked Bartola.

"Oh, it's the old village witches," I said. I used the Italian word *strega*. "Every now and then, one goes too far, there's a fight, but mostly it's just charms to cure a fever and such."

I thought my mother would hush me up, but she stood in the narrow stone stairs of the tower looking up at me with marked relief on her face, and she said:

"Yes, yes, Vittorio, you are so right. In Florence, people laugh at those old women. You know Gattena yourself; she never really did more then sell love potions to the girls."

"Surely we're not to drag her before a court!" I said, very happy that she was paying attention.

Bartola and Matteo were rapt.

"No, no, not Gattena, certainly not. Gattena's vanished. Run off."

"Gattena?" I asked, and then as my mother turned away, refusing, it seemed, to say another word, gesturing for me to escort my sister and brother safely to bed, I realized the gravity of this.

Gattena was the most feared and comical of the old witches, and if she had run off, if she was afraid of something, well, that was news, because she thought herself the one to be feared.

The following days were fresh and lovely and undisturbed by anything for me and my Bartola and Matteo, but when I looked back later, I recalled there was much going on.

One afternoon, I went up to the highest lookout window of the old tower where one guardsman, Tori, we called him, was falling asleep, and I looked down over all our land for as far as I could see.

"Well, you won't find it," he said.

"What's that?" I remarked.

"Smoke from a single hearth. There is no more." He yawned and leaned against the wall, heavily weighed down by his old boiled-leather jerkin, and sword. "All's well," he said, and yawned again. "So they like city life, or to fight for Francesco Sforza over the Duchy of Milan, so let them go. They didn't know how good they had it."

I turned away from him and looked over the woods again, and down into the valleys that I could see, and beyond to the slightly misty blue sky. It was true, the little hamlets seemed frozen in time down there, but how could one be so sure? It was not such a clear day. And besides, everything was fine within the household.

My father drew olive oil, vegetables, milk, butter and many such goods from these villages, but he didn't need them. If it was time for them to pass away, so be it.

Two nights later, however, it was undeniably obvious to me that everyone at supper was perpetually under a strain of sorts, which went entirely unvoiced, and that an agitation had gripped my mother, so that she was no longer engaging in her endless courtly chatter. Conversation was not impossible, but it had changed.

But for all the elders who seemed deeply and secretly conflicted, there were others who seemed relatively oblivious to such things, and the pages went about serving gaily, and a little group of musicians, who'd come up the preceding day, gave us a lovely series of songs with the viol and the lute.

My mother couldn't be persuaded to do her old slow dances, however.

It must have been very late when an unexpected visitor was announced. No one had left the main hall, except Bartola and Matteo, who had been taken off to bed by me earlier and left in the care of our old nurse, Simonetta.

The Captain of my father's Guard came into the hall, clicked his heels and bowed to my father and said:

"My Lord, it seems there is a man of great rank come to the house, and he will not be received in the light, or so he says, and demands that you come out to him."

Everyone at the table was at once alert, and my mother went white with anger and umbrage.

No one ever used the word "demand" to my father.

Also it was plain to me that our Captain of the Guard, a rather prepossessing old soldier who'd seen many battles with the wandering mercenaries, was himself overvigilant and a little shaken.

My father rose to his feet. He did not speak or move, however.

"Would you do that, my Lord, or should I send this Signore away?" the Captain asked.

"Tell him that he is most welcome to come into my house as my guest," said my father, "that we extend to him in the name of Christ Our Lord our full hospitality."

His very voice seemed to have a calming effect on the whole table, except perhaps for my mother, who seemed not to know what to do.

The Captain looked almost slyly at my father, as if to convey the secret message that this would never do, but he went off to deliver the invitation.

My father did not sit down. He stood staring off, and then he cocked his head, as though listening. He turned and snapped his fingers, drawing to attention the two guards slumbering at the ends of the hall.

"Go through the house, see to everything," he said in a soft voice. "I think I hear birds which have entered the house. It's the warm air, and there are many open windows."

These two went off, and immediately two other soldiers appeared to take their place. That in itself was not usual, for it meant that there were many men on duty.

The Captain came back alone, and once more bowed.

"My Lord, he will not come into the light, he says, but that you must come out to him, and he has little time to wait on you."

This was the first time I had ever seen my father really angry. Even when he whipped me or a peasant boy, he was rather lazy about it. Now the fine lineaments of his face, so given to reassurance by their very proportions, became absolutely wrathful.

"How dare he?" he whispered.

Yet he strode around the table, came in front of it and marched off with the Captain of the Guard hastening behind him.

I was out of my chair at once and after him. I heard my mother cry out softly, "Vittorio, come back."

But I stole down the stairs after my father, and into the courtyard, and only when he himself turned around and pressed my chest hard with his hand did I halt.

"Stay there, my son," he said with his old kindly warmth. "I shall see to it."

I had a good vantage point, right at the door of the tower, and there across the courtyard, at the gates in the full light of the torches, I saw this strange Signore who would not come into the light of the hall, for he did not seem to mind this outdoor illumination.

The huge gates of the arched entrance were

locked and bolted for the night. Only the small man-sized gate was opened, and it was there that he stood, with the blazing crackling fire on either side of him, glorying in it, it seemed to me, in his splendid raiment of dark, wine-red velvet.

From head to toe he was dressed in this rich color, hardly the current style, but every detail of him, from his bejeweled doublet and blown-up sleeves of satin and velvet stripes, was this same hue, as though carefully dyed in the best fullers in Florence.

Even the gems sewn into his collar and hanging about his neck on a heavy golden chain were wine red—most likely rubies or even sapphires.

His hair was thick and black, hanging sleekly onto his shoulders, but I couldn't see his face, no, not at all, for the velvet hat he wore overshadowed it, and I caught but a glimpse of very white skin, the line of his jaw and a bit of his neck, for nothing else was visible. He wore a broadsword of immense size, with an antique scabbard, and casually over one shoulder was a cloak of the same wine-dark velvet trimmed in what seemed to my distant eyes to be ornate gilt symbols.

I strained, trying to make them out, this border of signs, and I thought I could see a star and crescent moon worked into his fancy adornments, but I was really too far away.

The man's height was impressive.

My father stopped quite far short of him, yet when he spoke his voice was soft and I couldn't hear it, and out of the mysterious man, who still revealed nothing now of his face but his smiling mouth and white teeth, there came a silky utterance that seemed both surly and charming.

"Get away from my house in the name of God and Our Holy Redeemer!" my father cried out suddenly. And with a quick gesture, he stepped forward and powerfully thrust this splendid figure right out of the gate.

I was amazed.

But from the hollow mouth of darkness beyond the opening there came only a low satin laughter, a mocking laughter, and this it seemed was echoed by others, and I heard a powerful thundering of hooves, as though several horsemen had commenced at once to ride off.

My father himself slammed the gate. And turned and made the Sign of the Cross, and pressed his hands together in prayer.

"Dear Lord God, how dare they!" he said, looking up.

It was only now, as he stormed back towards me and towards the tower itself, that I realized the Captain of the Guard was paralyzed with seeming terror.

My father's eye caught mine as soon as he came into the light from the stairs, and I gestured to the Captain. My father spun round.

"Batten down my house," my father called out. "Search it from top to bottom and batten it down and call out the soldiery and fill the night with torches, do you hear? I will have men in every tower and on the walls. Do it at once. It will give peace and calm to my people!"

We had not yet reached the supper room when

an old priest living with us then, a learned Domini-can named Fra Diamonte, came down with his white hair all mussed, and his cassock half unbut-toned, and his prayer book in his hand.

"What is it, my Lord?" he asked. "What in the name of God has happened?"

"Father, trust in God and come and pray with me in the chapel," said my father to him. He then pointed to another guard who was fast approach-ing. "Light up the chapel, all its candles, for I want to pray. Do it now, and have the boys come down and play for me some sacred music."

He then took my hand and that of the priest. "It's nothing, really, you must both of you know that. It's all superstitious foolishness, but any excuse which makes a worldly man like me turn to his God is a good one. Come on, Vittorio, you and Fra Diamonte and I will pray, but for your mother put on a good face."

I was much calmer, but the prospect of being up all night in the lighted chapel was both wel-come and alarming.

I went off to get my prayer books, my Mass books and books of other devotions, fine vellum books from Florence, with gilt print and beauti-fully edged illustrations.

I was just coming out of my room when I saw my father there with my mother, saying to her, "And do not leave the children alone for a moment, and you, you in this state, I will not tolerate this distress."

She touched her belly.

I realized she was with child again. And I realized, too, that my father was really alarmed about something. What could it mean, "Do not leave the children alone for a moment"? What could this mean?

The chapel was comfortable enough. My father had long ago provided some decent wooden and velvet-padded prie-dieux, though on feast days everyone stood. Pews didn't exist in those times.

But he also spent some of the night showing me the vault beneath the church, which opened by means of a ring handle on a trapdoor, faced in stone, the ring itself fitted down flat beneath what appeared to be only one of many marble inlaid ornaments in the floor tiles.

I knew of these crypts but had been whipped for sneaking into them when I was a child, and my father had told me back then how disappointed in me he'd been that I couldn't keep a family secret.

That admonition had hurt far more than the whipping. And I'd never asked to go with him into the crypts, which I knew he had done over the years now and then. I thought treasure was down there, and secrets of the pagans.

Well, I saw now there was a cavernous room, carved high and deep out of the earth, and faced with stone, and that it was full of varied treasure. There were old chests and even old books in heaps. And two bolted doorways.

"Those lead to old burial places that you don't need to go to," he said, "but you need to know of this place now. And remember it."

When we came back up into the chapel, he put the trapdoor right, laid down the ring, relaid the marble tile, and the whole was quite invisible.

Fra Diamonte pretended not to have seen. My mother was asleep and so were the children.

We all fell asleep before dawn in the chapel.

My father walked out in the courtyard at sunup, when the cocks were crowing all over the villages inside the walls, and he stretched and looked up at the sky and then shrugged his shoulders.

Two of my uncles ran at him, demanding to know what Signore from where dared to propose a siege against us and when we were supposed to have this battle.

"No, no, no, you've got it all wrong," my father said. "We're not going to war. You go back to bed."

But he had no sooner spoken these words than a ripping scream brought us all around, and through the opening courtyard gates there came one of the village girls, one of our near and dear girls, shrieking the terrible words:

"He's gone, the baby's gone, they've taken him."

The rest of the day was a relentless search for this missing child. But no one could find him. And it was soon discovered that one other child had also vanished without a trace. He had been a half-wit, rather beloved because he caused no harm, but so addle-brained he couldn't even much walk. And everyone was ashamed to say that they did not even know how long that half-wit had been missing.

By dusk, I thought I would go mad if I didn't

get to see my father alone, if I couldn't push my way into the locked chambers where he sat with his uncles and the priests arguing and fighting. Finally, I hammered so loudly on the door and kicked so much that he let me in.

The meeting was about to break up and he drew me down by himself, and he said with wild eyes:

"Do you see what they've done? They took the very tribute they demanded of me. They took it! I refused it and they took it."

"But what tribute? You mean the children?"

He was wild-eyed. He rubbed his unshaven face, and he crashed his fist down on his desk, and then he pushed over all his writing things.

"Who do they think they are that they come to me by night and demand that I tender to them those infants unwanted by anyone?"

"Father, what is this? You must tell me."

"Vittorio, you will tomorrow be off to Florence, at the first light, and with the letters I mean to write tonight. I need more than country priests to fight this. Now get ready for the journey."

He looked up quite suddenly. He appeared to listen, and then to look about. I could see the light was gone from the windows. We ourselves were just dim figures, and he had thrown the candelabra down. I picked it up.

I watched him sidelong as I took one of the candles and lighted it by the torch at the door and brought it back, and then lighted the other candles.

He listened, still and alert, and then without

making a sound he rose to his feet, his fists on the desk, seemingly uncaring of the light that the candles threw on his shocked and wary face.

"What do you hear, my Lord?" I said, using the formal address for him without so much as realizing it.

"Evil," he whispered. "Malignant things such as God only suffers to live because of our sins. Arm yourself well. Bring your mother, your brother and your sister to the chapel, and hurry. The soldiers have their orders."

"Shall I have some supper brought there as well, just bread and beer, perhaps?" I asked.

He nodded as though that were scarcely a concern.

Within less than an hour we were all gathered inside the chapel, the entire family, which included then five uncles and four aunts, and with us were two nurses and Fra Diamonte.

The little altar was decked out as if for Mass, with the finest embroidered altar cloth and the thickest golden candlesticks with blazing candles. The Image of Our Crucified Christ shone in the light, an ancient colorless and thin wooden carving that had hung on the wall there since the time of St. Francis, when the great saint was supposed to have stopped at our castle two centuries ago.

It was a naked Christ, common in those times, and a figure of tortured sacrifice, nothing as robust and sensual as those crucifixes made these days, and it stood out powerfully in contrast to the parade of freshly painted saints on the walls in their brilliant scarlet and gold finery.

We sat on plain brown benches brought in for us, nobody speaking a word, for Fra Diamonte had that morning said Mass and bestowed into the Tabernacle the Body and Blood of Our Lord in the form of the Sacred Host, and the chapel was now, as it were, put to its full purpose as the House of God.

We did eat the bread, and drink a little bit of the beer near the front doors, but we kept quiet.

Only my father repeatedly went out, walking boldly into the torch-lighted courtyard and calling up to his soldiers in the towers and on the walls, and even sometimes being gone to climb up and see for himself that all was well under his protection.

My uncles were all armed. My aunts said their rosaries fervently. Fra Diamonte was confused, and my mother seemed pale to death and sick, perhaps from the baby in her womb, and she clung to my sister and brother, who were by this time pretty frankly frightened.

It seemed we would pass the night without incident.

It couldn't have been two hours before dawn when I was awakened from a shallow slumber by a horrid scream.

At once my father was on his feet, and so were my uncles, drawing out their swords as best they could with their knotted old fingers.

Screams rose all around in the night, and there came the alarms from the soldiers and the loud riotous clanging of old bells from every tower.

My father grabbed me by the arm. "Vittorio, come," he said, and at once, pulling up the handle

49

of the trapdoor, he threw it back and thrust into my hand a great candle from the altar.

"Take your mother, your aunts, your sister and your brother down, now, and do not come out, no matter what you hear! Do not come out. Lock the trapdoor above you and stay there! Do as I tell you!"

At once I obeyed, snatching up Matteo and Bartola and forcing them down the stone steps in front of me.

My uncles had rushed through the doors into the courtyard, shouting their ancient war cries, and my aunts stumbled and fainted and clutched to the altar and would not be moved, and my mother clung to my father.

My father was in a very paroxysm. I reached out for my eldest aunt, but she was in a dead faint before the altar, and my father thundered back to me, forced me into the crypt and shut the door.

I had no choice but to latch the trapdoor as he had shown me how to do, and to turn with the flickering candle in my hand and face the terrified Bartola and Matteo.

"Go down all the way," I cried, "all the way."

They nearly fell, trying to move backward down the steep narrow steps that were by no means easy to descend, their faces turned towards me.

"What is it, Vittorio, why do they want to hurt us?" Bartola asked.

"I want to fight them," Matteo said. "Vittorio, give me your dagger. You have a sword. It's not fair."

"Shhh, be quiet, do as our father said. Do you think it pleases me that I can't be out there with the men? Quiet!"

I choked back my tears. My mother was up there! My aunts!

The air was cold and damp, but it felt good. I broke out in a sweat, and my arm ached from holding the big golden candlestick. Finally we sank down in a huddle, the three of us at the far end of the chamber, and it felt soothing to me to touch the cold stone.

But in the interval of our collective silence I could hear through the heavy floor howls from above, terrible cries of fear and panic, and rushing feet, and even the high chilling whinnies of the horses. It sounded as if horses had come crashing into the chapel itself over our heads, which was not at all impossible.

I rose to my feet and rushed to the two other doors of the crypt, those which led to the burial chambers or whatever they were, I didn't care! I moved the latch on one, and could see nothing but a low passage, not even tall enough for me, and barely wide enough for my shoulders.

I turned back, holding the only light, and saw the children rigid with fear, gazing up at the ceiling as the murderous cries continued.

"I smell fire," Bartola whispered suddenly, her face wet at once with tears. "Do you smell it, Vittorio? I hear it."

I did hear it and I did smell it.

"Both of you make the Sign of the Cross; pray

now," I said, "and trust in me. We will get out of here."

But the clamor of the battle went on, the cries did not die out, and then suddenly, so suddenly it was as wondrous and frightful as the noise itself, there fell a silence.

A silence fell over all, and it was too complete to spell victory.

Bartola and Matteo clung to me, on either side.

Above, there was a clatter. The chapel doors were being thrown back, and then quite suddenly the trapdoor was yanked up and open, and in the glimmer of firelight beyond I saw a dark slender long-haired figure.

In the gust my candle went out.

Except for the infernal flicker above and beyond, we were committed unmercifully to total darkness.

Once again distinctly, I saw the outline of this figure, a tall, stately female with great long locks and a waist small enough for both my hands as she appeared to fly down the stairs soundlessly towards me.

How in the name of Heaven could this be, this woman?

Before I could think to pull my sword on a female assailant or make sense of anything at all, I felt her tender breasts brushed against my chest, and the cool of her skin as she seemed to be throwing her arms about me.

There was a moment of inexplicable and strangely sensuous confusion when the perfume of her tresses and her gown rose in my nostrils, and I fancied I saw the glistening whites of her eyes as she looked at me.

I heard Bartola scream, and then Matteo also.

I was knocked to the floor.

The fire blazed bright above.

The figure had them both, both struggling screaming children in one seemingly fragile arm, and stopping, apparently to look at me, a raised sword in her other hand, she raced up the stairway into the firelight.

I pulled my sword with both hands, rushed after her, up and out into the chapel, and saw that she had somehow by the most evil power all but reached the door, an impossible feat, her charges wailing and crying out for me, "Vittorio, Vittorio!"

All the upper windows of the chapels were full of fire, and so was the rose window above the crucifix.

I could not believe what I beheld, this young woman, who was stealing from me my sister and brother.

"Stop in the name of God!" I shouted at her. "Coward, thief in the night."

I ran after her, but to my utter astonishment she did stop, still, and turned to look at me again, and this time I saw her full in all her refined beauty. Her face was a perfect oval with great benign gray eyes, her skin like the finest Chinese white enamel. She had red lips, too perfect even for a painter to make by choice, and her long ashen blond hair was gray like her eyes in the light of the fire, sweeping down her back in a pampered swaying mass. Her gown, though stained dark with what must have been blood, was the same wine-red color I had seen in the apparel of the evil visitor of the night before.

With the most curious and then poignant face, she merely stared at me. Her right hand held her sword upraised, but she didn't move, and then she released from the powerful grip of her left arm my struggling brother and sister.

Both tumbled sobbing to the floor.

"Demon. Strega!" I roared. I leapt over them and advanced on her, swinging the sword.

But she dodged so swiftly that I didn't even see it. I couldn't believe that she was so far from me, standing now with the sword down, staring at me still and at the sobbing children.

Suddenly her head turned. There was a whistling cry, and then another and another. Through the door of the chapel, seeming to leap from the fires of Hell itself, there came another red-clad figure, hooded in velvet and wearing gold-trimmed boots, and as I swung my sword at him, he threw me aside and, in one instant, cut off the head of Bartola and then severed the head of the screaming Matteo.

I went mad. I howled. He turned on me. But from the female there came a sudden firm negation.

"Leave him alone," she cried in a voice that was both sweet and clear, and then off he went, this murderer, this hooded fiend in his gold-trimmed boots, calling back to her.

"Come on, now, have you lost your wits? Look at the sky. Come, Ursula."

She didn't move. She stared at me as before.

I sobbed and cursed and, grabbing my sword, ran at her again, and this time saw my blade descend to cut off her right arm, right below the elbow. The white limb, small and seemingly fragile like all of her parts, fell to the paved floor with her heavy sword. Blood spurted from her.

She did no more than look at it. And then at me with the same poignant, disconsolate and near heartbroken face.

I lifted my sword again. "Strega!" I cried, clenching my teeth, trying to see through my tears. "Strega!"

But in another feat of evil, she had moved back, far away from me, as if pulled by an invisible force, and in her left hand she now held her right, which still clutched her sword as if it were not severed. She replaced the limb I had cut off. I watched her. I watched her put the limb in place and turn it and adjust it until it was as it should be, and then before my astonished eyes, I saw the wound I had made utterly seal up in her white skin.

Then the loose bell sleeve of her rich velvet gown fell down again around her wrist.

In a twinkling she was outside the chapel, only a silhouette now against the distant fires burning in the tower windows. I heard her whisper:

"Vittorio."

Then she vanished.

I knew it was vain to go after her! Yet still I ran

out and swung my sword around in a great circle, crying out in rage and bitterness and mad menace at all the world, my eyes now blinded with tears, and my throat full to choking.

Everything was still. Everyone was dead. Dead. I knew it. The courtyard was strewn with bodies.

I ran back into the chapel. I grabbed up the head of Bartola and the head of Matteo into my arms. I sat down and held them in my lap, and I sobbed.

They seemed still alive, these severed heads, their eyes flashing, and their lips even moving with hopeless attempts to speak. Oh, God! It was beyond all human endurance. I sobbed.

I cursed.

I laid them side by side, these two heads in my lap, and I stroked their hair and stroked their cheeks and whispered comforting words to them, that God was close, God was with us, God would take care of us forever, that we were in Heaven. Oh, please, I beg you, God, I prayed in my soul, don't let them have the feeling and the consciousness which they still seem to possess. Oh, no, not such. I can't bear it. I cannot. No. Please.

At dawn, finally, when the sun poured arrogantly through the door of the chapel, when the fires had died away, when the birds sang as if nothing had happened, the innocent little heads of Bartola and Matteo were lifeless and still, and very obviously dead, and their immortal souls were gone from them, if they had not flown at the moment when the sword had severed these heads from the bodies.

I found my mother murdered in the courtyard. My father, covered with wounds on his hands and arms, as if he had grabbed at the very swords that struck him, lay dead on the stairs of the tower.

The work all around had been swift. Throats cut, and only here and there the evidence, as with my father, of a great struggle.

Nothing was stolen. My aunts, two dead in the far corner of the chapel, and two others in the yard, wore still all their rings and necklets and circlets about their hair.

Not a jeweled button had been ripped away.

It was the same throughout the entire compound.

The horses were gone, the cattle had roamed into the woods, the fowl flown. I opened the little house full of my hunting falcons, took off their hoods and let them all go into the trees.

There was no one to help me bury the dead.

By noon, I had dragged my family, one by one, to the crypt and tumbled them unceremoniously down the steps, and then laid them all out, side by side in the room, as best I could.

It had been a backbreaking task. I was near to fainting as I composed the limbs of each person, and last of all my father.

I knew that I could not do it for everyone else here in our compound. It was simply impossible. Besides, whatever had come might well come again, as I had been left alive, and there was a hooded demon man who had witnessed it, a vicious hooded assassin who had slaughtered two children piteously.

And whatever was the nature of this angel of death, this exquisite Ursula, with her barely tinted white cheeks and her long neck and sloping shoulders, I didn't know. She herself might come back to avenge the insult I had done her.

I had to leave the mountain.

That these creatures were not anywhere around now I felt instinctively, both in my heart and from the wholesomeness of the warm and loving sun, but also because I had witnessed their flight, heard their whistles to one another and heard the ominous words of the demon man to the woman, Ursula, that she must hurry.

No, these were things of the night.

So I had time to climb the highest tower and look at the country round.

I did. I confirmed that there was no one who could have seen the smoke of our few burning wooden floors and torched furniture. The nearest castle was a ruin, as I have said. The lower hamlets were long abandoned.

The nearest village of any size was a full day's walk, and I had to be off if I meant to get to any kind of hiding place by nightfall.

A thousand thoughts tormented me. I knew too many things. I was a boy; I could not even pass for a man! I had wealth in the Florentine banks but it was a week's ride from where I was! These were demons. Yet they had come into a church. Fra Diamonte had been struck dead.

Only one thought finally was possible for me.

Vendetta. I was going to get them. I was going

to find them and get them. And if they couldn't come out by the light of day, then it would be by that means that I would get them! I would do it. For Bartola, for Matteo, for my father and mother, for the humblest child who had been taken from my mountain.

And they had taken the children. Yes, that they had done. I confirmed it before I left, for it was slow to dawn on me with all my concerns, but they had. There was not a corpse of a child on the place, only those boys of my age had been killed, but anything younger had been stolen away.

For what! For what horrors! I was beside myself.

I might have stood in the tower window, with clenched fist, consumed with anger and the vow for vendetta, if a welcome sight hadn't distracted me. Down in the closest valley, I saw three of my horses wandering about, aimlessly, as though wanting to be called home.

At least I should have one of my finest to ride, but I had to get moving. With a horse I might just reach a town by nightfall. I didn't know the land to the north. It was mountain country, but I had heard of a fair-sized town not too far away. I had to get there, for refuge, to think and to consult with a priest who had a brain in his head and knew demons.

My last task was ignominious and revolting to me, but I did it. I gathered up all the wealth I could carry.

This meant that I retired first to my own room,

as if this were an ordinary day, dressed myself in my best dark hunter's green silk and velvet, put on my high boots and took up my gloves, and then taking the leather bags which I could affix to my horse's saddle, I went down into the crypt and took from my parents and my aunts and uncles their very most treasured rings, necklaces and brooches, the buckles of gold and silver which had come from the Holy Land. God help me.

Then I filled my purse with all the gold ducats and florins I could find in my father's coffers, as if I were a thief, a very thief of the dead it seemed to me, and hefting these heavy leather bags, I went to get my mount, saddle him and bridle him and start off, a man of rank, with his weaponry, and his mink-edged cape, and a Florentine cap of green velvet, off into the forest.

4

IN WHICH I COME UPON FURTHER
MYSTERIES, SUFFER SEDUCTION
AND CONDEMN MY SOUL TO
BITTER VALOR

OW, I was too full of rancor to
be thinking straight, as I've already
described, and surely you will understand this. But it wasn't smart of me
to go riding through the woods of Tuscany dressed
so richly, and by myself, because any woods in Italy
was bound to have its bandits.

On the other hand, playing the poor scholar
wouldn't have been the best choice either, it
seemed to me.

I can't claim to have made a real decision. The
desire for vengeance upon the demons that had
destroyed us was the only central passion I could
abide.

So there I was, riding steadily by mid-afternoon,
trying to keep to the valley roads as I lost sight of
our towers, trying not to cry anymore like a child,
but being drawn off into the mountainous land
over and over again.

My head was swimming. And the landscape gave me little time to think.

Nothing could have been more forlorn.

I came within sight of two huge ruined castles very soon after my departure, copings and ramparts lost in the greedy forest, which made me mindful that these had been the holdings of old Lords who had been fool enough to resist the power of Milan or Florence. It was enough to make me doubt my sanity, enough to make me think that we had not been annihilated by demons but that common enemies had made the assault.

It was utterly grim to see their broken battlements looming against the otherwise cheerful and brilliant sky, and to come upon the overgrown fragments of villages with their tumbledown hovels and forgotten crossroads shrines in which stone Virgins or saints had sunk into spiderwebs and shadows.

When I did spy a high distant well-fortified town, I knew well it was Milanese and had no intention of going up there. I was lost!

As for the bandits, I only ran into one little ragged band, which I took on immediately with a deluge of chatter.

If anything, the little pack of idiots gave me some distraction. My blood ran as fast as my tongue:

"I'm riding in advance of a hundred men," I declared. "We search for a band of outlaws claiming to be fighting for Sforza when they're nothing but rapists and thieves; you seen any of them? I have a florin for each of you if you can tell me anything. We mean to cut them down on sight. I'm tired. I'm sick of this."

I tossed them some coins.

They were off immediately.

But not before they let slip in talk of the country round that the nearest Florentine town was Santa Maddalana, which was two hours up ahead, and that it would close its gates at night, and nobody could talk his way into it.

I pretended to know all about that and to be on the way to a famous monastery that I knew lay farther north, which I couldn't possibly have reached, and then threw more money over my shoulder as I raced off, hollering out that they ought to ride on to meet the band coming behind who would pay them for their service.

I know they were debating all the time whether to kill me and take everything I had or not. It was a matter of stares and bluffs and fast talking and standing one's ground, and they were just utter ruffians, and somehow I got out of it.

I rode off as quickly as I could, left the main road and cut towards the slopes from which I could see in the far distance the vague outline of Santa Maddalana. A big town. I could see four massive towers all gathered near the obvious front gates, and several distinct church steeples.

I had hoped for something before this Santa Maddalana, something small, less fortified. But I couldn't remember names or was too lost now to go looking further.

The afternoon sunshine was brilliant but now at a slant. I had to make for Santa Maddalana.

When I reached the mountain proper on which this town was built, I went up sharply on the small paths used by the shepherds.

The light was fading fast. The forest was too thick to be safe so near a walled town. I cursed them that they didn't keep the mountain cleared, but then I had the safety of cover.

There were moments amid the deepening darkness when it seemed virtually impossible to reach the summit; the stars now lighted a glowing sapphirine sky, but that only made the venerable town in all its majesty seem ever more unattainable.

Finally the heedless night did plunge down amongst the thick trunks of the trees, and I was picking my way, counting on the instincts of my horse more than my own failing vision. The pale half-moon seemed in love with the clouds. The sky itself was nothing but bits and pieces thanks to the canopy of foliage above me.

I found myself praying to my father, as if he were safely with my guardian angels about me, and I think I believed in him and his presence more surely than I had ever believed in angels, saying, "Please, Father, help me get there. Help me get to safety, lest those demons render my vengeance impossible."

I gripped my sword hard. I reminded myself of the daggers I wore in my boots, in my sleeve, in my jacket and in my belt. I strained to see by the light of the sky, and had to trust my horse to pick his way through the thick tree trunks.

At moments I stopped very still. I heard no unusual sound. Who else would be fool enough to be out in the night of this forest? At some point very near the end of the journey, I found the main road, the forest thinned and then gave way to smooth fields and meadows, and I took the twists and turns at a gallop.

At last the town rose right up in front of us, as it happens when you reach the gates by a final turn, you seem to have been thrown up on the ground at the foot of a magic fortress—and I took a deep breath of thanks, no matter that the giant gates were firmly shut as if a hostile army were camped beneath it.

This had to be my haven.

Of course the Watch, a sleepy soldier hollering down from above, wanted to know who I was.

Once again the effort of making up something good distracted me from wayward, near uncontrollable, images of the fiend Ursula and her severed arm, and the decapitated bodies of my brother and sister fallen on the chapel floor in mid-gesture.

I cried out, in a humble tone but with pretentious vocabulary, that I was a scholar in the employ of Cosimo de' Medici come on a search for books in Santa Maddalana, in particular old prayer books pertaining to the saints and appearances of the Blessed Virgin Mary in this district.

What nonsense.

I had come, I declared, to visit the churches and schools and whatever old teachers the town might shelter, and to take back what I could purchase with good gold Florentine coin to my master in Florence.

"Yes, but your name, your name!" the soldier insisted as he opened the small lower gate only a crack, his lantern held high to inspect me.

I knew I made a good picture on my horse.

"De' Bardi," I declared. "Antonio De' Bardi, kinsman of Cosimo," I said with fierce nerve, naming the family of Cosimo's wife because it was the only name that came into my head. "Look, kindly man, take this payment for me, have a good supper with your wife as my guests, here, I know it's late, I'm so tired!"

The gate was opened. I had to dismount to lead my horse with lowered head through it and into the echoing stone piazza right inside.

"What in the name of God," asked the Watchman, "were you doing in these woods after dark alone? Do you know the dangers? And so young? What is the Bardi these days that they let their secretaries go riding all over unescorted?" He pocketed the money. "Look at you, a mere child! Somebody could murder you for your buttons. What's the matter with you?"

This was an immense piazza, and I could see more than one street leading off. Good luck. But what if the demons were here too? I had no clue as to where such things might roost or hide! But I went on talking.

"It's all my fault. I got lost. Tell on me and you'll get me in trouble," I said. "Show me to the Albergo. I'm so tired. Here, take this, no, you must." I gave him more money. "I got lost. I didn't listen. I'm about to faint. I need wine and supper and a bed. Here, good man, no, no, no, take more, I insist. The Bardi would not have it otherwise."

He ran out of pockets for the money, but managed somehow to stuff it in his shirt and then led me by torchlight to the Inn, banging on the door, and a sweet-faced old woman came down, grateful for the coins I thrust into her hand at once, to show me to a room.

"High up and looking out over the valley," I said, "if you please, and some supper, it can be stone cold, I don't care."

"You're not going to find any books in this town," said the Watchman, standing about as I beat it up the stairs after the woman. "All the young people go off; it's a peaceable place, just happy little shopkeepers. Young men today run off to universities. But this is a beautiful place to live, simply beautiful."

"How many churches do you have?" I asked the old woman when we'd reached the room. I told her that I must keep the lighted candle for the night.

"Two Dominican, one Carmelite," said the Watchman, slouching in the little door, "and the beautiful old Franciscan church, which is where I go. Nothing bad ever happens here."

The old woman shook her head and told him to be quiet. She set the candle down and gestured that it could stay.

The Watchman went on chattering as I sat on the bed, staring at nothing, until she'd brought a plate of cold mutton and bread, and a pitcher of wine.

"Our schools are strict," the man went on.

Again the old woman told him to hush up.

"Nobody dares to make trouble in this place," he said, and then both of them were gone.

I fell on my plate like an animal. All I wanted was strength. In my grief I couldn't even think of pleasure. I looked out on a tiny bit of high star-sprinkled sky for a little while, praying desperately to every saint and angel whose name I knew for help, and then I locked up the window tight.

I bolted the door.

And making sure that the candle was well sheltered in the corner, and plenty big enough to last until dawn, I fell into the lumpy little bed, too exhausted to remove boots or sword or daggers or anything else. I thought I'd fall into a deep sleep, but I lay rigid, full of hatred, and hurt, and swollen broken soul, staring into the dark, my mouth full of death as if I'd eaten it.

I could hear distantly the sounds of my horse being tended to downstairs, and some lonely steps on the deserted stone street. I was safe, at least that much was so.

Finally sleep came. It came totally and completely and sweetly; the net of nerves which had held me suspended and maddened simply dissolved, and I sank down into a dreamless darkness.

I was conscious of that sweet point where nothing for the moment matters except to sleep, to replenish and to fear yet no dreams, and then nothing.

A noise brought me around. I was immediately awake. The candle had gone out. I had my hand on my sword before my eyes opened. I lay on the narrow bed, back to the wall, facing the room and in a seemingly sourceless light. I could just make out the bolted door, but I couldn't see the window above me unless I turned my head to look up, and I knew, positively knew, that this window, heavily barred, had been broken open. The little light which fell on the wall came from the sky outside. It was a fragile, weak light, slipping down against the wall of the town and giving my little chamber the attitude of a prison cell.

I felt the cool fresh air come down around my neck and felt it on my cheek. I clutched the sword tight, listening, waiting. There were small creaking sounds. The bed had moved ever so slightly, as if from a pressure.

I couldn't focus my eyes. Darkness suddenly obscured everything, and out of this darkness there rose a shape before me, a figure bending over me, a woman looking right into my face as her hair fell down on me.

It was Ursula.

Her face was not an inch from mine. Her hand, very cool and smooth, closed over my own, on the hilt of my sword, with a deadly force, and she let her eyelashes stroke my cheek and then kissed my forehead.

I was enveloped in sweetness, no matter how hot my rebellion. A sordid flood of sensation penetrated to my very entrails.

"Strega!" I cursed her.

"I didn't kill them, Vittorio." Her voice was imploring but with dignity and a curious sonorous strength, though it was only a small voice, very young in tone and feminine in timbre.

"You were taking them," I said to her. I tried in a violent spasm to free myself. But her hand held me powerfully fast, and when I tried to free my left arm from under me, she caught my wrist and held me there too, and then she kissed me.

There came that magnificent perfume from her which I had breathed in before, and the stroking of her hair on my face and neck sent shameless chills through me.

I tried to turn my head, and she let her lips touch my cheek gently, almost respectfully.

I felt the length of her body against me, the definite swell of her breasts beneath costly fabric, and the smooth length of her thigh beside me in the bed, and her tongue touched my lips. She licked at my lips.

I was immobilized by the chills that went through me, humiliating me and kindling the passion inside me.

"Get away, strega," I whispered.

Filled with rage, I couldn't stop the slow smolder that had caught hold in my loins; I couldn't stop the rapturous sensations that were passing over my shoulders and down my back, and even through my legs.

Her eyes glowed above me, the flicker of her lids more a sensation than a spectacle I could see with my own eyes, and again her lips closed over mine, sucking at my mouth, teasing it, and then she drew back and pressed her cheek against me.

Her skin, which had looked so like porcelain, felt softer than a down feather against me, ah, all of her seemed a soft doll, made of luscious and magical materials far more yielding than flesh and blood yet utterly on fire with both, for a heat came out of her in a rhythmic throb, emanating right from the coolness of her fingers stroking my wrists as they held them, and then the heat of her tongue shot into my lips, against my will, with a wet, delicious and vehement force against which I could do nothing.

There formed in my crazed mind some realization that she had used my own hot desire to render me helpless, that carnal madness had made of me a body constructed about metal wires that could not help but conduct the fire she poured into my mouth.

She drew her tongue back and sucked with her lips again. My entire face was tingling. All my limbs were struggling both against her and to touch her, yes, embrace her yet fight her.

She lay against the very evidence of my desire. I couldn't have hidden it. I hated her.

"Why? What for!" I said, tearing my mouth

loose. Her hair descended on both sides as she lifted her head. I could scarcely breathe for the unearthly pleasure.

"Get off me," I said, "and go back into Hell. What is this mercy to me! Why do this to me?"

"I don't know," she answered in her clever, tremulous voice. "Maybe it's only that I don't want you to die," she said, breathing against my chest. Her words were rapid, like her heated pulse. "Maybe more," she said, "I want you to go away, go south to Florence, go away and forget all that's happened, as if it were nightmares or witches' spells, as if none of it took place; leave this town, go, you must."

"Stop your foul lies," I said before I could stop myself. "You think I'll do that? You murdered my family, you, you and yours, whatever you are!"

Her head dipped, her hair ensnaring me. I fought vainly to get loose. It was out of the question. I couldn't budge her grip.

All was blackness, and indescribable softness. I felt a sudden tiny pain in my throat, no more than the prick of pins, and my mind was suddenly flooded with the most tranquil happiness.

It seemed I'd stumbled into a blowing meadow of flowers, quite far away from this place and from all woes, and she lay with me, fallen against silently crushed stems and uncomplaining irises, Ursula, with her undone ashen hair, and she smiled with the most engaging and demanding eyes, fervent, perhaps even brilliant, as if ours were a sudden and total infatuation of mind as well as body. On my

chest she climbed, and though she rode me, looking down at me with exquisite smiling lips, she
parted her legs gently for me to enter her.

It seemed a delirious blending of elements, the
wet contracting secretive pocket between her legs
and this great abundance of silent eloquence pouring from her gaze as she looked lovingly down
at me.

Abruptly it stopped. I was dizzy. Her lips were
against my neck.

I tried with all my might to throw her off.

"I will destroy you," I said. "I will. I vow it. If I
have to chase you into the mouth of Hell," I whispered. I strained against her grasp so hard that my
own flesh burned against hers. But she wouldn't
relent. I tried to clear my mind. No, no dreams of
sweetness, no.

"Get away from me, witch."

"Hush, be quiet," she said sorrowfully. "You are
so young and so stubborn, and so brave. I was
young like you. Oh, yes, and so determined and
such a fearless paragon."

"Don't talk your filth to me," I said.

"Hush," she said again. "You'll wake the house.
What good will that do?" How painful, earnest and
enticing she sounded. Her voice itself could have
seduced me from behind a curtain. "I cannot make
you safe forever," she said, "or even for very long.
Vittorio, go."

She drew back so that I could see her sincere and
large yielding eyes all the better. She was a masterpiece. And such beauty, the perfect simulacrum of

the fiend I'd seen in the firelight of my chapel, needed no potions or spells to advance her cause. She was flawless and intimately magnificent.

"Oh, yes," she confessed, her half-visible eyes searching my face, "and I do find such beauty in you it pulls on my heart," she said. "Unfairly, unjustly. How am I to suffer this as well as all else?"

I struggled. I wouldn't answer. I wouldn't feed this enigmatic and infernal blaze.

"Vittorio, get out of here," she said, lowering her voice ever more delicately and ominously. "You have a few nights, maybe not even that. If I come to you again, I may lead them to you. Vittorio—. Don't tell anyone in Florence. They'll laugh at you."

She was gone.

The bed creaked and rocked. I was on my back, and my wrists ached from the pressure of her hands, and above me the window gaped on the gray featureless light, the wall beside the Inn rising up towards a sky I couldn't quite see from this helpless vantage point.

I was alone in the room. She was nowhere.

All of a sudden, I willed my limbs to action, but before I could so much as move, she appeared again, above in the window, visible from the waist to the top of her bowed head, peering down at me, and with her hands she tore loose the low embroidered border of her gown and bared her naked white breasts before me—tiny, rounded, very close together and with piquant nipples visible only in their darkness. With her right hand she scratched

74

her left breast, just above the little nipple, made it bleed.

"Witch!"

I rose up to grab hold of her, to kill her, and instead felt her hand grasp my head, and there came the pressure of her left breast into my very mouth, irresistibly frail yet firm. Once again, all that was real melted and was swept away like so much idle smoke rising from a fire, and we were together in the meadow which belonged only to us, only to our diligent and indissoluble embraces. I sucked the milk from her, as if she was maiden and mother, virgin and queen, all the while I broke with my thrusts whatever flower remained inside of her to be torn open.

I was let go. I fell. Helpless, unable even to raise a hand to keep her from flying, I fell down, weak and stupid onto the bed, my face wet and my limbs trembling.

I couldn't sit up. I could do nothing. I saw in flashes our field of tender white irises and red irises, the loveliest flowers of Tuscany, the wild irises of our land, blowing in the greenest grass, and I saw her running away from me. Yet all this was transparent, half-tinted, and could not mask the tiny cell of a room as it had done before, only linger, like a veil drawn across my face, to torment me with its tickling weightless silkiness.

"Spells!" I whispered. "My God, if you have ever committed me to guardian angels, will you spur them on now to cover me with their wings!" I sighed. "I need them."

Finally, shakily and with dim vision, I sat up. I rubbed at my neck. Chills ran up and down my spine, and the backs of my arms. My body was still full of desire.

I squeezed my eyes shut, refusing to think of her yet wanting anything, any source of stimulation, that would soothe this awful need.

I lay back again, and was very still until this carnal madness had left me.

I was a man again then, for not having been, at random, a man.

I got up, ready for tears, and I took my candle down to the main room of the Inn, trying not to make a sound on the crooked winding stone stairs, and I got a light from a candle there on a hook on the wall, at the mouth of the passage, and I went back up, clinging to this comforting little light, shielding the shuddering flame with my cupped hand and praying still, and then I set down the candle.

I climbed up and tried to see what I could from the window.

Nothing, nothing but an impossible drop beneath me, a sloping wall up which a flesh-and-blood maiden could never have climbed, and higher, the mute, passive sky, in which the few stars had been covered by fleecy clouds as if not to acknowledge my prayers or my predicament.

It seemed absolutely certain I was going to die.

I was going to fall victim to these demons. She was right. How could I possibly exact the revenge they deserved? How in Hell could I do it! Yet I believed in my purpose utterly. I believed in my revenge as completely as I believed in her, this witch whom I had touched with my very own fingers, who had dared to kindle a wanton conflict in my soul, who had come with her comrades of the night to slaughter my family.

I couldn't overmaster the images of the night before, of her standing bewildered in the chapel door. I couldn't get the taste of her off my lips. All I had to do was think of her breasts, and my body would weaken as if she were feeding my desire from her nipple.

Make this subside, I prayed. You cannot run. You cannot go off to Florence, you cannot live forever with nothing but the memory of the slaughter you saw, that is impossible, unthinkable. You cannot.

I wept when I realized that I wouldn't be alive now if it had not been for her.

It was she, the ashen-haired one I was cursing with every breath, who had stopped her hooded companion from killing me. It would have been a complete victory!

A calm came over me. Well, if I was going to die, there was no choice, really. I would get them first. I would somehow do it.

As soon as the sun was up, so was I, and walking around the town, my saddlebags over my shoulder casually, as if they didn't contain a fortune, I sized up quite a portion of Santa Maddalana, with its treeless, narrow-stoned streets, built centuries before, perhaps some of its buildings with their wild patternless mortared stones going back even to Roman times.

It was a marvelously peaceful and prosperous town.

The forges were already at work, and so were the cabinetmakers and also the saddlemakers; there were several shoemakers dealing in some fine slippers as well as the workaday boots, and quite a cluster of jewelers and men who worked in a great variety of precious metals, as well as the usual swordmakers, men who made keys and the like and those who dealt in hides and furs.

I passed more fancy shops than I could count. One could buy fancy fabrics here, right from Florence, I supposed, and lace from north and south it seemed, and Oriental spices. The butchers were having a time of it with the abundance of fresh meat. And there were many wine shops, and I passed at least a couple of busy notaries, letter writers and the like, and several doctors or, rather, apothecaries.

Carts were rolling through the front gates, and there was even a little crush in the streets now and then before the sun was even high enough to come fiercely down over the close-tiled roofs and hit the bare stones on which I plodded uphill.

The churches rang their bells for Mass, and I saw plenty of schoolchildren rushing past me, all rather clean and neatly dressed, and then two little crews being paraded by monks into the churches, both of which were quite antique and had no ornament on the front at all, save for statues deep in niches—saints who scarcely had any features left to them at all—the heavily patched stones of the facades obviously having weathered the frequent earthquakes of this region.

There were two rather ordinary bookshops that had almost nothing much, except the prayer books one would expect to find, and these at very high prices. Two merchants sold really fine wares from the East. And there was a cluster of carpet sellers, too, who dealt in an impressive variety of country-made goods and intricate carpets from Byzantium.

Lots of money was changing hands. There were well-dressed people showing off their fine clothes. It seemed a self-sufficient place, though there were travelers coming uphill with the clop of horses' hooves echoing on the barren walls. And I think I spied one neglected and very much fortified convent.

I passed at least two more inns, and as I criss-crossed through the barely passable alleyways here and there, I ascertained that there were actually three basic streets to the town, all running parallel up and down the hill.

At the far deep end were the gates by which I had entered, and the huge farmers' markets opened now in the piazza.

At the high end was the ruined fortress or castle where once the Lord had lived—a great cumbersome mass of old stones, of which only a part was visible from the street, and in the lower floors of this complex there were the town's governing offices.

There were several small grottoes or piazzas,

and old fountains almost crumbled away but still giving forth their gurgling water. Old women were busy, shuffling along with their market baskets and their shawls in spite of the warmth; and I saw beautiful young girls about giving me the eye, all of them very young.

I didn't want any part of them.

As soon as Mass was over and school had begun, I went to the Dominican church—the largest and most impressive of the three I could readily see—and asked at the rectory for a priest. I had to go to Confession.

There came out a young priest, very handsome with well-formed limbs and a healthy look to his complexion and a truly devout manner to him, his black and white robes very clean-looking. He looked at my attire, and my sword, indeed he took me in very respectfully but quite comprehensively, and obviously presuming me to be a person of importance, invited me into a small room for the Confession.

He was gracious more than servile. He had no more than a crown of golden hair clipped very short around the top of his bald head, and large almost shy eyes.

He sat down, and I knelt close to him on the bare floor, and then out of me came the whole lurid tale.

With bowed head, I went on and on with it, rushing from one thing to another, from the first hideous happenings that had so stirred my curiosity and alarm, to my father's fragmented and mysterious words and at last to the raid itself and

the dreadful assassination of everyone in our compound. By the time I came to the death of my
brother and sister, I was gesticulating madly, and all
but shaping my brother's head with my hands in
the empty air, and gasping and unable to catch my
breath.

Only when I was utterly finished with every last
word did I look up and realize that the young priest
was staring down at me in perfect distress and
horror.

I didn't know what to make of his expression.
You could have seen the very same face on a man
startled by an insect or an approaching battalion of
bloody murderers.

What had I expected, for the love of God?

"Look, Father," I said. "All you have to do is
send someone up that mountain and see for yourself!" I shrugged, and implored him with my open
hands. "That's all! Send someone to look. Nothing's stolen, Father, nothing's taken, but what I
took! Go look! I'll wager nothing has been disturbed except by ravens and buzzards if such are
like to go up there."

He said nothing. The blood was palpitating in
his young face, and his mouth was open and his
eyes had a dazed, miserable look.

Oh, this was too marvelous. A silky boy of a
priest, probably fresh out of the seminary, used to
hearing nuns tell of evil thoughts, and men once a
year muttering resentfully about vices of the flesh
because their wives had dragged them to their
duty.

I became incensed.

"You are under the Seal of the Confessional," I said, trying to be patient with him, and not to play the Lord too much, because I could do that with priests if I wasn't careful; they made me so mad when they were stupid. "But I will give you permission, under the Seal, to send a messenger up that mountain to see with your own eyes . . ."

"But son, don't you see," he said, speaking with surprising resolve and firmness in his low voice. "The Medici themselves may have sent this band of assassins."

"No, no, no, Father," I pleaded, shaking my head. "I saw her hand fall. I cut off the creature's hand, I tell you. I saw her put it back. They were demons. Listen to me. These are witches, these are from Hell, these beings, and there's too many of them for me to fight alone. I need help. There's no time for disbelief. There's no time for rational reservations. I need the Dominicans!"

He shook his head. He didn't even hesitate.

"You are losing your mind, son," he said. "Something dreadful has happened to you, there's no doubt of that, and you believe all this, but it didn't happen. You are imagining things. Look, there are old women around who claim they make charms . . ."

"I know all that," I said. "I know an ordinary alchemist or witch when I see one. This was no side-street magic, Father, no country bunch of curses. I'm telling you, these demons slaughtered everyone in the castle, in the villages. Don't you see?"

I went into the lurid particulars again. I told how she had come into the window of my room, but then when I was halfway through it, I realized how utterly worse I was making it by going on about Ursula.

Why, this man thought I'd woken in a hot dream, imagining a damned succubus. This was futile, this entire enterprise.

My heart was hurting me in my chest. I was sweating all over. This was a waste of time.

"Give me absolution, then," I said.

"I want to ask something of you," he said. He touched my hand. He was trembling. He looked more dazed and perplexed than even before, and very concerned, for my state of mind, I assumed.

"What is that?" I said coldly. I wanted to get away. I had to find a monastery! Or a damned alchemist. There were alchemists in this town. I could find someone, someone who had read the old works, the works of Hermes Trismegistus or Lactantius or St. Augustine, somebody who knew about demons.

"Have you read St. Thomas Aquinas?" I asked, choosing the most obvious demonologist of whom I could think. "Father, he talks all about demons. Look, you think I would have believed all this myself last year at this time? I thought all sorcery was for backdoor swindlers. These were demons!" I could not be deterred. I went at him.

"Father, in the *Summa Theologica*, the first book, St. Thomas talks of the fallen angels, that some of them are allowed to be here on earth, so that all of these fallen angels don't just fall out of the natural scheme of things. They are here, allowed to be useful, to tempt men, and Father, they carry the fire of Hell about with them! It's in St. Thomas. They are here. They have . . . have . . . bodies we can't understand. The *Summa* says so. It says that angels have bodies which are beyond our understanding! That's what this woman possesses." I struggled to remember the actual argument. I struggled in Latin. "This is what she does, this being! It's a form, it's a limited form, but one that I can't understand, but she was there, and I know it on account of her actions."

He put up his hand for my patience.

"Son, please," he said. "Allow me to confide what you have confessed to me to the Pastor," he asked me. "You understand, if I do this, he too will be bound by the same Seal of Confession as I am bound. But let me ask him to come in and let me tell him what you have said, and let me ask that he speak to you. You understand, I cannot do any of this without your solemn permission."

"Yes, I know all that," I said. "What good will this do? Let me see this Pastor."

Now I was being too haughty entirely, too impertinent. I was exhausted. I was doing the old Signore trick of treating a country priest like he was a servant. This was a man of God, and I had to get a grip on myself. Maybe the Pastor had read more, understood more. Oh, but who would understand who had not seen?

There came back to me a fleeting yet vivid and

searing memory of my father's anxious face on the night before the demons had struck. The pain was inexpressible.

"I'm sorry, Father," I said to the priest. I winced, trying to contain this memory, this awful drench of misery and hopelessness. I wondered why any of us were alive, ever, for any reason!

And then the words of my exquisite tormentor came back, her own tortured voice of the last night saying that she had been young too, and such a paragon. What had she meant, speaking of herself with such sorrow?

My study of Aquinas came back to haunt me. Were not demons supposed to remain absolutely confirmed in their hatred of us? In the pride which had made them sin?

That was not the sinuous luscious creature who had come to me. But this was folly. I was feeling for her, which is what she had wanted me to do. I had only so many hours of daylight to plan her destruction and must be on with it.

"Please, yes, Father, as you wish," I said. "But bless me first."

This drew him out of his troubled ruminations. He looked at me as if I'd startled him.

At once he gave his blessing and his absolution.

"You can do what you wish with the Pastor," I said. "Yes, please, ask the Pastor if he will see me. And here, for the church." I gave him several ducats.

He stared at the money. But he didn't touch it. He stared at this gold as if it were hot coals.

"Father, take it. This is a tidy little fortune. Take it."

"No, you wait here—or I tell you what, you come out into the garden."

The garden was lovely, a little old grotto, from which you could see the town sneaking up on the right all the way to the castle, and then you could see over the walls far out over the mountains. There was an antique statue of St. Dominic there, a fountain and a bench, and some old words carved into the stone about a miracle.

I sat down on the bench. I looked up at the healthy blue sky and the virgin white clouds, and I tried to catch my breath inside of myself. Could I be mad? I wondered. That was ridiculous.

The Pastor startled me. He came plunging out of the low arched doorway of the rectory, an elderly man with almost no hair at all, and a small bulging nose and ferocious large eyes. The younger priest was running to keep up with him.

"Get out of here," the Pastor said to me in a whisper. "Get out of our town. Get clear away from it, and don't tell your stories to anybody in it, you hear me?"

"What?" I asked. "What sort of solace is this!"

He was steaming. "I'm warning you."

"Warning me of what?" I demanded. I didn't bother to get up from the bench. He glowered over me. "You're under the Seal of Confession. What are you going to do if I don't leave?" I asked.

"I don't have to do anything, that's just it!" he said. "Go away and take your misery with you." He stopped, clearly at a loss, embarrassed perhaps, as if he'd said something he regretted. He ground his teeth and looked off and then back at me.

"For your own sake, leave," he said in a whisper. He looked at the other priest. "You go," he said, "and let me talk to him."

The young priest was in a total fright. He left immediately.

I looked up at the Pastor.

"Leave," he said to me in his low, mean voice, his lower lip drawing back to reveal his lower teeth. "Get out of our town. Get out of Santa Maddalana."

I looked at him with cold contempt. "You know about them, don't you?" I said in a low voice.

"You're mad. Mad!" he said. "If you speak of demons to people here you'll end up burnt at the stake yourself for a sorcerer. You think it can't happen?"

It was hatred in his eyes, shameless hatred.

"Oh, poor damned priest," I said, "you're in league with the Devil."

"Get out!" he growled.

I got up and looked down into his swelling eyes, his pouting, overworked mouth.

"Don't you dare break the Seal of my Confession, Father," I said. "If you do, I'll kill you."

He stood stock-still, staring at me.

I smiled very coldly and went to pass on through the rectory and away.

He ran after me, whispering like a steaming kettle. "You misunderstand everything. You're crazy, you're imagining things. I'm trying to save you from persecution and villainization."

I turned around at the door to the church and glared him into utter silence.

"You've tipped your hand," I said. "You're too merciless. Remember what I said. Break the Seal and I'll kill you."

He was as frightened now as the young priest had been.

I stood looking at the altar for a long while, ignoring him, forgetting him utterly, my mind pretending to have thoughts in it, to be construing and planning when all I could do was endure. Then I made the Sign of the Cross and I left the church.

I was in utter despair.

For a while I walked around. Once again, it was only the most pleasant town I had ever seen, with everyone happily at work, with best-swept cobbled streets, and pretty flower boxes under all the windows, and prettily dressed people going about their affairs.

It was the cleanest place I'd ever seen in my life, and the most contented. And the people, they were all eager to sell me their wares, but they didn't press it terribly much. But it was an awfully dull town in a way. There were no people my age, none at all that I saw. In fact, there weren't all that many children.

What should I do? Where should I go? What was I looking for?

I didn't quite know how to answer my own questions, but I was certainly on my guard for the slightest evidence that this town somehow harbored the demons, that Ursula had not found me here, but that I had found her.

The mere thought of her overcame me with a cool, inviting shock of desire. I saw her breasts, felt the taste of her, saw in a blurred flash the flowered meadow. No!

Think. Make some plan. As for this town, no matter what the priest knew, these people were too wholesome for harboring demons.

5

THE PRICE OF PEACE AND THE
PRICE OF VENGEANCE

S the heat of the day started to really rise, I went into the arbor of the Inn for the heavy noon meal and sat down by myself under the wisteria, which was blooming magnificently over the latticework. This place was on the same side of the town as the Dominican church, and it too had a lovely view of the town to the left and a view out over the mountains.

I closed my eyes, and putting my elbows on the table, I clasped my hands and I prayed. "God, tell me what to do. Show me what is to be done." And then I was quiet in my heart, waiting, thinking.

What were my choices?

Take this tale to Florence? Who would believe it? Go to Cosimo himself and tell him this story? Much as I admired and trusted the Medici, I had to realize something. Nobody of my family was living but me. I alone could lay claim to our fortunes in the Medici bank. I didn't think Cosimo would deny my signature or my face. He'd give over to me what was mine, whether I had kinsmen or not, but a story of demons? I'd wind up locked up somewhere in Florence!

And talk of the stake, of being burnt for a sorcerer, that was entirely possible. Not likely. But possible. It could happen very suddenly and spontaneously in a town like this, a mob gathering, denunciations by a local priest, people shouting and running to see what was up. This did now and then happen to people.

About this time, my meal was set out for me, a good meal with plenty of fresh fruit and well-cooked mutton and gravy, and as I started to dip my bread and eat, up came two men who asked to sit down with me and buy a cup of wine for me.

I realized one of them was a Franciscan, a very kindly-looking priest, poorer it seemed than the Dominicans, which was logical I suppose, and the other an elderly man with little twinkling eyes and long stiff white eyebrows, sticking up as if with glue, as if he were costumed as a cheerful elf to delight children.

"We saw you go in to the Dominicans," said the Franciscan quietly and politely and smiling at me. "You didn't look so happy when you came out." He winked. "Why don't you try us?" Then he laughed. It was no more than a good-natured joke and I knew it, about the rivalry of the two orders. "You're a fine-looking young man; you come from Florence?" he asked.

"Yes, Father, traveling," I said, "though where exactly, I don't know. I'm stopped here for a while, I think." I was talking with my mouth full, but I was too hungry to stop. "Sit down, please." I started to rise, but they sat down.

I bought another pitcher of red wine for the table.

"Well, you couldn't have found a finer place," said the little old man, who seemed to have his wits about him, "that is why I am so happy that God sent my own son, back here, to serve in our church, so that he could live out his days by his family."

"Ah, so you are father and son," I said.

"Yes, and I never thought I'd live so long," said the father, "to see such prosperity come to this town as has come. It's miraculous."

"It is, it is the blessing of God," said the priest innocently and sincerely. "It's a true wonder."

"Oh, really, instruct me in this, how so?" I asked. I pushed the plate of fruit to them. But they said they had eaten.

"Well, in my time," said the father, "you know we had more than our share of woes, or that's how it seemed to me. But now? It's utter bliss, this place. Nothing bad ever happens."

"It's true," said the priest. "You know, I remember the lepers we had in the old days, who lived outside the walls. They are all gone now. And then there were always a few really bad youths, young men causing trouble, you know, the really bad sort. You had them in every town. But now? You couldn't find one bad man in all of Santa Maddalana or in any of the villages around. It's as if people have returned to God with their whole hearts."

"Yes," said the old elfin man, shaking his head, "and God has been merciful in so many other ways."

I felt chills on my back again, as I had with Ursula, but it was not from pleasure.

"In what way is that, in particular?" I asked.

"Well, look around," said the old man. "Have you seen any cripples in our streets? Do you see any half-wits? When I was a child, why, when you, my son, were a child"—he said to the priest— "there were always a few unfortunate souls, born ill formed, or without good brains, you know, and one had to look out for them. I can remember a time when there were always beggars at the gates. We have no beggars, haven't had any for years."

"Amazing," I said.

"Yes, true," said the priest thoughtfully. "Everyone here is in good health. That's why the nuns left so long ago. Did you see the old hospital shut up? And the convent out of town, long abandoned. I think there are sheep in there now. The farmers use its old rooms."

"No one ever takes sick?" I asked.

"Well, they do," said the priest, taking a slow drink of his wine, as though he were a moderate man in this respect, "but they don't suffer, you know. It's not like the old days. It seems if a person is like to go, then he goes quickly."

"Yes, true, thanks be to God," said the elder.

"And the women," said the priest, "they are

lucky here in birth. They are not burdened with so many children. Oh, we have many whom God calls home to himself in the first few weeks—you know, it's the curse of a mother—but in general, our families are blessedly small." He looked to his father. "My poor mother," he said, "she had twenty babies all told. Well, that never happens now, does it?"

The little old man stuck out his chest and smiled proudly. "Aye, twenty children I reared myself; well, many have gone their way, and I don't even know what became of . . . but never mind. No, families are small here now."

The priest looked slightly troubled. "My brothers, maybe someday God will grant me some knowledge of what became of them."

"Oh, forget about them," said the old man.

"Were they a spirited bunch, might I ask?" I said under my breath, peering at both of them and trying to make it seem quite natural.

"Bad," muttered the priest, shaking his head. "But that's our blessing, see, bad people leave us."

"Is that so?" I asked.

The little old man scratched his pink scalp. His white hair was thin and long, sticking in all directions, rather like the hair of his eyebrows.

"You know, I was trying to remember," he said, "what did happen to those poor cripple boys, you remember, the ones born with such miserable legs, they were brothers . . ."

"Oh, Tomasso and Felix," said the priest.

"Yes."

"They were taken off to Bologna to be cured.

Same as Bettina's boy, the one born without his hands, remember, poor little child."

"Yes, yes, of course. We have several doctors."

"Do you?" I said. "I wonder what they do," I murmured. "What about the town council, the *gonfalonier*?" I asked. *Gonfalonier* was the name for the governor in Florence, the man who nominally, at least, ran things.

"We have a *borsellino*," said the priest, "and we pick a new six or eight names out of it now and then, but nothing much ever happens here. There's no quarreling. The merchants take care of the taxes. Everything runs smoothly."

The little elfin man went into laughter. "Oh, we have no taxes!" he declared.

His son, the priest, looked at the old fellow as though this was not something that ought to be said, but then he himself merely looked puzzled. "Well, no, Papa," he said, "it's only that the taxes are . . . small." He seemed perplexed.

"Well, then you are really blessed," I said agreeably, trying on the surface to make light of this utterly implausible picture of things.

"And that terrible Oviso, remember him?" the priest suddenly said to his father and then to me. "Now that was a diseased fellow. He nearly killed his son. He was out of his mind, roared like a bull. There was a traveling doctor who came through, said they would cure him at Padua. Or was it Assisi?"

"I'm glad he never came back," said the old man. "He used to drive the town crazy."

I studied them both. Were they serious? Were

they talking double-talk to me? I could see nothing cunning in either one of them, but a melancholy was coming over the priest.

"God does work in the strangest ways," he said. "Oh, I know that's not quite the proverb."

"Don't tempt the Almighty!" said his father, downing the dregs of his cup.

I quickly poured out the wine for both of them.

"The little mute fellow," said a voice.

I looked up. It was the innkeeper, with his hands on his hips, his apron stretching over his pot-belly, a tray in his hand. "The nuns took him with them, didn't they?"

"Came back for him, I think," said the priest. He was now fully preoccupied. Troubled, I would say.

The innkeeper took up my empty plate.

"The worst scare was the plague," he whispered in my ear. "Oh, it's gone now, believe you me, or I wouldn't utter the word. There's no word that will empty a town any faster."

"No, all those families, gone, just like that," said the old man, "thanks to our doctors, and the visiting monks. All taken to the hospital in Florence."

"Plague victims? Taken to Florence?" I asked, in obvious disbelief. "I wonder who was minding the city gates, and which gate it was by which they were admitted."

The Franciscan stared at me fixedly for a moment, as if something had disturbed him violently and deeply.

The innkeeper gave the priest's shoulder a

squeeze. "These are happy times," he said. "I miss the processions to the monastery—it's gone too, of course—but we have never been better."

I let my eyes shift quite deliberately from the innkeeper to the priest and found that the priest was gazing directly at me. There seemed a tremor to the edge of his mouth. He was sloppily shaven and had a loose jaw, and his deeply creased face looked sad suddenly.

The very old man chimed in that there had been a whole family down with the plague out in the country not very long ago, but they had been taken to Lucca.

"It was the generosity of . . . who was it, my son, I don't . . ."

"Oh, what does it matter?" said the innkeeper. "Signore," he said to me, "some more wine."

"For my guests," I gestured. "I have to be off. Restless limbs," I said. "I must see what books are for sale."

"This is a fine place for you to stay," said the priest with sudden conviction, his voice soft as he continued to gaze at me, his eyebrows knitted. "A fine place indeed, and we could use another scholar. But—."

"Well, I'm rather young myself," I said. I made ready to rise, putting one leg over the bench. "There are no young men here of my age?"

"Well, they go off, you see," said the elfin one. "There are a few, but they are busy at the trades of their fathers. No, the rapscallions don't hang around here. No, young man, they do not!"

The priest studied me as if he didn't hear his father's voice.

"Yes, and you're a learned young man," said the priest, but he was clearly troubled. "I can see that, and hear it in your voice, and all about you is thoughtful and clever—." He broke off. "Well, I guess you'll be on your way very soon, won't you?"

"You think I should?" I asked. "Or stay, which is it?" I made my manner mild, not unkind.

He gave me a half-smile. "I don't know," he said. Then he looked dour again and almost tragic. "God be with you," he whispered.

I leant towards him. The innkeeper, seeing this confidential manner, turned away and busied himself somewhere else. The old elfin one was talking to his cup.

"What is it, Father?" I asked in a whisper. "Is the town too well-off, is that it?"

"Go on your way, son," he said almost wistfully. "I wish I could. But I'm bound by my vow of obedience and by the fact that this is my home, and here sits my father, and all the others have vanished into the wide world." He became suddenly hard. "Or so it seems," he said. And then, "If I were you, I wouldn't stay here."

I nodded.

"You look strange, son," he said to me in the same whisper. Our heads were right together. "You stand out too much. You're pretty and encased in velvet, and it's your age; you're not really a child, you know."

"Yes, I see, not very many young men in the

town at all, not the sort who question things. Just the old and the complacent and those who accept and who don't see the tapestry for the one small monkey embroidered in the corner."

He didn't answer this overzealous streak of rhetoric, and I was sorry I'd said it. In that little lapse perhaps my anger and my pain had flashed through. Disgusting! I was angry with myself.

He bit his lip, anxious for me, or for himself, or for both of us.

"Why did you come here?" he asked sincerely, almost protectively. "By which way did you come? They said you came in the night. Don't leave by night." His voice had become such a whisper I could scarcely hear him.

"You don't need to worry about me, Father," I said. "Pray for me," I said. "That's all."

I saw in him a species of fear as real as that which I had seen in the young priest, but it was even more innocent, for all his age, and all his wrinkles, and the wetness of his lips with the wine. He looked fatigued by that which he couldn't comprehend.

I stepped free of the bench and was on my way when he grasped my hand. I bent my ear to his lips.

"My boy," he said, "there's something . . . something . . ."

"I know, Father," I said. I patted his hand.

"No, you don't. Listen. When you leave, take the main road south, even if it's out of your way. Don't go north; don't take the narrow road north."

"Why not?" I demanded.

Doubting, silent, utterly stricken, he let go of me.

"Why not?" I said in his ear.

He was no longer facing me. "Bandits," he said. "Toll bandits who control the road; they'll make you pay to go through. Go south." He turned sharply away from me and began to speak to his father in a soft gentle scolding manner as if I was already on my way.

I left.

I was stunned as I set foot in the hollow street. "Toll bandits?"

Many shops were shut now, as was definitely the custom after the heavy meal, but others were not.

My sword weighed a ton on my hip, and I felt feverish from the wine and dizzy from all these people had revealed to me.

So, I thought, my face burning, we have a town here with no young men, no cripples, no half-wits, no diseased people and no unwanted children! And on the road north we have dangerous bandits.

I moved downhill, walking faster and faster, and went out the wide-open gates and into the open country. The breeze was at once magnificent and welcome.

All around me lay rich, well-tended fields, vineyards, patches of orchard and farmhouses—lush and fertile vistas which I couldn't see when I had come in by darkness. As for the road north, I could see nothing of it due to the immense size of the town, whose uppermost fortifications were northward.

I could see, below on a ridge, what must have

been the ruins of the convent and, way down the mountain and far off to the west, what might have been the monastery.

I made my way to two farms within the hour, having a cup of cool water with both farmers.

It was all the same, talk of a paradise here, free of miscreants and the horror of executions, absolutely the most peaceful place in the world, and only well-formed children everywhere.

It had been years since any bandits had dared to linger in the woods. Of course you never knew who might pass through, but the town was strong and kept the peace.

"Oh, not even on the north road?" I asked.

Neither farmer knew anything about any north road.

When I asked what became of the unhealthy, the lame, the injured, it was the same. Some doctor or other, or priest, or order of friars or nuns, had taken them off to a university or city. The farmers sincerely couldn't remember.

I came back into the town well before twilight. I went poking around, in and out of every shop, in a near systematic manner, eyeing everyone as closely as I might without attracting undue attention.

Of course I couldn't hope to cover even one street of the place, but I was determined to discover what I could.

In the booksellers, I went through the old *Ars Grammatica* and *Ars Minor*, and the big beautiful Bibles that were for sale, which I could only see by asking that they be taken out of the cabinets.

"How do I go north from here?" I asked the

bored man who leaned on his elbow and looked at me sleepily.

"North, nobody goes north," he said, and yawned in my face. He wore fine clothes without a sign of mending, and good new shoes of well-worked leather. "Look, I have much finer books than that," he said.

I pretended interest, then explained politely that all were more or less what I had and did not need, but thank you.

I went into a tavern where men were busy at dice and shouting over the game, lustily, as though they had nothing better to do. And then through the bakers' district, where the bread smelled wondrously delicious, even to me.

I had never felt so utterly alone in my life, as I walked among these people listening to their pleasant talk and hearing the same tale of safety and blessings over and over again.

It froze my blood to think of nightfall. And what was this mystery of the road north? Nobody, nobody but the priest, even raised an eyebrow at the mention of that point of the compass.

About an hour before dark, I happened into one shop where the proprietor, a dealer in silks and lace from Venice and Florence, was not so patient with my idle presence, as others had been, in spite of the fact that I obviously had money.

"Why are you asking so many questions?" she said to me. She seemed tired and worn out. "You think it's easy to take care of a sick child? Look in there."

I stared at her as if she'd lost her mind. But then it dawned on me, clear and cold. I knew exactly what she meant. I poked my head through a curtained doorway and saw a child, feverish and sick, slumbering in a dirty narrow bed.

"You think it's easy? Year after year she doesn't get better," said the woman.

"I'm sorry," I said. "But what's to be done?"

The woman tore out her stitches and put down her needle. She seemed past all patience. "What's to be done? You mean to tell me you don't know!" she whispered. "You, a clever man like you!" She bit into her lip. "But my husband says, No, not yet, and so we go on with it."

She went back to her work, muttering to herself, and I, horrified and struggling to keep a straight face, made my way on. I went into a couple more shops. Nothing special happened. Then in the third on my way, I found an old man very out of his wits and his two daughters both trying to keep him from tearing his clothes off.

"Here, let me help you," I said at once.

We got him down in the chair, got his shirt over his head, and finally he stopped making incoherent noises. He was very wizened and drooling.

"Oh, thank God, this won't go on long," said one of the daughters, wiping her brow. "It's a mercy."

"Why won't it go on long?" I asked.

She glanced up at me, and away, and then back again. "Oh, you're a stranger here, Signore, forgive me, you are so young. I only saw a boy when I looked at you. I mean God will be merciful. He's very old."

"Hmmm, I see," I said.

She looked at me with cold cunning eyes, as if they were made of metal.

I bowed and went out. The old man had started to take off his shirt again, and the other sister, who had been silent all the time, slapped him.

I winced at it, and kept walking. I meant to see as much as I could right now.

Passing through rather peaceful little tailors' shops I came at last to the district of the porcelain dealers, where two men were having an argument about a fancy birthing tray.

Now, birthing trays, once used in practicality to receive the infant as it came from the womb, had become by my time fancy gifts given after the child was born. They were large platters painted with lovely domestic designs, and this shop had an impressive display of them.

I heard the argument before I was seen.

One man said to buy the damned tray, while the other said the infant wouldn't even live and the gift was premature, and a third man said the woman would welcome the beautiful gorgeously painted birthing tray anyway.

They stopped when I entered the shop proper to look at all the imported wares, but then when I turned my back, one of the men uttered under his breath, "If she has a brain in her head, she'll do it."

I was struck by the words, so struck that I

turned at once to snatch a handsome plate from the shelf and pretend to be much impressed with it. "So lovely," I said, as if I hadn't heard them.

The merchant got up and started to extol the contents on display. The others melted into the gathering evening outside. I stared at the man.

"Is the child sick?" I asked in the smallest most childish voice that I myself could muster.

"Oh, no, well, I don't think so, but you know how it is," said the man. "The child's smallish."

"Weak," I volunteered.

In a very clumsy way, he said, "Yes, weak." His smile was artificial, but he thought himself quite successful.

Then both of us turned to fussing over the wares. I bought a tiny porcelain cup, very beautifully painted, which he claimed to have bought from a Venetian.

I knew damned good and well I should leave without a word, but I couldn't stop myself from asking him as I paid, "Do you think the poor smallish weak child will live?"

He laughed a rather deep coarse laugh as he took my money. "No," he said, and then he glanced at me as though he'd been in his thoughts. "Don't worry about it, Signore," he said with a little smile. "Have you come to live here?"

"No, Sir, only passing through, going north," I said.

"North?" he asked, a little startled but sarcastic. He shut up the cashbox and turned the key. Then shaking his head as he put the box into the cabinet and closed the doors, he said, "North, eh? Well, good luck to you, my boy." He gave a sour chuckle. "That's an ancient road. You better ride as fast as you can from sunup."

"Thank you, Sir," I said.

Night was coming on.

I hurried into an alleyway and stood there, against the wall, catching my breath as though someone were chasing me. I let the little cup fall and it shattered loudly, the noise echoing up the towering buildings.

I was half out of my wits.

But instantly, and fully aware of my situation, and convinced of the horrors I had discovered, I made an inflexible decision.

I wasn't safe in the Inn, so what did this matter? I was going to do it my way and see for myself.

This is what I did.

Without going back to the Inn, without ever officially leaving my room in the Inn, I turned uphill when the shadows were thick enough to cover me, and I climbed the narrowing street towards the old ruined castle.

Now all day I had been looking at this imposing collection of rock and decay, and could see that it was indeed utterly ruined and empty of all save the birds of the air, except, as I have said, for the lower floors, which supposedly held offices.

But the castle had two standing towers remaining to it, one that faced over the town, and another, much fallen away, beyond and remote on the edge of a cliff, as I had seen from the lower farmland.

Well, I made for the tower that overlooked the town.

The government offices were shut up of course already, and the curfew soldiers would soon be out, and there was noise from only a couple of taverns that obviously stayed open no matter what the law was.

The piazza before the castle was empty, and because the three streets of the town took many a curve in their way downhill, I could see almost nothing now but a few dim torches.

The sky, however, was wondrously bright, clear of all but the most rounded and discreetly shaped clouds, very visible against the deeper blue of the night, and the stars seemed exquisitely numerous.

I found old winding stairs, too narrow almost for a human being, that curved around the useful part of the old citadel and led up to the first platform of stone, before an entrance to the tower.

Of course this architecture was no stranger to me whatsoever. The stones were of a rougher texture than those of my old home, and somewhat darker, but the tower was broad and square and timelessly solid.

I knew that the place was ancient enough that I would find stone stairways leading quite high, and I did, and soon came to the end of my trek in a high room which gave me a view of the entire town stretched out before me.

There were higher chambers, but they had been accessible in centuries past by wooden ladders that could be pulled up, to defeat an enemy and isolate him below, and I couldn't get to them. I could hear the birds up there, disturbed by my presence. And I could hear the breeze moving faintly.

However, this was fine, this height.

I had a view all around from the four narrow windows of this place, looking in all directions.

And most especially, and important to me, I could see the town itself, directly below me, shaped like a great eye—an oval with tapered ends—with random torches burning here and there, and an occasional dimly lighted window, and I could see a lantern moving slowly as some-one walked in a leisurely pace down one of the thoroughfares.

No sooner had I seen this moving lantern than it went out. It seemed the streets were utterly deserted.

Then the windows too went dark, and very shortly there were not four torches that I could see anywhere.

This darkness had a calming effect on me. The open country sank into a deep dark tinge of blue beneath the pearly heavens, and I could see the forests encroaching on the tilled land, creeping higher here and there, as the hills folded over one another or sank steeply into valleys of pure blackness.

I could hear the total emptiness of the tower.

Nothing stirred now, not even the birds. I was quite alone. I could have heard the slightest footfall on the stairs down below. No one knew I was here. All slept.

I was safe here. And I could keep a vigil.

I was too full of misery to be frightened, and frankly I was prepared to take my stand against Ursula in this spot, preferred it, in fact, to the confines of the Inn, and I feared nothing as I said my prayers and laid my hand on my sword as usual.

What did I expect to see in this sleeping town? *Anything that happened in it.*

Now, what did I think that was to be? I couldn't have told anyone. But as I circled the room, as I glanced again and again down at the few scattered lights below and the hulk of the descending ramparts beneath the glowing summer sky, the place seemed loathsome, full of deceit, full of witchcraft, full of payment to the Devil.

"You think I don't know where your unwanted babies are taken?" I muttered in a rage. "You think that people who are down with the plague are welcomed right through the open gates of your neighboring cities?"

I was startled by the echoes of my own murmurings off the cold walls.

"But what do you do with them, Ursula? What would you have done with my brother and sister?"

My ruminations were madness perhaps, or might have seemed so to some. But I learnt this. Revenge takes one's mind from the pain. Revenge is a lure, a mighty molten lure, even if it is hopeless.

One blow from this sword and I can strike off her head, I thought, and heave it out that window, and then what will she be but a demon stripped of all worldly power?

Now and then I half-drew my sword, then put

it back. I took out my longest dagger and slapped the palm of my left hand with its blade. I never stopped walking.

Suddenly, as I made one of my boring circumlocutions, I happened to spy far away, on a distant mountain, in which direction I really didn't know—but not the direction by which I had come—a great quantity of light playing behind the mesh of the sylvan darkness.

At first I thought this might be a fire, there was so much light, but as I narrowed my eyes and focused my mind, I saw that this was out of the question.

There was no riotous glare on the few visible clouds above, and the illumination, for all the breadth of it, was contained as if it emanated from a vast congregation gathered together with a fantastical quantity of candles. How steady yet pulsing was this orgy of fierce light!

I felt a chill in my bones as I looked at it. It was a dwelling! I leant over the window edge. I could see its complex and sprawling outline! It stood out from all the land, this one luxuriantly lighted castle, all by itself, and obviously visible from one entire side of this town, this spectacle of forest-shrouded house in which some celebration appeared to require that every torch and taper be lighted, that every window, battlement and coping be hung with lanterns.

North, yes, north, for the town dropped straight off behind me, and this castle lay north, and it was that direction of which I'd been warned, and who in this town could not have known of this place, yet there had not been one single solitary mention save for the whisper of the terrified Franciscan in the Inn at my table.

But what was I looking at? What could I see? Thick woods, yes; it was very high but surrounded by close and concealing woods, through which its light again and again palpitated like a great menace, but what was that coming from it, what was that wild, half-visible movement in the darkness, over the slopes that fell away from the mysterious promontory?

Were there things moving in the night? Moving from that very distant castle right towards this village? Amorphous black things, as if they were great soft shapeless birds following the alignment of the land but free of its gravity. Were they coming towards me? Had I been charmed?

No, I saw this. Or did I?

There were dozens of them!

They were coming closer and closer.

They were tiny shapes, not large at all, the largeness having been a delusion caused by the fact that they traveled in packs, these things, and now, as they came near to the town, the packs broke apart and I saw them springing up to the very walls beyond me on either side like so many giant moths.

I turned around and ran to the window.

They had descended in a swarm upon the town! I could see them dip down and vanish in the blackness. Below me on the piazza, there appeared two black shapes, men in streaming capes, who ran or rather leapt into the mouths of the streets, issuing from their lips an audible and audacious laughter.

I heard crying in the night, I heard sobs.

I heard a thin wail, and a muffled groan.

No lights appeared in the town.

Then out of the darkness, these evil things appeared again, on the tops of the walls, running right on the edge and then leaping free.

"God, I see you! Curse you!" I whispered.

There was a sudden loud noise in my ears, a great brush of soft cloth against me, and then the figure of a man reared up before my face.

"Do you see us, my boy?" It was a young man's voice, hearty, full of merriment. "My very curious little boy?"

He was too close for my sword. I could see nothing but rising garments.

With my elbow and shoulder and all my strength, I went for his groin.

His laughter filled the tower.

"Ah, but that does not hurt me, child, and if you're so curious, well then, we'll take you too with us to come and see what you long to see."

He caught me in a suffocating swaddle of fabric. And suddenly I felt myself lifted off the floor, encased in a sack, and I knew we had left the tower!

I was head down, sick to nausea. It seemed he flew, carrying me on his back, and his laughter was now half blown away by the wind, and I could not free my arms. I could feel my sword, but couldn't reach the handle.

Desperately I felt for my dagger, not the one which I must have dropped when I had been caught by him, but the other in my boot, and then having that, I twisted and turned towards the rough back on which I rode, bouncing and growling, and plunged the dagger through the cloth over and over again.

He gave a wild scream. I stabbed him again.

My whole body, inside the sack, was whipped up into the air, away from him.

"You little monster," he cried. "You wretched impudent child."

We descended sharply, and then I felt myself hit the ground, the rocky grassy ground, and I rolled over, tearing at the fabric of the blinding sack with my knife.

"You little bastard," he cursed.

"Are you bleeding, you filthy devil?" I called out. "Are you?" I ripped at the sack, lost in it, rolling over and over, then feeling the wet grass with my naked hand.

I saw the stars.

Then the cloth was torn free of my struggling limbs.

I lay at his feet, but only for a moment.

6

THE COURT OF THE RUBY GRAIL

OTHING could have wrenched the dagger from my hand. I cut deep into his legs, bringing forth another riot of screams from him. He picked me up, indeed hurled me high in the air, and I fell, stunned, onto the dewy ground.

This gave me my first blurred but imperative glimpse of him. A great rush of red light illuminated him, a hooded and cloaked figure dressed as a knight, in long old-fashioned tunic and sleeves of shining mail. He twisted his torso, his golden hair tangling over his face, obviously in pain from the wounds inflicted on his back, and now stomped his wounded leg.

I rolled over twice, holding tight to the dagger, as I freed my sword sufficiently to draw it out of the scabbard. I was on my feet before he even so much as moved, and swung the sword with one hand, clumsily, but with all my force, hearing it smash into his side with a sickening moist slosh of a sound. The gush of blood in the bright light was horrific and monstrous.

There came his worst cry. He fell to his knees.

"Help me, you imbeciles; he's a devil!" he screamed. His hood fell back.

I scanned the immense fortifications rising to my right, the high crenelated towers with their fluttering flags in the unsteady glow of countless lights, just as I'd glimpsed from the distance of the town. It was a fantastical castle of pointed roofs, sharply broken arched windows, and high battlements crowded with dark figures moving in silhouette as they looked down on our struggle.

There came rushing down the wet grass the figure of Ursula in a red gown, cloakless, her hair in long braids with red ribbon, rushing towards me.

"Don't hurt him, I charge you," she screamed. "Don't touch him."

A group of male figures, all got up in the same old-fashioned knightly tunics, down to their knees, with somber pointed steel helmets, followed her. They had bearded faces all, and ghastly white skin.

My adversary pitched forward on the grass, sprouting blood as if he were a hideous fountain.

"Look what he's done to me, look!" he shouted.

I stuck my dagger in my belt, grabbed the sword with two hands and went at his neck, letting a roar escape my teeth as I did, and saw the head roll over and over and down the hill. "Ah, now you're dead, you're bloody dead!" I cried out. "You murderous fiend, you're dead. Go get your head. Put that back on!"

Ursula flung her arms around me, her breasts

sealed against my back. Her hand imprisoned mine once more and forced me to bow the tip of the sword to the ground.

"Don't touch him," she screamed again, with a threat in her voice. "Don't come near, I charge you."

One of the others had recovered the shaggy blond head of my foe and held it up as the others watched the body twitch and writhe.

"Oh, no, it's too late," said one of the men.

"No, put it back, put it on his neck," cried another.

"Let me go, Ursula," I said. "Let me die with honor, will you do me that courtesy!" I struggled. "Let me free, to die in my own way, will you do that much?"

"No," she said hotly into my ear. "I will not."

I was absolutely powerless against her strength, no matter how soft the cushion of her breasts or how cool and soft her fingers. She had complete mastery of me.

"Go to Godric," cried one of the men.

The other two had picked up the writhing, kicking, headless man. "Take him to Godric," said the one who carried the head. "Only Godric can pronounce on this."

Ursula let out a loud wail. "Godric!" It was like the howl of the wind or a beast, it was so shrill, so immense, echoing off the walls.

High up, against the wide gaping arched doorway of the citadel, his back to the light, there stood a slender elderly figure, limbs bent with age.

"Bring them both," he called out. "Ursula, quiet yourself, lest you frighten everyone."

I made a swift bid for freedom. She tightened her grip. There came the pinprick of her teeth in my neck. "Oh, no, Ursula, let me see what's to happen!" I whispered. But I could feel the murky clouds rising about me, as though the air itself had thickened and was enfolding me with scent and sound and the sensuous force.

Oh, love you, want you, yes, I did and can't deny it. I felt myself holding her in the high moist grasses of the field, and she lay beneath me, but these were dreams and there were no wild red flowers, and I was being taken somewhere, and she had but weakened me, pulled on my heart with the force of her own.

I tried to curse her. All around us lay the flowers and the grasses, and she said, "Run," but this was quite impossible because it was not made of truth, but of fantasy and the sucking of her mouth on me and her limbs entwining me as if she were a serpent.

A French castle. It was as though I had been transported to the north.

I had opened my eyes.

All the accoutrements of a French court.

Even the dim sedate music which I could hear made me think of old-fashioned French songs sung at suppers in long-ago childhood.

I awoke, sitting cross-legged on a carpet, slumped over, and came to myself rubbing my neck and feeling about desperately for weapons which had all been taken from me. I nearly lost my balance and fell backward.

The music was repetitive and dull and pounding as it rose up from some faraway place below, with too many muffled drums and the thin nasal whine of horns. It had no melody.

I looked up. French, yes, the high narrow pointed archway that led to a long balcony outside, below which some great celebration was in noisy progress. Fancy French, the tapestries of the ladies with their tall cone-shaped hats, and their snow-white unicorns.

Quaint antique, like the illustrations in prayer books of courts in which poets sat reading aloud the boring and tedious *Roman de la Rose*, or the fables of Reynard the Fox.

The window was draped in blue satin covered in the fleurs-de-lys. There was old filigree crumbling about the high doorway and what I could see of the window frame. And cabinets were gilded and painted in the French style, decayed and stiff.

I turned around.

There stood the two men, their long tunics streaked with blood, and their mail sleeves coarse and thick. They had taken off their pointed helmets, and they stared at me with icy pale eyes, each a solemn bearded figure. The light positively glinted on their hard white skin.

And there stood Ursula, a silver-framed jewel upon the shadows, gazing down at me, her gown high-waisted and soft-falling and old-fashioned as their clothes, as though she too had come from some long-ago kingdom of the French, her snow-white breasts bare almost to her nipples, beneath a rich full little bodice of flowered red-and-gold velvet.

At a desk, on an X-shaped chair, there sat the Elderly one, his age quite true to the posture I had glimpsed silhouetted against the castle light, and he was pale as they, of the same deadly white complexion, both beautiful yet awful and monstrous.

Turkish lamps hung on chains about the room, flames glittering deep inside them, giving off a hurtful light against my dazed eyes, and also a fragrance as of roses and summer fields, something alien to heat and burnt things.

The Elderly one had a bald head, as ugly as the unearthed bulb of an iris, upended and shaved of all root, and implanted with two gleaming gray eyes, and a long narrow solemn uncomplaining and unjudging mouth.

"Ah, so," he said to me in a soft voice, lifting one eyebrow, which was scarcely visible except for the sharp arching wrinkle of his perfect white flesh. He had thick slanting lines for cheeks. "You realize you've killed one of us, don't you?"

"I hope so," I said. I climbed to my feet. I nearly lost my balance. Ursula reached out, then stepped back, as though she had caught herself in a breach of decorum.

I righted myself, glaring at her quite ferociously and then at the bald Elderly one, who looked up at me with unbroken calm.

"Do you care to see what you've done?" he asked of me.

"Why should I?" I asked. But I did see.

On a great trestle-board table to my left lay the dead blond thief who had hefted me body and soul into his big cloth sack. Ah, the debt was paid in full.

He lay still, shrunken horridly, as if his limbs had collapsed upon themselves, and his bloodless white head, lids open on dark clotted eyes, lay against his roughly torn neck. What a delight. I stared at one skeletal hand of the being, which hung over the edge of the table, white and like some shriveling creature of the sea beneath a merciless sun on sand by the oceanside.

"Ah, excellent," I said. "This man who dared to abduct me and bring me here by force, quite dead, thank you for the sight of it." I looked at the Elderly one. "Honor demands nothing less. We don't even have to talk of common sense, do we? And what others did you take from the village? The wild old man who tore at his shirt? The infant born small? The weak, the infirm, the sick, whatever they'd give you, and what do you give them in exchange?"

"Oh, do be quiet, young one," said the Elderly solemn male. "You are courageous beyond honor or common sense, that's plain enough."

"No, it isn't. Your sins against me demand I fight you with my last breath, you, all of you." I pivoted and stared at the open door. The plodding music in itself sickened me and threatened to make me dizzy from all the blows and falls I'd suffered. "Such noise from below. What are you, a bloody court?"

All three men broke into laughter.

"Well, you've very nearly got it right," said one of the bearded soldiers in a deep bass of a voice. "We are the Court of the Ruby Grail, that's our very name, only we prefer that you say it properly in Latin or in French, as we say it."

"The Court of the Ruby Grail!" I said. "Leeches, parasites, blood drinkers, that's what you all are. What is the Ruby Grail? Blood?"

I struggled to remember the prick of her teeth against my throat without the spell which had always come with them, but there it was, threatening to swallow me, the drifting, fragrant memory of meadows and her tender breasts. I shook myself all over. "Blood drinkers. Ruby Grail! Is that what you do with all of them, the ones you take? Drink their blood?"

The Elderly one looked pointedly at Ursula. "What is it you're asking of me, Ursula?" he put the question to her. "How can I make such a choice?"

"Oh, but Godric, he's brave and fine and strong," said Ursula. "Godric, if you but say yes, no one will go against it. No one will question it. Please, I beg you, Godric. When have I ever asked—."

"Asked for what?" I demanded, looking from her solicitous and heartbroken face to the Elderly man. "For my life? Is that what you ask? You'd better kill me."

The old man knew that. I didn't have to tell him. There was no way I could be given mercy at this juncture. I would merely fling myself against them again, seeking to bring down another or another.

Suddenly, as if quite angry and impatient, the Elderly figure rose with surprising agility and grabbed me by the collar as he swept past me in a great graceful rustle of red robes, and dragged me with him, as if I weighed nothing, out through the archway and to the edge of the stone railing.

"Look down on the Court," he said.

The hall was immense. The overhang on which we stood ran all around, and below there was scarcely a foot of bare stone, so rich were the hangings of gold and burgundy. The long table below hosted a string of Lords and Ladies, all in the requisite burgundy-red cloth, the color of blood, not wine, as I had believed, and before them glared the bare wood, with not a plate of food nor a cup of wine, but all were content and watching with cheerful eyes, as they chattered, the dancers who covered the great floor, dancing deftly on thick carpets as though they liked this padding beneath their slippered feet.

There were so many interlocking circles of figures moving to the throb and beat of the music that they made a series of arabesques. The costumes embraced a great nationality of styles, from the very French to the modern Florentine, and everywhere there were gay circles of red-dyed silk or the red field covered with flowers or some other design which looked very like stars or crescent moons, I could not quite see it.

It was a somber yet tantalizing picture, all of

them in this same rich color which held sway some-where between the putrid ghastliness of blood and the stunning splendor of scarlet.

I noted the sconces, candlesticks, torches ga-lore. How easy it would be to set their tapestries afire. I wondered if they could burn, they them-selves, like other witches and heretics.

I heard Ursula let out a little gasp. "Vittorio, be wise," she whispered.

At her whisper, the man at the center of the table below—he who held that very high-backed chair of honor, which my father would have held at home—looked up at me. He was blond-haired, blond as the shaggy one I'd slain, but his long locks were pampered and silky on his broad shoulders. His face was youthful, far more so than my father's yet plenty older than my own, and as inhumanly pale as all the rest, his searing blue eyes fixing upon me. He returned at once to his study of the dance.

The whole spectacle seemed to shiver with the hot smoking quaver of the flames, and as my eyes watered, I realized with a start that the figures worked into the tapestry were not the quiet ladies and unicorns of the small studious chamber from which we'd come, but devils dancing in Hell. Indeed, there were quite hideous gargoyles in the most violent and cruel style, carved beneath the porch all around, on which we stood, and I could see at the capitals of the branching columns that held up the ceiling above us more of the demonic and winged creatures carved into the stone.

Grimaces of evil were emblazoned on the walls

behind me, across from me. In one tapestry below, the circles of Dante's Hell climbed one upon another ever higher and higher.

I stared at the shining bare table. I was dizzy. I was going to be sick, lose consciousness.

"Make you a member of the Court, that is what she asks," said the Elder, pushing me hard against the rail, not letting me free, not letting me turn away. His voice was unhurried and low and without the slightest opinion on the matter. "She wants us to bring you into our Court as a reward for the fact that you slew one of us, that is her logic."

His glance to me was thoughtful, cool. His hand on my collar was neither cruel nor rough, merely simple.

I was a tempest of half-uttered words and curses, when suddenly I realized I was falling.

In the Elderly one's grasp, I had fallen over the rail, and in a second descended to the thick layers of carpet below, where I was yanked to my feet, as the dancers made way for us on either side.

We stood before the Lord in the high-backed chair, and I saw that the wood figures of his regal throne were, of course, animalian, feline and diabolical.

All was black wood, polished so that one could smell the oil, and it mingled sweetly with the perfume of all the lamps, and there came a soft crackling from the torches.

The musicians had stopped. I couldn't even see them. And then when I did, saw the little band quite high up in their own little balcony or loft, I perceived that they too had the porcelain-white skin and the lethal cats' eyes, as they gazed down at me, all of them slender males, modestly clothed, and seemingly apprehensive.

I stared at the Lord. He had not moved or spoken. He was a fine, imperial figure of a man, his thick bulky blondish hair combed back from his face and falling, as I had seen before, in carefully combed locks on his shoulders.

His clothes too were of the old fashion, a great loose tunic of velvet, not a soldier's tunic, but almost a robe unto itself, trimmed in darkly dyed fur to match its lurid color, and beneath it he wore big beautiful full sleeves ballooning out loosely over his elbows and then tapering around his long narrow forearms and wrists. A huge chain of medallions hung about his neck, each heavily worked circle of gold set with a cabochon stone, a ruby, red as his clothing.

He held one slender naked hand curled on the table, simply. The other I could not see. He gazed at me with blue eyes. There was something puritanical and scholarly about his bare hand, and the refinement and cleanliness of it.

Across the thick overlapping carpets, Ursula came with a quick step, holding her skirts in two dainty hands. "Florian," she said, making a deep bow to the Lord behind the table. "Florian, I am begging you for this one, on account of character and strength, that you bring him into the Court for my sake, for my heart. It's as simple as that."

Her voice was tremulous but reasoning.

"Into the Court? Into this Court?" I demanded. I felt the heat rise in my face. I looked from right to left. I stared at their white cheeks, their dark mouths, which were all too often the color of fresh wounds. I stared at the blanched and colorless expressions with which they regarded me. Were their eyes full of demonic fire, or was it only that every other bit of humanity had been taken from their countenances?

I saw my own hands as I looked down, my own clenching fists, very ruddy and human, and quite suddenly, as if I were meant to smell it, I caught my own scent, the scent of my sweat and the dust from the road clinging to me and mingling with whatever in me was simply human.

"Yes, you are quite the morsel to us," said the Lord himself, speaking from the table. "You are indeed, and the hall is filled with your scent. And it is too early for us to feast. We feast when the bell rings twelve times, that is our infallible custom."

It was a beautiful voice, a voice of ringing clarity and charm, tinged with the accent of the French, which can in itself be so beguiling. It was with a French restraint and regality that he expressed himself.

He smiled at me, and his smile was gentle, as was Ursula's smile, but not pitying, and not at all cruel or sarcastic.

I had no eyes now for the other faces to the left and the right of him. I knew only that there were many, and some were men and some women, and the women wore the stately French headdresses of olden times, and somewhere in the corner of my eye, I thought I saw a man got up like a jester.

"Ursula, such a thing as this," the Lord said, "requires long consideration."

"Does it!" I cried out. "You mean to make me one of your Court? That takes no consideration."

"Oh, come now, my boy," the Lord said in his soft, calming voice. "We are not subject to death or decay or disease here. You squirm on the end of a hook, you're a doomed catch from the sea, and you do not even know that you are no longer in the life-sustaining water."

"My Lord, I do not wish to be part of your Court," I said. "Spare yourself your kindnesses and your advice." I looked about. "Don't talk to me of your Feast."

These creatures had adopted an abominable stillness, a frozen regard which was in itself utterly unnatural and menacing. A wave of revulsion came over me. Or was it panic, panic which I would not allow to form inside of me, no matter how completely and hopelessly I was surrounded by them, and how alone I stood.

The figures at the table might have been made of china, so fixed they were. Indeed it seemed that the very act of posing to perfection was inherently part of their attentiveness.

"Oh, if I had but a crucifix," I said in a soft voice, not even thinking about what I was saying.

"That would mean nothing to us," said the Lord matter-of-factly.

"Oh, how well I know; your lady here came

into my very chapel to take my brother and sister prisoner! No, crosses mean nothing to you. But it would mean something to me just now. Tell me, do I have angels about me that protect me? Are you always visible? Or do you, now and then, melt with the night and vanish? And when that is so, can you see the angels that defend me?"

The Lord smiled.

The Elderly one, who had let go of my collar, for which I was very thankful, laughed softly under his breath. But there came no easy mirth from anyone else.

I glanced at Ursula. How loving and desperate she looked, how bold and steadfast as she glanced from me to this Lord, whom she had called Florian. But she was no more human than any of them; she was the deathly semblance of a young woman, past all description in gifts and graces but long out of life, as they were. Some grail was this Ruby Grail.

"Hear his words, Sir, in spite of what he actually says," she begged. "It's been so very long since there was a new voice within these walls, one that would remain with us, be one of us."

"Yes, and he almost believes in his angels, and you think him wondrously clever," said the Lord understandingly. "Young Vittorio, let me assure you, there are no guardian angels that I can see about you. And we are always visible, as you know, for you have seen us at our best and at our worst. No, not really truly at our best, not at our finest."

"Oh," I said, "and for that I can't wait, my Lord,

for I am so in love with you all, and your style of slaughtering, and there is of course the matter of what your corruption has done to the town below and how you've stolen the souls of the very priests themselves."

"Hush, you work yourself into a mortal fever," he said. "Your scent fills my nostrils as if the pot is boiling over. I might devour you, child, cut you up and give your pulsing parts up and down the table to be suckled while the blood is still very hot, and your eyes blink—."

On those words I thought I would go mad. I thought of my dead sister and brother. I thought of the hideous and hopeless tender expressions of their severed heads. I couldn't bear this. I shut my eyes tight. I sought for any image to banish these horrors. I raised from memory the spectacle of Fra Filippo Lippi's Angel Gabriel on his knees before the Virgin, yes, angels, angels, fold your wings about me, now, oh, God, send me your angels!

"I curse your damned Court, you sweet-tongued devil!" I cried out. "How did you get your foot into this land! How did it happen?" I opened my eyes, but I saw only Fra Filippo's angels in a great tumbling, falling spectacle of remembered works, radiant beings filled with the warm carnal breath of earth mingled with Heaven. "Did he go to Hell?" I cried out louder. "The one who's head I cut off? Is he burning?"

If silence can swell and fall back upon itself, then so did the silence of this great hall or solar, and I heard nothing but my own anxious breath.

But still the Lord remained unperturbed.

"Ursula," he said. "This can be considered."

"No!" I cried out. "Never! Join you? Become one of you?"

The Elder's hand held me powerless with clamped fingers on my neck. I would only make myself foolish if I struggled. Were he to tighten his grip, I would be dead. And maybe that was best. Only I had more to say:

"I will never, I won't. What? How dare you think my soul so cheap you can have it for the asking!"

"Your soul?" asked the Lord. "What is your soul that it does not want to travel centuries under the inscrutable stars, rather than a few short years? What is your soul that it will not seek for truth forever, rather than for one paltry common lifetime?"

Very slowly, with the muted rustle of garments, he rose to his feet, displaying for the first time a long full mantle of red which fell down, making a great patch of blood-colored shadow behind him. He bent his head ever so slightly, and lamps gave his hair a rich gilded look, and his blue eyes softened.

"We were here before you and your kindred," he said. His voice never broke decorum. He remained civil, elegant. "We were here centuries before you came to your mountain. We were here when all these mountains round were ours. It is you who are the invader." He paused and drew himself up. "It is your species that draws ever closer with farm and village and fortress and castle, and encroaches upon us, upon the forests which are ours, so that we must be cunning where we would be swift, and visible where we would be as the Gospel 'thief in the night.' "

"Why did you kill my father and my family!" I demanded. I could keep silent no longer, I didn't care how beguiling his eloquence, his soft purring words, his charmed face.

"Your father and his father," he said, "and the Lord before him—they cut down the trees that crowded your castle. And so I must keep back the forest of humans from mine. And now and then I must range wide with my ax, and so I have, and so it was done. Your father could have given tribute and remained as he was. Your father could have sworn a secret oath that required all but nothing of him."

"You can't believe he would have surrendered to you our babes, for what, do you drink their blood or sacrifice them to Satan on some altar?"

"You shall see by and by," he said, "for I think you must be sacrificed."

"No, Florian," Ursula gasped. "I beg you."

"Let me put a question to you, gracious Lord," I said, "since justice and history weigh so heavily with you. If this is a Court, a true Court, why have I no benefit of human defense? Or human peers? Or any humans to defend me?"

He seemed troubled by the question. Then he spoke.

"We are the Court, my son," he said. "You are nothing, and you know it. We would have let your father live, as we let the stag live in the forest so that it may breed with the doe. It's no more than that."

"Are there any humans here?"

"None that can help you," he said simply.

"No human guards by day?" I asked.

"No guards by day," he said, and for the first time he smiled a little proudly. "You think we require them? You think our small pigeon coop is not content by day? You think we need human guards here?"

"I certainly do. And you're a fool if you think I'd ever join your Court! No human guards, when right below is an entire village which knows what you are and who you are and that you come by night and cannot by day?"

He smiled patiently. "They are vermin," he said quietly. "You waste my time with those who are beneath contempt."

"Hmm, you do yourself wrong with such a harsh judgment. I think you have more love of them, in some way or another, my Lord, than that!"

The Elder laughed. "Of their blood perhaps," he said under his breath.

There was a bit of uneasy laughter from somewhere else in the hall, but it fell away, like a fragment of something broken.

The Lord spoke again:

"Ursula, I will consider but I do not—."

"No, for I will not!" I said. "Even if I were damned, I wouldn't join you."

"Hold your tongue," cautioned the Lord calmly.

"You are fools if you do not think the towns-people below will rise up and take this citadel by the light of the day and open your hiding places!"

There was a rustling and noise throughout the great hall, but no words, none at least that I could hear, but it was as if these pale-faced monsters were communing with each other by thought or merely exchanging glances which made their ponderous and beautiful garments shift and move.

"You are numb with stupidity!" I declared. "You make yourselves known to the whole daylight world, and you think this Court of the Ruby Grail can endure forever?"

"You insult me," said the Lord. A bit of rosy color came divinely and beautifully into his cheeks. "I ask you with courtesy to be quiet."

"Do I insult you? My Lord, allow me to advise you. You are helpless by day; I know you are. You strike by night and only by night. All signs and words point to it. I remember your hordes fleeing my father's house. I remember the warning, 'Look at the sky.' My Lord, you have lived too long in your country forest. You should have followed my father's example and sent off a few pupils to the philosophers and priests of the city of Florence."

"Don't mock me anymore," he said imploringly with the same well-bred restraint. "You are causing anger in me, Vittorio, and I have no room for it."

"Your time is short, old Demon," I said. "So make merry in your antiquated castle while you can."

Ursula cried out under her breath, but I wouldn't be stopped.

"You may have bought off the old generation of idiots who run the town right now," I said, "but if you don't think the worlds of Florence and Venice and Milan are not moving in on you more fiercely than you can ever prevent, you are dreaming. It's not men such as my father who are a threat to you, my Lord. It's the scholar with his books; it's the university astrologers and alchemists who'll move in on you; it's the modern age of which you know nothing, and they will hunt you down, like some old beast of legend, and drag you out of this lair in the heat of the sun and cut off your heads, all of you—."

"Kill him!" There came a female voice from those who watched.

"Destroy him now," said a man.

"He isn't fit for the coop!" screamed another.

"He's unworthy to be kept in the coop for a moment, or even to be sacrificed."

Then a whole chorus let loose with demands for my death.

"No," cried Ursula, throwing out her arms to the Lord. "Florian, I beg you!"

"Torture, torture, torture," they began to chant, first two and three and then four.

"My Lord," said the Elder, but I could scarce hear his voice, "he's only a boy. Let us put him in the coop with the rest of the flock. In a night or two he won't remember his name. He'll be as tame and plump as the others."

"Kill him now," screamed one voice over all. And: "Be done with him," cried others, their demands rising ever louder in volume.

There came a piercing shout seconded at once: "Tear him limb from limb. Now. Do it."

"Yes, yes, yes!" It was like the beat of battle drums.

7

THE COOP

ODRIC, the Elder, shouted loudly for silence, right at the moment that numerous rather glacial hands had tightened on my arms.

Now, once in Florence I had seen a man torn apart by a mob. I'd been far too close for my own desire to the spectacle, and had been nearly trampled in the efforts of those who, like me, wanted to get away.

So it was no fantasy to me that such could happen. I was as resigned to it as I was to any other form of death, believing, I think, as powerfully in my anger and my rectitude as I did in death.

But Godric ordered the blood drinkers back, and the entire pallid-faced company withdrew with a courtly grace that bordered upon the coy and the cloying, heads bowed or turned to one side, as if a moment before they had not been party to a rabble.

I kept my eyes fixed on the Lord, whose face now showed such a heat that it appeared near human, the blood pulsating in his thin cheeks, and his mouth as dark as a dried blood scar, for all its pleasing shape. His dark golden hair seemed almost brown, and his blue eyes were filled with pondering and concern.

"I say that he be put in with the others," said Godric, the bald Elder.

At once, Ursula's sobs broke forth, as though she could not restrain herself any longer. I looked over to see her, her head bowed, her hands struggling to completely shield her face, and, through the creases of her long fingers, droplets of blood falling as though her tears were made of it.

"Don't cry," I said, not even thinking about the wisdom of it. "Ursula, you have done all you can. I am impossible."

Godric turned and looked at me with one thickly creased raised eyebrow. This time I was close enough to see that his bald white head did have such hairs to it, scant eyebrows of gray as thick and ugly as old splinters.

Ursula brought up a rose-colored napkin from the fold of her long high-waisted French gown, a pale pink tissue of a thing stitched on the edges with green leaves and pink flowers, and on this she wiped her lovely red tears and looked at me, as if she were crushed with longing.

"My predicament is impossible," I said to her. "You've done all you can to save me. If I could, I would put my arms around you to protect you from this pain. But this beast here is holding me hostage."

There were outraged gasps and murmurs from

the still dark-garbed company, and in a blur I allowed myself to see the thin, gaunt, bone-white faces that lined the long board on either side of the Lord, to glance at some of the Ladies who were so Frenchified in their old headdresses and wimples of rose red that they had not a single hair visible. There seemed both a Frankish absurdity and delicacy to them, and of course they were all demons.

The bald Elder, Godric, only chuckled.

"Demons," I said, "such a collection."

"The coop, my Lord," said Godric, the bald one. "With the others, and then I may make my suggestions to you in private, and with Ursula we shall talk. She grieves unduly."

"I do!" she cried. "Please, Florian, if only because I have never asked anything of this sort, and you know it."

"Yes, Ursula," said the Lord, in the softest voice which had issued from his lips yet. "I know that, my loveliest flower. But this boy is recalcitrant, and his family, when from time to time they had the advantage over those of us who wandered from here to hunt, destroyed those unfortunate members of our tribe. It happened more than once."

"Marvelous!" I cried out. "How brave, how wondrous, what a gift you give me."

The Lord was astonished and annoyed.

But Ursula hurried forward, in a flurry of dark shadowy velvet skirts, and leaned over the polished table to be close to him. I could see only her hair in its long thick braids, twined exquisitely with red velvet ribbons, and the shape of her gorgeous arms, so perfectly narrow and plump at the same time, enchanted me against my own will.

"To the coop, please, my Lord," she begged, "and let me have him at least for so many nights as I need to reconcile my heart to this. Let him be admitted tonight for the Midnight Mass, and let him wonder."

I made no answer to this. I merely memorized it.

Two of the company, clean-shaven men in court dress, suddenly appeared at my side, to assist Godric, it seemed, in having me taken off.

Before I knew what was to befall me, a soft binding of cloth was put over my eyes. I was sightless.

"No, let me see!" I cried out.

"The coop then, it is, very well," came the Lord's voice, and I felt myself being taken away from the room, fast, as if the feet of those who escorted me scarcely needed to touch the floor.

The music rose again, in an eerie throb, but I was mercifully being escorted away from it. Only Ursula's voice accompanied me as I was carried up staircases, my feet now and then bruised coarsely on the steps, and the fingers that held me carelessly hurting me.

"Be quiet, please, Vittorio, don't struggle, be my brave one now in silence."

"And why, my love?" I asked. "Why set your heart on me? Can you kiss me without your stinging teeth?"

"Yes, and yes, and yes," she said in my ear.

I was being dragged along a passage. I could hear a loud mingled chorus of voices, common ordinary speech, and the wind of the outdoors and a wholly different kind of music.

"What is this? Where do we go?" I asked.

Behind me, I heard doors shut, and then the blindfold was ripped from my eyes.

"This is the coop, Vittorio," she said, pressing her arm against mine and trying to whisper in my ear. "This is where victims are kept until needed."

We stood on a high barren stone landing, the stairs leading down and at a curve into the huge courtyard, which contained so much activity and of such bizarre sorts that I could not possibly comprehend all of it immediately.

We were high within the walls of the castle, that I knew. And the courtyard itself was enclosed on all four sides, and I could see as I looked up that the walls were faced in white marble and there were everywhere the narrow pointed twin-arched windows of the French style. And above, the heavens had a bright pulsing glow, fed no doubt by countless fluttering torches on the roofs and abutments of the castle.

This was all nothing much to my eyes, except that it meant escape was impossible, for the nearest windows were far too high, and the marble too smooth to be scaled in any physical way.

There were many tiny balconies overhanging above, and they too were impossibly high. I saw the pale red-clothed demons on those balconies looking down at me, as though my introduction were a spectacle. There were some very large porches, and these too had their idle gloating and merciless occupants.

Damn them all, I thought.

What stunned me and fascinated me was the great jumble of human beings and dwellings which I saw crowding the courtyard before me.

First of all, it was far more fiercely illuminated than the ghastly Court, where I had just stood trial, if it could be called such, and it was an entire world unto itself—a rectangular court planted with dozens of olive trees and other flowering trees, orange trees, lemon trees, and all of these strung with lanterns.

It was an entire little world full of what seemed to be drunken and confused persons. Bodies, some half-naked, others fully and even richly clothed, shuffled, stumbled or lay about with no purpose. Everyone was filthy, disheveled, degraded.

There were hovels all over, like old-fashioned peasant huts of mere straw, and open wooden shacks, and little stone enclaves, and trellised gardens and countless circuitous pathways.

It was a drunken labyrinth of a garden gone wild under the naked night.

The fruit trees grew thick in clusters and then broke open to reveal grassy places where people merely lay staring at the stars, as if they were dozing, though their eyes were open.

Myriad flowering vines covered wire enclosures that seemed to have no purpose but to create some alcove of privacy, and there were giant cages full of fat birds, aye, birds, and cooking fires scattered about—and big kettles simmering on beds of coals, from which a deeply spiced fragrance arose.

Kettles! Yes, full of broth.

I saw that a foursome of demons roamed about—there may have been more—scrawny-limbed and bleached as their Lords, and forced to the same blood-red dress, only they were in shape-less garments no better than rags—peasant garb.

Two tended a pot of the simmering broth or soup or whatever it was, whilst another swept with a big old broom, and yet another carried on his hip indifferently a small mewling human toddler, whose head rolled painfully on his weak neck.

It was more grotesque and disturbing than the hideous Court below, with its stately cadaverous mock aristocrats.

"It's stinging my eyes," I said. "I can feel the smoke rising from the kettles." It was a pungent delicious mingling of fragrances. I could identify many of the rich cooking spices, and the smell of mutton and beef, but there were other more exotic flavors intermingled with it.

Everywhere human beings were in this hope-less daze. Children, old women, the famed cripples who never appeared in the town below, hunch-backs, and little twisted bodies which had never grown to full size, and big hulking men as well, bearded and swart, and boys my age or older—all of them shuffling about or lying about, but dazed, and crazy, and looking up at us, and blink-ing and pausing as though our presence should mean something though they could not make out what.

I swayed on the landing, and Ursula held my arm. I felt ravenous as the heavy fumes filled my nostrils. Hunger, hunger such as I'd never known. No, it was a pure thirst for the soup, as though there were no food that was not liquid.

Suddenly the two gaunt and aloof men who had not left us—they who had blindfolded me and dragged me here—turned and went down the steps, letting their heels make a sharp marching sound on the stones.

A few eager cries came up from the great mottled and scattered assemblage. Heads turned. Sluggish bodies tried to rouse themselves from the vaporous torpor.

The two Lords, with their long trailing sleeves and stiff backs, marched together as if they were kinsmen as they approached the first of the visible cauldrons.

I watched as drunken mortals gathered themselves up and stumbled towards the red-clad Lords. As for the red-clad Lords, they seemed to glory in mystifying all.

"What are they doing? What will they do?" I was sick. I was going to fall. Yet how sweet this soup smelled, and how much I wanted it. "Ursula," I said. But I didn't know what words to make to follow this prayer of her name.

"I'm holding you, my love, this is the coop. Look, do you see?"

Through a haze, I saw the Lords pass beneath

the jagged thorny branches of the blooming orange trees, where fruit hung still, as though none of these swollen, lethargic souls needed such a fresh and bright thing as an orange.

The Lords took up a stance on either side of this first kettle, and each, extending a right hand, slashed his right wrist with a knife which he held in his left hand, and let the blood flow copiously into the brew.

A weak happy cry rose from those humans gathering meekly around them.

"Oh, damnable, it's the blood, of course," I whispered. I would have fallen if Ursula had not taken hold of me. "The brew is spiced with blood."

One of the Lords turned away, as though the smoke and the fumes disgusted him, yet he allowed himself to bleed into the mix. Then turning swiftly, almost crossly, he reached out to snatch by the arm one of the thin, weak-looking white demons in peasant garb.

He caught the poor fellow and dragged him to the kettle. The thin paltry demon begged and whined to be allowed to be free, but his wrists were both slashed, and now, though he turned his bony face away, he was bled furiously into the soup.

"Ah, you are better than Dante with your circles of Hell, aren't you?" I said. But it hurt me that I had taken such a tone with her.

She supported me utterly.

"They are peasants, yes, they dream of being Lords, and if they obey, they might."

I recalled now that the demon soldiers who had

brought me back to the castle had been rude huntsmen. How well it was all thought out, but this, my narrow-shouldered love, with her soft yielding arms and her shining tear-stained face, was a pure Lady, was she not?

"Vittorio, I want so badly for you not to die."

"Do you, dearest?" I said. I had my arms around her. I could no longer stand without this support.

My vision was fading.

Yet with my head against her shoulder, my eyes directed to the crowd below, I could see the human beings surrounding the kettles and dipping their cups into the brew, dipping their cups right where the blood had fallen, and then blowing on the hot liquid to cool it before they drank.

A soft, horrid laughter echoed up the walls. I think it came from those spectators above on the balconies.

There was a sudden swirl of red color, as if a giant unfurling flag had fallen.

But it was a Lady dropping down from the remote heights above, to land amid the worshipful hordes of the coop.

They bowed and saluted her, and backed away from her, and gave forth loud gasps of awe as she too approached the kettle and, with a loud rebellious laugh, cut her wrist and fed her blood into it.

"Yes, my darlings, my little chicks," she declared. She looked up at us.

"Come down, Ursula, have pity on our hungry little world; be generous tonight. So it is not your night to give; give in honor of our new acquisition."

Ursula seemed shamed by all of this, and held me gently with her long fingers. I looked into her eyes.

"I'm drunk, drunk merely from the fragrance."

"My blood is only for you now," she whispered.

"Give it to me then, I hunger for it, I'm weak to dying," I said. "Oh, God, you've brought me to this. No, no, I did it myself."

"Sshhh, my lover, my sweet," she said.

Her arm coiled about my waist, and there came just under my ear her tender lips sucking on the flesh, as if she meant to make a pucker there on my neck, warm it with her tongue, and then the prick of her teeth.

I felt ravaged, and with both hands in a fantasy I reached out for her figure as we ran together through the meadow which belonged only to us and to which these others could never be admitted.

"Oh, innocent love," she said even as she drank from me, "oh, innocent innocent love."

Then a sudden icy hot fire entered the wound in my neck, and I felt it as if it were a delicate parasite of long tendrils that once inside my body could find the most remote reaches of me.

The meadow spread out around us, vast and cool, and utterly given over to the blowing lilies. Was she with me? Beside me? It seemed in one radiant instant I stood alone and heard her cry out as if she were behind me.

I meant, within this ecstatic dream, this fluttering cooling dream of blue skies and tender breaking stems, to turn and go to her. But out of the corner of my eyes, I beheld something of such splendor and magnificence that my soul leapt.

"Look, yes, you see!"

My head fell back. The dream was gone. The high white marble walls of the prison castle rose above my hurting gaze. She held me and stared down at me, bewildered, her lips bloody.

She hoisted me in her arms. I was as helpless as a child. She carried me down the stairs, and there was nothing I could do to rouse my limbs.

It seemed all the world above was tiny figures ranging on balconies and battlements and laughing and pointing with their tiny outstretched hands, so dark against the torches all around them.

Blood red, smell it.

"But what was it; did you see it in the field?" I asked her.

"No!" she cried. She looked so frightened.

I lay on a heap of hay, a makeshift bed, and the poor underfed demon peasant boys stared stupidly down at me with bloodshot eyes, and she, she wept, her hands again to her face.

"I cannot leave him here," she said.

She was far, far away. I heard people crying. Was there a revolt among the drugged and the damned? I heard people weeping.

"But you will, and come to the kettle first and give your blood."

Who spoke those words?

I didn't know.

". . . time for the Mass."

"You won't take him tonight."

"Why are they crying?" I asked. "Listen, Ursula, they've all started crying."

One of the scrawny boys stared right into my eyes. He had a hand on the back of my neck and a warm cup of brew to my mouth. I didn't want it to slop down my chin. I drank and drank. It filled my mouth.

"Not tonight," came Ursula's voice. Kisses on my forehead, on my neck. Someone snatched her away. I felt her hand hold tight to mine, then I felt her pulled away.

"Come now, Ursula, leave him."

"Sleep, my darling," she cried in my ear. I felt her skirts brushing me. "Vittorio, sleep."

The cup was thrown aside. Stupidly, in utter intoxication I watched the contents spill and sink darkly into the mounded hay. She knelt before me, her mouth open and tender and luscious and red.

She took my face in her cool hands. The blood poured out of her mouth and into mine.

"Oh, love," I said. I wanted to see the field. It didn't come. "Let me see the field! Let me see it!"

But there was no meadow, only the shocking sight of her face again, and then a dimming light, a gathering embrace of darkness and sound. I could no longer fight. I could no longer speak. I could no longer remember . . . But someone had said that very thing.

And the crying. It was so sad. Such crying, such doleful, helpless weeping.

When next I opened my eyes, it was morning. The sun hurt me, and my head ached unbearably.

A man was on top of me, trying to get my clothes off me. Drunken fool. I turned over, dizzy and sick, sick to vomiting, and threw him off, and with a sound blow knocked him senseless.

I tried to get up but I couldn't. The nausea was intolerable. All around me others slept. The sun hurt my eyes. It scalded my skin. I snuggled into the hay. The heat beat down on my head, and when I ran my own fingers through my hair, my hair felt hot. The pain in my head throbbed in my ears.

"Come into the shelter," a voice said. It was an old crone, and she beckoned to me from beneath a thatched roof. "Come in, where it's cool."

"Curse you all," I said. I slept. I drifted.

Sometime during the late afternoon I came to my senses.

I found myself on my knees near one of the kettles. I was drinking in a slovenly wretched manner from a bowl of brew. The old woman had given it to me.

"The demons," I said. "They are asleep. We can . . . we can . . ." but then the futility of it overcame me. I wanted to throw away the cup, but I drank the hot brew.

"It's not just blood, it's wine, it's good wine," said the old woman. "Drink it, my boy, and feel no pain. They'll kill you soon enough. It's not so terrible."

When it was dark again, I knew it.

I rolled over.

I could fully open my eyes, and they did not hurt as they had in the day.

I knew that I had lost the whole arc of the sun in this drugged and stupid and disastrous languor. I had fallen into their plans. I had been helpless when I should have been trying to rouse these useless ones around me to mutiny. Good God, how could I have let it happen! Oh, the sadness, the dim distant sadness . . . And the sweetness of slumber.

"Wake, boy."

A demon voice.

"They want you tonight."

"Oh, and who wants me for what?" I asked. I looked up. The torches were alight. All was twinkling and glowing, and there came the soft rustle of green leaves overhead—the sharp sweet smell of the orange trees. The world was woven of dancing flames above and the entrancing patterns of the black leaves. The world was hunger and thirst.

The brew simmered, and that scent blotted out all else. I opened my mouth for it, though there was none of it near me.

"I'll give it to you," said the demon voice. "But sit up. I must clean you up. You must look good for tonight."

"For what?" I said. "All of them are dead."

"Who?"

"My family."

"There is no family here. This is the Court of the Ruby Grail. You are the property of the Lord of the Court. Now, come, I have to prepare you."

"For what do you prepare me?"

"For the Mass, you're to go, get up," said the demon, who stood wearily over me, leaning on his broom, his shining hair an elfin mess around his face. "Get up, boy. They'll want you. It's almost midnight."

"No, no, not almost midnight, no!" I cried out. "No!"

"Don't be afraid," he said, coldly, wearily. "It's useless."

"But you don't understand, it's the loss of time, the loss of reason, the loss of hours during which my heart beat and my brain slept! I'm not afraid, you miserable demon!"

He held me flat to the hay. He washed my face.

"There, there, you are a handsome fine one. They always sacrifice those such as you right away. You're too strong, too fine of limb and face. Look at you, and the Lady Ursula dreaming of you and weeping for you. They took her away."

"Ah, but I was dreaming too . . ." I said. Was I talking to this monstrous attendant as though he and I were friends? Where was the great magnificent web of my dreams, the immense and luminous majesty?

"You can talk to me, why not?" he said. "You will die in rapture, my pretty young Lord," he said. "And you'll see the church all alight, and the Mass; you'll be the sacrifice."

"No, I dreamed of the meadow," I said. "I saw something in the meadow. No, it wasn't Ursula." I was talking to myself, to my own sick bedeviled mind, talking to my wits to make them listen. "I saw someone in the meadow, someone so . . . I can't . . ."

"You make things so painful for yourself," said the demon soothingly. "Here, I have all your buttons and buckles right. What a fine Lord you must have been."

Must have been, must have been, must have been . . .

"You hear that?" he asked.

"I hear nothing."

"It's the clock, striking the third quarter of the hour. It's almost time for the Mass. Don't pay attention to the noise. It's the others who'll be sacrificed. Don't let it unnerve you. Just so much common weeping."

8

REQUIEM, OR THE HOLY
SACRIFICE OF THE MASS AS I
HAD NEVER SEEN IT

AD ever a chapel been more beautiful? Had ever white marble been used to such an advantage, and from which fount of eternal gold had come these glorious curlicues and serpentine adornments, these high-pointed windows, illuminated from without by fierce fires that brought into the perfection of jewels their tiny thick facets of tinted glass to form their solemn narrow and seemingly sacred pictures?

But they were not sacred pictures.

I stood in the choir loft, high above the vestibule, looking down over the great nave and at the altar at the far end. Once again I was flanked by ominous and regal Lords, who seemed now to be absolutely fervent in their duty as they held me firm and standing by the arms.

My mind had cleared, but only somewhat. The wet cloth was once again pressed to my eyes and forehead. The water was as if from a mountain stream of flowing melted snow.

In my sickness, in my fever, I saw everything.

I saw the demons fashioned in the glittering windows, as artfully put together of red and gold and blue glass as any angels or saints. I saw their leering faces as they peered down, these monsters with their webbed wings and clawlike hands, upon the congregation.

Below, allowing a broad central aisle, was gathered in its ruby dark finery the great Court on either side, standing to face the long heavily carved and broad Communion Rail and the high altar behind it.

Paintings covered the cove behind the altar. Demons dancing in Hell, graceful among the flames as though they bathed in a welcome radiance, and strung above them on loose and unfurling banners the golden letters from St. Augustine's words, so familiar to my study, that these flames were not the flames of real fire but only the absence from God, but the word "absence" had been replaced by the Latin word for "freedom."

"Freedom" was the word in Latin worked into the high white marble walls, in a frieze that ran beneath the balconies on either side of the church, on the same level as this, my place, in which more of the Court beheld the spectacle.

Light rose to flood the high-groined arches of the roof.

And what was this spectacle?

The high altar was draped in crimson trimmed in gilt fringe, its abundant cloths short enough to reveal the tableau in white carving of figures prancing in Hell, though from this great distance my eyes might have deceived me as to their levity.

What I did see with perfection were the thick candlesticks before not a crucifix but a huge carved stone replica of Lucifer, the fallen angel, long locks aflame, and garments too a torrent of rising fire, frozen in marble, and in his upraised hands the symbols of death—in the right the scythe of the grim reaper—and in the other the sword of the executioner.

I gasped when I beheld the image! Monstrous, it was positioned precisely where I wanted so to see my Crucified Christ, and yet in a moment of delirium and agitation, I felt my lips curl in a smile, and I heard my own mind tell me cunningly that there was nothing less grotesque about the Crucified God if He Himself had been there.

My guards held me firm. Had I tottered?

From the assemblage around me and behind me, from those whom I had not even regarded, there came suddenly the muted roll of drums, ominous and slow, mournful and beautiful in their own muffled simplicity.

At once there followed a deep-throated chorus of horns, in lovely weaving song and effortless sweet intermingling, playing not the repetitious chord music of the night before, but a strong plaintive and imploring polyphony of melodies so sad that they flooded my heart with sadness, stroked my heart and made the tears nearly spring to my eyes.

Oh, what is this? What is this blended and rich

music, surrounding me and pouring forth into the nave to echo off the satiny marble and rebound gently and with perfect modulation to the place where I stood, staring, rapt at the distant figure of Lucifer?

At his feet, all flowers laid out in vessels of silver and gold were red, the red of roses and carnations, the red of the iris, the red of wildflowers I could not name, an altar alive and decked and crawling with all those things which were high color, his glorious tint, the one color left to him that might rise from his inevitable and unredeemable darkness.

I heard the dusty, sonorous songs of the reed shawm, the small oboe and the reed dulcian, and other small reed organs played by mouth, and then the more ringing tone of the brass sackbut horn, and perhaps even the light singing of the hammers striking the taut strings of the dulcimer.

This music alone might have engaged me, filled my soul, its threads of melody interweaving, overlapping, harmonizing and then drifting apart. It left me no breath to speak or eyes for other things. Yet I beheld the statues of the demons who ran from right to left—so like the Lords and Ladies of the Courtly table of last night—from the imposing figure of their Devil.

Were they blood drinkers all, these terrible gaunt saints of Hell, carved from hardwood with its own reddish mahogany glint, in their stark stylized garments, cleaving to thin bodies, their eyes half-lidded, their mouths open, and against each lower lip two white fangs, as if made from tiny bits of snow-white ivory to mark the purpose of each individual monster.

Oh, Cathedral of horrors. I tried to turn my head, to close my eyes, and yet the monstrosity of it enthralled me. Pathetic unformed thoughts never reached my lips.

The horns died around me, and the reedy woodland instruments died away. Oh, don't go, sweet music. Don't leave me here.

But what came was a chorus of the sweetest softest tenor voices; they called out the Latin words that I could not follow, an anthem for the dead, an anthem on the mutability of all things, and at once came a full lustrous harmonizing chorus of sopranos male and female, of basses and baritones, singing heartily in splendid polyphony in answer to these lone tenors:

"I go now to the Lord, for He has allowed these Creatures of Darkness to answer my supplications . . ."

What nightmarish words were these?

Once again there came the rich thick chorus of many voices to underscore the tenors:

"The instruments of death await me in their warm and devout kiss, and into their bodies, by the will of God, they shall take my life's blood, my rapture, my soul's ascent through their own, so as better to know both Heaven and Hell in their Dark Service."

The reed organ played its solemn song.

Into the Sanctuary of the church, there proceeded now, to the fullest most lustrous strength of the polyphony yet, a stream of priestly figures.

I saw the Lord Florian in a rich red chasuble as if he were the bishop of Florence himself, only this garment bore the Cross of Christ impudently upside down in honor of the Damned One, and on his untonsured head of dark blond hair he wore a gilded jeweled crown as if he were both Frankish monarch and servant of the Dark Lord.

The strong piercing notes of the horns dominated the song. A march had begun. The drums rumbled beneath, hushed and steady.

Florian had taken his place before the altar with his face to the congregation, and on one side of him stood the fragile Ursula, her hair full and loose and down on her shoulders, though shrouded like a Mary Magdalene in a scarlet veil which hung to the very edge of the hem of her tapering gown.

Her upturned face was directed to me, and I could see even from this great airy span that her hands, shaped as a steeple, with fingers pressed together, trembled.

On the other side of this high priest Florian stood his bald Elder, in his own chasuble and thick embroidered lace sleeves, another priestly assistant.

Acolytes came from either side, tallish young demons with faces of the usual chiseled ivory, and the simple surplices of those who attend the Mass. They took their positions ranked down the long marble Communion Rail.

Once again, there rose the magnificent chorus of voices around me, falsettos mingling with true sopranos and the throbbing basses of the males, as redolent of the woodlands as the wooden horns, and beneath it all the heavy driving brass declaration.

What did they mean to do? What was this hymn which now the tenors sang, and what was the answer that came from all the voices so close to me, the words in Latin unstrung and only incoherently enveloping me:

"Lord, I am come into the Valley of Death; Lord, I am come to the end of my Sorrow; Lord, in thy deliverance I give life to those who would be idle in Hell were it not for thy divine plan."

My soul rebelled. I loathed it, and yet I could not look away from the spectacle below. My eyes swept the church. I saw for the first time the gaunt, demonic fanged demons on their pedestals rising between the narrow windows, and everywhere the glint of racks upon racks of tiny candles.

The music broke again for the solemn declaration of the tenors:

"Let the fount be brought forward, that those who are our sacrifices should be washed clean."

And it was done.

Ranks of young demons in their guise as Altar Boys came forward, carrying with them in their preternaturally strong hands a magnificent baptismal fount of deep-pink Carrara marble. This they set some ten feet before the Communion Rail.

"Oh, abominations, to make it so beautiful," I whispered.

"Quiet now, my young one," said the regal

guard beside me. "Watch, for what you see here you will never see between Heaven and Earth again, and as you will go unconfessed to God, you will burn in darkness forever."

He sounded as if he believed it.

"You have no power to damn my soul," I whispered, trying in vain to clear my eyes, not to so love the weakness that still caused me to depend upon their clamping hands.

"Ursula, farewell," I whispered, making of my lips a kiss.

But in this miraculous and private little moment, seemingly unnoticed by the whole congregation, I saw her head shake in a small secretive negation.

No one saw because all eyes were now on another spectacle, far more tragic than any of the controlled and modulated ritual we had beheld.

Up the aisle, driven by acolyte demons in tunics of red and lace sleeves trimmed in red and gold, there came a poor wretched sampling of the lost ones of the coop, shuffling old women, drunken men and little boys, mere children, clinging to the very demons who escorted them to their deaths, like piteous victims of some horrid old trial where the offspring of the condemned are led to execution with their parents. Horror.

"I curse you all. I damn you. God, bring down your justice on this," I whispered. "God, bring down your tears. Weep for us, Christ, that this is happening."

My eyes turned up in my head. It seemed I

dreamed, and once again came the bright green limitless meadow to my eyes, and once again, as Ursula ran from me, as her spirited young form rushed across the high breaking field of grass and lilies, there rose another figure, another familiar figure—.

"Yes, I see you!" I cried out to this vision in my half-rescued dream.

But no sooner had I recognized it, locked to it, than it vanished; it was gone, and with it was gone all comprehension of it, all memory of its exquisite face and form and its meaning, its pure and powerful meaning. Words fled from me.

From below I saw the Lord Florian look up, angered, silent. The hands beside me dug into my flesh.

"Silence," said the guards next to me, their commands overlapping one another.

The lovely music rose higher and higher, as though the climbing soprano voices and the throbbing, winding horns would hush me now and pay tribute only to the unholy baptism.

The baptism had begun. The first victim, an ancient woman of bent and bony back, had been stripped of her poor garments and washed with handfuls of water in the fount, and now was led to the Communion Rail, oh, so frail, so unprotected by her kith and kin and her guardian angels!

Oh, and now to see the children stripped, to see their tiny little legs and buttocks bare, to see their bony shoulders, those tiny parts where it seemed the winglets of baby angels once sprouted from their backs, to see them washed and then delivered to stand trembling along the stretch of marble balustrade.

It happened very fast.

"Cursed animals, for that is what you are, not airy demons, no!" I muttered, struggling in the grasp of the two loathsome minions. "Yes, cowardly minions, both of you, to be a party to this evil."

The music drowned out my prayers. "Dear God, send my angels to me," I said to my heart, my secret heart, "send my wrathful angels, send them with your fiery sword. God, this cannot be borne."

The Communion Rail now had its full complement of victims, naked and trembling all, and blazing with carnal human color against the luminous marble and the colorless priests.

The candles flickered on the giant Lucifer, with its great webbed wings, who presided over all.

The Lord Florian now stepped down to take the first Communicant in his hands, and lowered his lips to drink.

The drums beat fierce and sweet, and the voices twined and reached to Heaven. But there was no Heaven here beneath these branching white columns, these groined arches. There was nothing but death.

All the Court had begun to make two streams along the sides of the chapel marching silently up to come behind the Communion Rail, where each might take a victim from those who stood helpless and ready, and now Lord and Lady chose which they wanted, and some shared, and one victim was passed from one to another, and so on it went, this mockery, this lurid, predatory Communion.

Only Ursula did not move.

The Communicants were dying. Some were already dead. None struck the floor. Their pliant dried-up limbs were captured silently and deftly by the attendant demons, and bodies were whisked away.

More victims were still being bathed. Others were taken to the Rail. On it went.

The Lord Florian drank again and again, one child after another put before him, his slender fingers capturing the small neck and holding it as he bent his lips.

I wonder what Latin words he dared to speak.

Slowly the members of the Court slipped out of the Sanctuary, moving down the side aisles again to pivot and take their old stance. They had had their fill.

All through the room the color of blood infused once pallid faces, and it seemed to my misted vision, to my head so full of the loveliness of song, that they all were human now, human for this little while.

"Yes," said Florian, his voice arching out soft and sure to my ears over the length of the nave. "Human now for this one instant, with the blood of the living, incarnated again, we are, young prince. You have understood it."

"Ah, but Lord," I said, in my exhausted whisper, "I do not forgive it."

An interval of silence fell. Then the tenors declared:

"It is time, and the midnight hour is not finished."

The sure and tight hands in which I was held focused me now to the side. I was spirited out of the choir loft and down the winding screw stairs of white marble.

As I came to myself, still supported, staring up the center aisle, I saw that only the baptistry fount remained. All victims were gone.

But a great cross had been brought into the hall. It had been positioned *upside down*, to one side of the altar, and forward, at the Communion Rail.

The Lord Florian held up for me to see five huge iron nails in his hand, and beckoned for me to come.

The cross was anchored into place, as though it had often been brought to this spot. It was made of rich hardwood, thick, heavy and polished smooth, though it bore the marks of other nails, and no doubt the stains of other blood.

The very bottom of it fitted right at the Railing itself against the marble banister, so that he who was to be crucified would be three feet above the floor and visible to all the worshippers.

"The worshippers, you filthy lot!" I laughed. Thank God and all his angels that the eyes of my father and mother were filled with celestial light and could see nothing of this crude degradation.

The Elder revealed to me in his outstretched hands two golden goblets.

I knew the meaning. With these, to catch my blood as it gushed from the wounds made by the nails.

He bowed his head.

I was forced up the aisle. The statue of Lucifer grew immense behind the glittering pontifical figure of Florian. My feet did not touch the marble. All around me the members of the Court turned to attend my progress, but never so much that their eyes were not upon their Lord.

Before the baptismal fount my face was washed.

I tossed my head, twisting my neck, throwing the water impudently on those who tried to bathe me. The acolytes were in fear of me. They approached and reached hesitantly for my buckles.

"Strip him," said the Lord, and once again he held up the nails for me to see.

"I see well enough, my cowardly Lord," I said. "It is nothing to crucify a boy such as me. Save your soul, Lord, do that! And all your Court will wonder."

The music swelled from the loft above. The chorus came again, answering and underscoring the anthem of the tenors.

There were no words for me now; there was only candlelight and the knowledge that my clothes were about to be taken from me, and that this horror would take place, this evil inverted crucifixion, never sanctified by St. Peter himself, for the inverted cross not now to be a symbol of the Evil One.

Suddenly the trembling hands of the acolytes withdrew.

Above, the horns played their most beautiful poignant melody.

The tenors hurled out their question, in flawless voices, from the loft above:

"Can this one not be saved? Can this one not be delivered?"

The chorus rose, in unison:

"Can this one not be released from the power of Satan?"

Ursula stepped forward and drew from her head the immense long red veil that hung to her feet, and threw it out so that it descended like a cloud of red around her. Beside her, an acolyte appeared with my very sword in his hand, and my daggers.

Once again the tenor voices implored:

"One soul released to go forth into the world, mad, and bearing witness only to the most patient ears to the power of Satan."

The chorus sang, a riot of melody erupting from them, and it seemed a swift affirmation had overtaken their song.

"What, not to die!" I said. I strained to see the face of the Lord in whose hands all of this rested. But he was blocked from my view.

Godric the Elder had come between. Opening the gate of the marble Communion Rail with his knee, he moved down the aisle towards me. He thrust one of his golden cups to my lips.

"Drink and forget, Vittorio, else we lose her heart and her soul."

"Oh, but then you must lose it!"

"No!" she screamed. "No." Over his shoulder, I could see her snatch three of the nails from Florian's left hand and fling them out on the marble. The singing rose high and rich under the arches. I couldn't hear the nails strike the stone.

The sound of the choir was jubilant, celebratory. The mournful tones of requiem were gone.

"No, God, if you would save her soul, then take me to the cross, take me!"

But the golden cup was forced to my lips. My jaws were opened by Ursula's hand, and the liquid poured down my throat. I saw my sword lifted before my closing eyes as if it were a cross, the long hilt, the handles.

Soft mocking laughter rose and blended with the magical and indescribable beauty of the choir.

Her red veil swirled about me. I saw the red fabric rise up in front of me. I felt it come down around me like a spellbinding shower, full of her perfume, soft with her tenderness.

"Ursula, come with me . . ." I whispered.

Those were my last words.

"Cast out," cried the swelling voices above. "Cast out . . ." cried the huge choir, and it seemed the Court sang with the chorus, "Cast out," and my eyes closed as the red fabric covered my face, as it came down like a witch's web over my struggling fingers and sealed itself over my open mouth.

The horns blared forth the truth. "Forgiven! Cast out!" sang the voices.

"Cast out to madness," whispered Godric in my

ear. "To madness all of your days, and you, you might have been one of us."

"Yes, one of us," came Florian's smooth unperturbed whisper.

"Fool that you were," said Godric. "You might have been immortal."

"One of us forever, immortal, imperishable, to reign here in glory," said Florian.

"Immortality or death," said Godric, "and these were choices royal, but you shall wander witless and scorned through the world."

"Yes, witless and scorned," came a childish voice at my ear. And then another, "Witless and scorned."

"Witless and scorned," said Florian.

But the choir sang on, obliterating all sting from their words, its delirious hymn growing ever more tremendous in my half-slumber.

"A fool to wander the world in contempt," said Godric.

Blinded, sealed in the softness of the veil, intoxicated by the drink, I could not answer them. I think I smiled. Their words were too senselessly mingled with the sumptuous soothing voices of the choir. And fools that they were, they had never known that what they said simply had not mattered.

"And you could have been our young prince." Was it Florian at my side? Cool, dauntless Florian. "We could have loved you as she loves you."

"A young prince," said Godric, "to rule here with us forever."

"Become the jester of alchemists and old wives," said Florian sadly, solemnly.

"Yes," said a childish voice, "fool to leave us."

How wondrous were the anthems that made their words mere sweet and contrapuntal syllables.

I think I felt her kiss through the silk. I think I felt it. I think. It seemed in the tiniest of feminine whispers, she said simply, without ceremony:

"My love." It had her triumph and her farewell within it.

Down, down, down into the richest, kindest sleep that God can give, I sank. The music gave a shape to my limbs, gave air to my lungs, when all other senses had been abandoned.

9

IT was pouring down rain. No, the rain had stopped. They still couldn't understand me.

I was surrounded by these men. We were right near Fra Filippo's workshop. I knew this street. I'd just been here with my father a year ago.

"Speak more slowly. Corrr . . . blub, it doesn't make sense!"

"Look," said the other one. "We want to help you. Tell me your father's name. Speak it slowly."

They shook their heads. I thought I was making perfect sense, I could hear it, Lorenzo di Raniari, why couldn't they hear it, and I was his son, Vittorio di Raniari. But I could feel my lips, how swollen they were. I knew I was filthy from the rain.

"Look, take me to Fra Filippo's shop. I know them there," I said. My great painter, my passionate and tormented painter, his apprentices would know me. He would not, but the helpers who had seen me weep that day at his work. And then, then, these men would take me to the house of Cosimo in the Via del Largo.

"Fee, fee?" they said. They repeated my clumsy attempts at speech. I had failed again.

I started towards the workshop. I staggered and almost fell. These were honest men. I had the heavy bags over my right shoulder, and my sword was clanking against me, practically throwing me off balance. The high walls of Florence were closing in on me. I almost hit the stones.

"Cosimo!" I shouted at the top of my voice.

"We can't take you to Cosimo like this! Cosimo won't see you."

"Ah, you understand; you heard me."

But the man now cocked his ear. An honest merchant, drenched to the skin in his somber green robes, and all because of me no doubt. I wouldn't come in out of the rain. No sense. They'd found me lying in the rain right in the middle of the Piazza della Signoria.

"It's coming back, it's coming clear."

I saw the entrance to Fra Filippo's workshop up ahead. The shutters were being taken down. They were opening it up now that the thunderous storm had ceased, and the water was drying up on the stone streets. People were coming out.

"Those men in there," I shouted.

"What, what are you saying?"

Shrugs all around, but they aided me. An old man held my elbow.

"We should take him to San Marco, let the monks care for him."

"No, no, no, I need to talk to Cosimo!" I shouted.

Again, they shrugged and shook their heads.

Suddenly I stopped. I rocked and steadied myself by rudely grabbing hold of the younger man's shoulder.

I stared at the distant workshop.

The street was no more than an alleyway here, barely sufficient for horses to pass and for the pedestrians not to be injured, and the stone facades all but closed out the slate-gray sky above. Windows were opened, and it seemed that a woman could reach across upstairs and touch the house opposite her.

But look what was there, right before the shop.

I saw them. I saw the two of them! "Look," I said again. "Do you see them?"

The men couldn't see. Lord, the two figures before the shop were bright as if illuminated from within their flushed skin and loosely girdled robes.

I held the shoulder bags over my left shoulder and put my hand on my sword. I could stand, but my eyes must have been wide as plates staring blindly at what I beheld.

The two angels were arguing. The two angels, with their wings moving ever so slightly in time with their words and their gestures, were arguing with each other where they stood, right before the shop.

They stood oblivious to all humans who passed them and couldn't see them, and they argued one with another, both angels blond, both angels I knew, I knew these angels, I knew them from the paintings of Fra Filippo, and I could hear their voices.

I knew the rolled curls of the one, whose head was crowned with a wreath of small perfectly matched flowerlets, his loose mantle crimson, his undergarment a bright clear sky blue trimmed in gold.

And the other, I knew him as well, knew his bare head and soft shorter hair, and his golden collar, and the insignia on his mantle, and the thick bands of ornament on his wrists.

But above all I knew their faces, their innocent pink-tinged faces, their serene full yet narrow eyes.

The light melted down, somber and stormy still, though the sun was burning up there behind the gray sky. My eyes began to water.

"Look at their wings," I whispered.

The men couldn't see.

"I know the wings. I know them both, look, the angel with the blond hair, the ringlets in rows coming down his head, it's from the *Annunciation*, and the wings, his wings are made like the peacock, brilliantly blue, and the other, his feathers are tipped in the purest dust of gold."

The angel with the crown of flowers gestured excitedly to the other; from a mortal man, the gestures, the posture, would have evinced anger, but it was nothing so heated as that. The angel was only seeking to be understood.

I moved slowly, pulling loose of my helpful companions, who couldn't see what I saw!

What did they think I stared at? The gaping shop, the apprentices in the deep shadows within, the meager half-tinted flashes of canvases and panels, the yawning mouth beyond which the work was carried out.

The other angel shook his head somberly. "I don't go along with it," he said in the most serene and lilting voice. "We can't go that far. Do you think this doesn't make me weep?"

"What?" I cried out. "What makes you weep?"

Both angels turned. They stared at me. In unison, they collected their dark, multicolored and spectacled wings close to themselves, as though they meant to shrink thereby into invisibility, but they were no less visible to me, shining, both so fair, so recognizable. Their eyes were full of wonder as they gazed at me. Wonder at the sight of me?

"Gabriel!" I cried out. I pointed, "I know you, I know you from the *Annunciation*. You are both Gabriel, I know the paintings, I have seen you, Gabriel and Gabriel, how can it be?"

"He can see us," said the angel who had been gesturing so pointedly. His voice was subdued but seemed to reach my ears effortlessly and gently. "He can hear us," he said, and the wonder in his face increased, and he looked above all innocent and patient, and ever so gently concerned.

"What in the name of God are you saying, boy?" asked the old man beside me. "Now, collect your wits. You're carrying a fortune in your bags. Your hands are covered in rings. Now speak sensibly. I'll take you to your family, if you'll only tell me who they are."

I smiled. I nodded, but I kept my eyes fixed on the two startled and amazed angels. Their clothes appeared light, near translucent, as though the fabric were not of a natural weave any more than their incandescent skin was natural. All of their makeup was more rarefied, and fine-woven with light.

Beings of air, of purpose, made up of presence and of what they do—were these the words of Aquinas coming back to me, the *Summa Theologica* on which I had learnt my Latin?

Oh, how miraculously beautiful they were, and so safely apart from all around them, standing transfixed in the street in their quiet wide-eyed simplicity, pondering as they gazed with compassion and interest at me.

One of them, the one crowned with flowers, the one who wore the sky-blue sleeves, the one who had so caught my heart when I had seen him in the *Annunciation* with my father, the one with whom I had fallen in love, moved towards me.

He became larger as he drew closer, taller, slightly larger all over than an ordinary being, and so full of love in the soundless shuffle of his loose and gracefully spilling clothes that he seemed more immaterial and monumentally solid, more perhaps the very expression of God's creation, than anything of flesh and blood might be.

He shook his head and smiled. "No, for you are yourself the very finest of God's creation," he said in a low voice that stole its way through the chatter that surrounded me.

He walked as if he were a mortal being, with clean naked feet over the wet dirty stones of the

Florentine street, oblivious to the men who could not see him as he stood now so close to me, letting his wings spread out and then folding them again tight, so that I only saw the high feathered bones of them above his shoulders, which were sloped like those of a young boy.

His face was brilliantly clean and flushed with all the radiant color Fra Filippo had painted. When he smiled, I felt my entire body tremble violently with unadulterated joy.

"Is this my madness, Archangel?" I asked. "Is this their curse come true, that I shall see this as I gibber and incur the scorn of learned men?" I laughed out loud.

I startled the gentlemen who had been trying so much to help me. They were thoroughly flustered. "What? Speak again?"

But in a shimmering instant, a memory descended upon me, illuminating my heart and soul and mind all in one stroke, as though the sun itself had flooded a dark and hopeless cell.

"It was you I saw in the meadow, you I saw when she drank my blood."

Into my eyes he looked, this cool collected angel, with the rows and rows of immaculate blond curls and the smooth placid cheeks.

"Gabriel, the Archangel," I said in reverence. The tears flooded to my eyes, and it felt like singing to cry.

"My boy, my poor wretched boy," said the old merchant. "There is no angel standing in front of you. Pay attention, now, please."

"They can't see us," said the angel to me simply. Again came his smooth easy smile. His eyes caught the light falling from the brightening sky as he peered into me, as if he would see deeper with every moment of his study.

"I know," I answered. "They don't know!"

"But I am not Gabriel, you must not call me that," he said very courteously and soothingly. "My young one, I am very far from being the Archangel Gabriel. I am Setheus, and I'm a guardian angel only." He was so patient with me, so patient with my crying and with the collection of blind and concerned mortals around us.

He stood close enough for me to touch, but I didn't dare.

"My guardian angel?" I asked. "Is it true?"

"No," said the angel. "I am not your guardian angel. Those you must somehow find for yourself. You've seen the guardian angels of another, though why and how I don't know."

"Don't pray now," said the old man crankily. "Tell us who you are, boy. You said a name before, your father, tell us."

The other angel, who stood as if too shocked to move, suddenly broke his reserve and he too came forward in the same silent barefooted style, as though the roughened stones and the wet and dirt could not mar him or harm him.

"Can this be good, Setheus?" he asked. But his pale iridescent eyes were focused on me with the same loving attention, the same rapt and forgiving interest.

"And you, you are in the other painting, I know you too, I love you with my whole heart," I said.

"Son, to whom are you speaking?" demanded the younger man. "Whom do you love with your whole heart?"

"Ah, you can hear me?" I turned to the man. "You can understand me."

"Yes, now tell me your name."

"Vittorio di Raniari," I said, "friend and ally of the Medici, son of Lorenzo di Raniari, Castello Raniari in the north of Tuscany, and my father is dead, and all my kinsmen. But—."

The two angels stood right before me, together, one head inclined towards the other as they regarded me, and it seemed that the mortals, for all their blindness, could not block the path of the angels' vision or come between me and them. If only I had the courage. I so wanted to touch them.

The wings of the one who'd spoken first were rising, and it seemed a soft shimmer of gold dust fell from the awakening feathers, the quivering, sparkling feathers, but nothing rivaled the angel's meditative and wondering face.

"Let them take you to San Marco," said this angel, the one named Setheus, "let them take you. These men mean well, and you will be put in a cell and cared for by the monks. You cannot be in a finer place, for this is a house under Cosimo's patronage, and you know that Fra Giovanni has decorated the very cell in which you'll stay."

"Setheus, he knows these things," said the other angel.

"Yes, but I am reassuring him," said the first

angel with the simplest shrug, looking wonderingly at his companion. Nothing characterized their faces so much as subdued wonder.

"But you," I said, "Setheus, may I call you by name, you'll let them take me away from you? You can't. Please don't leave me. I beg you. Don't leave me."

"We have to leave you," said the other angel. "We are not your guardians. Why can't you see your own angels?"

"Wait, I know your name. I can hear it."

"No," said this more disapproving angel, waving his finger at me as if correcting a child.

But I would not be stopped. "I know your name. I heard it when you were arguing, and I hear it now when I look at your face. Ramiel, that's your name. And both of you are Fra Filippo's guardians."

"This is a disaster," whispered Ramiel, with the most touching look of distress. "How did this occur?"

Setheus merely shook his head, and smiled again generously. "It has to be for the good, it must be. We have to go with him. Of course we do."

"Now? Leave now?" demanded Ramiel, and again, for all the urgency, there was no anger. It was as though the thoughts were purified of all lower emotions, and of course it was so, it was perfectly so.

Setheus leaned close to the old man, who couldn't of course either see him or hear him, and he said in the old man's ear:

"Take the boy to San Marco; have him put in a

goodly cell, for which he has plenty of money, and have him nursed to health."

Then he looked at me. "We'll go with you."

"We can't do that," said Ramiel. "We can't leave our charge; how can we do such a thing without permission?"

"It's meant to be. This is permission. I know that it is," said Setheus. "Don't you see what's happened? He's seen us and he's heard us and he's caught your name, and he would have caught mine if I hadn't revealed it. Poor Vittorio, we are with you."

I nodded, almost ready to weep at the sound of myself addressed. The whole street had gone drab and hushed and indistinct around their large, quiet and flushed figures, the finespun light of their garments stirring about them as if the celestial fabric were subject to the invisible currents of the air which men cannot feel.

"Those are not our real names!" said Ramiel scoldingly to me, but gently, as one would scold an infant.

Setheus smiled. "They are good enough names by which to call us, Vittorio," he said.

"Yes, take him to San Marco," said the man beside me. "Let's go. Let the monks handle all this."

The men rushed me towards the mouth of the street.

"You'll be very well cared for at San Marco," said Ramiel, as though he were bidding me farewell, but the two angels were moving beside us, and only falling a little behind.

"Don't you leave me, either of you, you can't!" I said to the angels.

They seemed perplexed, their lovely folded gossamer robes unstained by rain, the hems clean and shining as if they had not touched the street, and their bare feet looking so exquisitely tender as they followed at our pace.

"All right," said Setheus. "Don't worry so, Vittorio. We're coming."

"We can't simply leave our charge like this for another man, we can't do it," Ramiel continued to protest.

"It's God's will; how can it be otherwise?"

"And Mastema? We don't have to ask Mastema?" asked Ramiel.

"Why should we ask Mastema? Why bring care to Mastema? Mastema must know."

And there they were, arguing again, behind us, as I was hurried through the street.

The steel sky gleamed, then grew pale and gave way above to blue as we came to an open piazza. The sun shocked me, and made me sicken, yet how I wanted it, how I longed for it, and yet it rebuked me and seemed to scourge me as if it were a whip.

We were only a little ways from San Marco. My legs would soon give out. I kept looking over my shoulder.

The two lustrous, gilded figures came on, silently, with Setheus gesturing for me to go along.

"We're here, we're with you," said Setheus.

"I don't know about this, I don't know!" said Ramiel. "Filippo has never been in such trouble, he has never been subjected to such temptation, such indignity—."

"Which is why we have been drawn off now, so that we do not interfere with what must take place with Filippo. We know we were on the very verge of getting into trouble on account of Filippo and what Filippo has done now. Oh, Filippo, I see this, I see the grand design."

"What are they talking about?" I demanded of the men. "They're saying something about Fra Filippo."

"And who would that be, who is talking, may I ask?" said the old man, shaking his head as he escorted me along, the young madman in his charge with the clanking sword.

"My boy, be quiet now," said the other man, who took the larger burden of supporting me. "We can understand you only too well now, and you are making less sense than ever, talking to people that no one can see and hear."

"Fra Filippo, the painter, what's happening with him?" I demanded. "There's some trouble."

"Oh, it is unbearable," said the angel Ramiel behind me. "It is unthinkable that this should happen. And if you ask me, which no one has and no one will, I believe that if Florence were not at war with Venice, Cosimo de' Medici would protect his painter from this."

"But protect him from what?" I demanded. I looked into the eyes of the old man.

"Son, obey me," said the old man. "Walk straight, and stop banging me with that sword. You are a great Signore, I can see this, and the name of the Raniari rings loud in my ears from the distant mountains of Tuscany, and the gold on your right hand alone weighs more than the dowry of both of my daughters put together, not to mention the gems, but don't shout in my face."

"I'm sorry. I didn't mean to. It's only, the angels won't say precisely."

The other man who led me so kindly, who helped me honestly with the saddlebags in which was my fortune, and did not even seek to steal anything from me, began to speak:

"If you're asking about Fra Filippo, he's deep into trouble again. He's being put to the torture. He's on the rack."

"No, that can't happen, not to Filippo Lippi!" I stopped dead and shouted. "Who would do such a thing to the great painter?"

I turned, and the two angels suddenly covered their faces, as tenderly as ever Ursula had covered hers, and they started weeping. Only their tears were marvelously crystalline and clear. They merely looked at me. Oh, Ursula, I thought with excruciating pain suddenly, how beautiful are these creatures, and in what grave do you sleep beneath the Court of the Ruby Grail that you cannot see them, cannot see their silent secret progress through the city streets?

"It's true," said Ramiel. "It's all too terribly true. What have we been, what sort of guardians, that Filippo has gotten himself into this trouble, that he is so contentious and deceiving, and why have we been so helpless?"

"We are only angels," said Setheus. "Ramiel,

we do not have to accuse Filippo. We are not accusers, we are guardians, and for the sake of the boy who loves him, don't say such things."

"They can't torture Fra Filippo Lippi," I cried out. "Who did he deceive?"

"He did it to himself," said the old man. "He's into fraud this time. He sold off a commission, and everybody knows that one of his apprentices painted too much of the work. He's been put on the rack, but he didn't really get hurt."

"Didn't really hurt him! He's only magnificent!" I said. "You tell me they tortured him. Why was he tortured, how can anyone justify such a stupidity, such an insult, it's an insult to the Medici."

"Silence, child; he confessed," said the younger of the two mortal men. "It's almost over. Some monk if you ask me, Fra Filippo Lippi; if he isn't chasing women, he's in a brawl."

We had come to San Marco. We stood in the Piazza San Marco right before the doors of the monastery, which were flush with the street, as was the case with all such buildings in Florence, as if the Arno never overflowed its banks, which it did. And I was glad, oh, so glad to see this haven.

But my mind was rampant. All memories of demons and horrid murder had been swept clean from me in an instant by the horror that the artist whom I cherished most in all the world had been put on the rack like a common criminal.

"He sometimes . . . well," said Ramiel, "behaves like a common . . . criminal."

"He'll get out of it, he'll pay a fine," said the old

man. He rang the bell for the monks. He patted me with a long, tired, dry hand. "Now stop crying, child, stop. Filippo is a nuisance, everybody knows it. If only there were a little of the saintliness of Fra Giovanni in him, only a little!"

Fra Giovanni. Of course, by this man, Fra Giovanni, they meant the great Fra Angelico, the painter who in centuries to come would bring the awestruck to all but kneel before his paintings, and it was in this monastery that Fra Giovanni worked and lived, it was here that, for Cosimo, he painted the very cells of the monks.

What could I say? "Yes, yes, Fra Giovanni, but I don't . . . I don't . . . love him." Of course I loved him; I honored him and his wondrous work, but it was not like my love for Filippo, the painter I had glimpsed only once—. How explain these strange things?

A surge of nausea caused me to bend double. I backed away from my kindly helpers. I heaved up the contents of my stomach into the street, a bloody stream of filth from the demons who had fed me. I saw it drip and flow into the street. I smelled the putrid stench of it, and I saw it spill from me into the cracks between the cobblestones, this mess of half-digested wine and blood.

The whole horror of the Court of the Ruby Grail seemed manifest in this moment. Hopelessness seized me, and I heard the whisper of demons in my ear, *witless and scorned,* and I doubted all that I'd seen, all that I was, all that had transpired only moments before. In a dreamy woodland, my father and I rode together and we talked of Filippo's paintings, and I was a student and a young lord and had all the world before me, and the strong good smell of the horses filled my nostrils with the smell of the woods.

Witless and scorned. Mad when you might have been immortal.

As I rose up again, I leant back against the wall of the monastery. The light of the blue sky was bright enough to shut my eyes, but I bathed in its warmth. Slowly, as my stomach settled, I tried to gaze steadily before me, to fight the pain of the light and love it and trust in it.

My vision was filled with the face of the angel Setheus right in front of me, only a foot from me, peering at me with the deepest concern.

"Dear God, you *are* here," I whispered.

"Yes," he said. "I promised you."

"You aren't leaving me, are you?" I asked.

"No," he said.

Over his shoulder, Ramiel peered at me closely, as if studying me at leisure and with commitment for the first time. His shorter looser hair made him seem younger, though such distinctions made no difference.

"No, none at all," he whispered, and for the first time, he too smiled.

"Do as these gentle people tell you," said Ramiel. "Let them take you inside, and then you must sleep a natural sleep, and when you wake we'll be with you."

"Oh, but it's a horror, a story of horrors," I whispered. "Filippo never painted such horrors."

"We are not painted things," said Setheus. "What God has in store for us we will discover together, you and Ramiel and I. Now you must go inside. The monks are here. Into their care we give you, and when you wake we will be at your side."

"Like the prayer," I whispered.

"Oh, yes, truly," Ramiel said. He raised his hand. I saw the shadow of his five fingers and then felt the silken touch of his fingers as he closed my eyes.

IN WHICH I CONVERSE WITH THE INNOCENT AND POWERFUL SONS OF GOD

WOULD sleep and deeply, yes, but not until much later. What came was a hazy, dreamlike wonderland of protective images. I was carried by a burly monk and his assistants into the monastery of San Marco.

There could be no place better for me in all of Florence—other than Cosimo's own house perhaps—than the Dominican Monastery of San Marco.

Now, in all of Florence, I know of many exquisite buildings and so much magnificence that even then, as a boy, I could not catalogue in my mind all the riches that lay before me.

But nowhere is there any cloister more serene, I think, than that of San Marco, which had only recently been renovated by the most humble and decent Michelozzo at the behest of Cosimo the Elder. It had a long and venerable history in Florence, but only in recent times had it been given over to the Dominicans, and it was endowed in certain sublime ways in which no other monastery was.

As all Florence knew, Cosimo had lavished a fortune on San Marco, maybe to make up for all the money he made by usury, for as a banker he was a taker of interest and therefore a usurer, but then so were we who had put money in his bank.

Whatever the case, Cosimo, our capo, our true leader, had loved this place and given to it many many treasures, but most of all perhaps its marvelously proportioned new buildings.

His detractors, the whiners, the ones who do nothing great, and suspect all that isn't in a state of perpetual disintegration, they said of him, "He even puts his coat of arms in the privies of the monks."

His coat of arms, by the way, is a shield with five protuberant balls on it, the meaning of which has been variously explained, but what these enemies actually said was: Cosimo had hung his balls over the monks' privies. Eh! That his enemies would be so lucky to have such privies, or such balls.

How much more clever it might have been for those men to point out that Cosimo often spent days at this monastery himself in meditation and prayer, and that the former Prior here, who was Cosimo's great friend and advisor, Fra Antonino, was now the Archbishop of Florence.

Ah, so much for the ignorant, who still to the day five hundred years from then tell lies about Cosimo.

As I passed under the door, I thought, What in

the name of God shall I say to these people in this House of God?

No sooner had that thought popped out of my sleepy head and, I fear, my drugged and sleepy mouth, than I heard Ramiel's laugh in my ear.

I tried to see if he was at my side. But I was blubbering and sick again, and dizzy, and could make out only that we had entered the most tranquil and pleasing cloister.

The sun so burnt my eyes that I couldn't thank God yet for the beauty of the square green garden in the center of this place, but I could see very starkly and sweetly the low rounded arches created by Michelozzo, arches which created gentle colorless and humble vaults over my head.

And the tranquillity achieved by the pure columns, with their small rolled Ionic capitals, all of this added to my sense of safety and peace. Proportions were always the gift of Michelozzo. He opened up things when he built them. And these wide spacious loggias were his stamp.

Nothing would erase the memory for me of the soaring dagger-tipped Gothic arches of the French castle in the North, of the filigreed stone peaks everywhere there that seemed to point in animosity at the Almighty. And though I knew I misjudged this architecture and its intent—for surely, before Florian and his Court of the Ruby Grail had taken hold of it, it had been born from the devotions of the French and the Germans—I still could not get the hated vision of it out of my head.

Trying desperately not to heave up my guts again, I relaxed all my limbs as I saw this Florentine enclosure.

Down around the cloister, down around the burning hot garden, the large monk, a bear of a man, beaming down at me in habitual and inveterate kindness, carried me in his burly arms, while there came others in their flowing black and white robes, with thin radiant faces seeming to encircle us even in our rapid progress. I couldn't see my angels.

But these men were the nearest to angels that the world provides.

I soon realized—due to my former visits to this great place—that I was not being taken to the hospice, where drugs were dispensed to the sick of Florence, or to the pilgrims' refuge, which was always swarming with those who come to offer and pray, but up the stairs into the very hall of the monks' cells.

In a glaze of sickness in which beauty brought a catch in my throat, I saw at the head of the stairway, spread out on the wall, the fresco of Fra Giovanni's *Annunciation*.

My painting, the *Annunciation*! My chosen favorite, the painting which meant more to me than any other religious motif.

And no, it wasn't the genius of my turbulent Filippo Lippi, no, but it was my painting, and surely this was an omen that no demon can damn a soul through the poison of forced blood.

Was Ursula's blood forced on you too? Horrid

thought. Try not to remember her soft fingers being pulled loose from you, you fool, you drunken fool, try not to remember her lips and the long thick kisslet of blood slipping into your own open mouth.

"Look at it!" I cried out. I pointed one flopping arm towards the painting.

"Yes, yes, we have so many," said the big smiling bear of a monk.

Fra Giovanni was of course the painter. Who could have not seen it in one glance? Besides, I knew it. And Fra Giovanni—let me remind you one more time that this is Fra Angelico of the ages— had made a severe, soothing, tender but utterly simple Angel and Virgin, steeped in humility and devoid of embellishments, the visitation itself taking place between low rounded arches such as made up the very cloister from which we had just come.

As the big monk swung me around to take me down the broad corridor—and broad it was, and so polished and austere and beautiful to me—I tried to form words as I carried the image of the angel in my mind.

I wanted to tell Ramiel and Setheus, if they were still with me, that look, Gabriel's wings had only simple stripes of color, and look, how his gown fell in symmetrical and disciplined folds. All of this I understood, as I understood the rampant grandeur of Ramiel and Setheus, but I was blubbering nonsense again.

"The halos," I said. "You two, where are you? Your halos hover over your heads. I saw them. I saw them in the street and in the paintings. But you see in the painting by Fra Giovanni, the halo is flat and surrounds the painted face, a disk hard and golden right on the field of the painting . . ."

The monks laughed. "To whom are you speaking, young Signore Vittorio di Raniari?" one of them asked me.

"Be quiet, child," said the big monk, his booming bass voice pushing against me through his barrel of a chest. "You're in our tender care. And you must hush now, see, there, that's the library, you see our monks at work?"

They were proud of it, weren't they? Even in our progress when I might have vomited all over the immaculate floor, the monk turned to let me see through the open door the long room crowded with books and monks at work, but what I saw too was Michelozzo's vaulted ceiling, again, not soaring to leave us, but bending gently over the heads of the monks and letting a volume of light and air rise above them.

It seemed I saw visions. I saw multiple and triple figures where there should only be one, and even in a flash a misty confusion of angelic wings, and oval faces turned, peering at me through the veil of supernatural secrecy.

"Do you see?" was all I could say. I had to get to that library, I had to find texts in it that defined the demons. Yes, I had not given up! Oh, no, I was no babbling idiot. I had God's very own angels at my assistance. I'd take Ramiel and Setheus in there and show them the texts.

We know, Vittorio, wipe the pictures from your mind, for we see them.

"Where are you?" I cried out.

"Quiet," said the monks.

"But will you help me go back there and kill them?"

"You're babbling," said the monks.

Cosimo was the guardian patron of that library. When old Niccolo de' Niccoli died, a marvelous collector of books with whom I had many times spoken at Vaspasiano's bookshop, all of his religious books, and maybe more, had been donated by Cosimo to this monastery.

I would find them in there, in that library, and find proof in St. Augustine or Aquinas of the devils with which I'd fought.

No. I was not mad. I had not given up. I was no gibbering idiot. If only the sun coming in the high little windows of this airy place would stop baking my eyeballs and burning my hands.

"Quiet, quiet," said the big monk, smiling still. "You are making noises like an infant. Hhhhh. Burgle, gurgle. Hear? Now, look, the library's busy. It's open to the public today. Everybody is busy today."

He turned only a few steps past the library to take me into a cell. "Down there . . ." he went on, as if cajoling an unruly baby. "Only a few steps away is the Prior's cell, and guess who is there this very minute? It's the Archbishop."

"Antonino," I whispered.

"Yes, yes, you said it right. Once our own Antonino. Well, he's here, and guess why?"

I was too groggy to respond. The other monks surrounded me. They wiped me with cool cloths. They smoothed back my hair.

This was a clean large cell. Oh, if the sun would only stop. What had those demons done to me, made me into a half-demon? Dare I ask for a mirror?

Set down on a thick soft bed, in this warm, clean place, I lost all control of my limbs. I was sick again.

The monks attended me with a silver basin. The sunlight pierced brilliantly upon a fresco, but I couldn't bear to look at the gleaming figures, not in this hurtful illumination. It seemed the cell was filled with other figures. Were they angels? I saw transparent beings, drifting, stirring, but I could catch hold of no clear outline. Only the fresco burned into the wall in its colors seemed solid, valid, true.

"Have they done this to my eyes forever?" I asked. I thought I caught a glimpse of an angelic form in the doorway of the cell, but it was not the figure of either Setheus or Ramiel. Did it have webbed wings? Demon wings? I started in terror.

But it was gone. Rustling, whispering. *We know.*

"Where are my angels?" I asked. I cried. I told out the names of my father and his father, and of all the di Raniari whom I could remember.

"Shhhhh," said the young monk. "Cosimo has been told that you are here. But this is a terrible day. We remember your father. Now let us remove these filthy clothes."

My head swam. The room was gone.

Sodden sleep, a glimpse of her, my savior Ursula. She ran through the blowing meadow. Who was this pursuing her, driving her out of the nodding, weaving flowers? Purple irises surrounded her, were crushed under her feet. She turned. Don't, Ursula! Don't turn. Don't you see the flaming sword?

I woke in a warm bath. Was it the cursed baptismal fount? No. I saw the fresco, the holy figures, dimly, and more immediately the real live monks who surrounded me on their knees on the stone, their big sleeves rolled back as they washed me in the warm, sweet-scented water.

"Ah, that Francesco Sforza . . ." they spoke in Latin to one another. "To charge into Milan and take possession of the Dukedom! As if Cosimo did not have enough trouble, without Sforza having done such a thing."

"He did it? He has taken Milan?" I asked.

"What did you say? Yes, son, he has. He broke the peace. And your family, all your poor family murdered by the freebooters; don't think they'll go unpunished, rampaging through that country, those damned Venetians . . ."

"No, you mustn't, you must tell Cosimo. It was not an act of war, what happened to my family, not by human beings . . ."

"Hush, child."

Chaste hands sponged the water over my shoulders. I sat slumped against the warm metal back of the tub.

". . . di Raniari, always loyal," said one of them to me. "And your brother was to come to study with us, your sweet brother, Matteo . . ."

I let out a terrible cry. A soft hand sealed my lips.

"Sforza himself will punish them. He'll clean out that country."

I cried and cried. No one could understand me. They wouldn't listen to me.

The monks lifted me to my feet. I was dressed in a long comfortable soft linen robe. It came to me that I was being dressed for execution, but the hour of such danger had passed.

"I am not mad!" I said clearly.

"No, not at all, only grief-stricken."

"You understand me!"

"You are tired."

"The bed is soft for you, brought specially for you, hush, don't rave anymore."

"Demons did it," I whispered. "They weren't soldiers."

"I know, son, I know. War is terrible. War is the Devil's work."

No, but it wasn't war. Will you listen to me?

Hush, this is Ramiel at your ear; didn't I tell you to sleep? Will you listen to us? We have heard your thoughts as well as your words!

I lay down on the bed flat on my chest. The monks brushed and dried my hair. My hair was so long now. Unkempt, country Lord hair. But this was an immense comfort to be bathed and gentlemanly clean.

"Those are candles?" I asked. "The sun has gone down?"

"Yes," said the monk beside me. "You have slept."

"May I have more candles?"

"Yes, I'll bring them to you."

I lay in the darkness. I blinked and tried to shape the words of the *Ave*.

Many lights appeared in the door, some six or seven in a cluster, each a sweet small perfectly shaped flame. Then they fluttered as the monk's feet came softly towards me. I saw him clearly as he knelt to place the candelabra beside my bed.

He was thin and tall, a sapling in hollow willowy robes. His hands were so clean. "You are in a special cell. Cosimo has sent men to bury your dead."

"Thanks be to God," I said.

"Yes."

So now I could speak!

"They are still talking down there, and it's late," said the monk. "Cosimo is troubled. He'll stay the night here. The whole city is filled with Venetian agitators stirring up the populace against Cosimo."

"Now hush," said another monk who appeared suddenly. He bent down and lifted my head to place another thick pillow beneath it.

What bliss this was. I thought of the damned ones imprisoned in the coop. "Oh, horrors! It's night, and they're waiting for the horrible Communion."

"Who, child? What Communion?"

Once again, I glimpsed figures moving, drifting, as it were, in the shadows. But they were too soon gone.

I had to vomit. I needed the basin. They held my hair for me. Did they see the blood in the candlelight? The pure streak of blood? It smelled so rotten.

"How can one survive such poison?" one monk whispered to the other in Latin. "Do we dare purge him?"

"You'll frighten him. Be quiet. He has no fever."

"Well, you're damned wrong if you think you took my wits," I declared suddenly. I shouted it to Florian and to Godric and to all of them.

The monks looked at me in urgent astonishment.

I laughed. "I only was talking to those who tried to hurt me," I said, again letting each word have a clear distinct shape.

The thin monk with the remarkably scrubbed hands knelt by me. He smoothed my forehead. "And the beautiful sister, the sister who was to be married, is she too . . . ?"

"Bartola! She was to be married? I didn't know. Well, he can have her head for a maidenhead." I wept. "The worms are at work in the dark. And the demons dance on the hill, and the town does nothing."

"What town?"

"You're raving again," said a monk who stood beyond the candles. How distinct he looked, though he was beyond the light, a round-shouldered individual with a hooked nose and thick somber heavy eyelids. "Don't rave anymore, poor child."

I wanted to protest, but I saw suddenly a giant soft wing, each feather tinged with gold, come down over me, enfolding me. I was tickled all over by the softness of the feathers. Ramiel said:

What must we do to make you shut up? Filippo needs us now; will you give us some peace and quiet for Filippo, whom God sent us to guard? Don't answer me. Obey me.

The wing crushed out all vision, all woe.

Shadowy pale darkness. Even and complete. The candles were behind me, set up high.

I woke. I rose up on my elbows. My head was clear. A lovely even illumination gave just the smallest tremble as it filled the cell. From the high window came the moon. The shaft of the moon struck the fresco on the wall, the fresco obviously painted by Fra Giovanni.

My eyes could see it with amazing clarity. Was this my demonic blood?

A strange thought came to me. It rung in my consciousness with the clarity of a golden bell. I myself possessed no guardian angels! My angels had left me; they had departed, because my soul was damned.

I had no angels. I had seen Filippo's because of the power the demons had given me, and because of something else. Filippo's angels argued so much with each other! That's how I had seen them. Some words came to me.

200

They came back to me from Aquinas, or was it Augustine? I'd read so much of both to learn my Latin, and their endless excursuses had so delighted me. The demons are full of passion. But angels are not.

But those two angels had such spirit. That's why they'd cut through the veil.

I pushed back the covers and set my bare feet on the stone floor. It was cool, and pleasing, because the room, having received the sun all day, was still warm.

No drafts swept the polished and immaculate floor.

I stood before the wall painting. I wasn't dizzy or sick, or like to fall. I was myself again.

What an innocent and untroubled soul Fra Giovanni must have been. All his figures were devoid of malice. I could see the figure of Christ seated before a mountain, round gold halo decorated with the red arms and top of a cross. Beside him stood ministering angels. One held bread for him, and the other, whose figure was cut off by the door that was cut into the wall, this other angel, whose wingtips were barely visible, carried wine and meat.

Above, on the mountain, I saw Christ also. It was a painting of different incidents, in sequence, and above, Christ was standing in His same smooth and multiwrinkled pink robes, but here He was agitated, as agitated as Fra Giovanni could make Him, and Christ had lifted His left hand, as if in wrath.

The figure who fled from Him was the Devil! It

was a horrid creature with the webbed wings I thought I'd glimpsed earlier, and it had hideous webbed feet. It had dewclaws on its webbed feet. Sour-faced and in a dirty gray robe, it fled from Christ, who stood firm in the Desert, refusing to be tempted, and, only after this confrontation, then had the ministering angels come, and had Christ taken His place with His hands clasped.

I sucked in my breath in terror as I beheld this image of the demon. But a great rush of comfort passed through me, causing my hair to tingle at its roots, causing my feet to tingle against the polished floor. I had routed the demons, I had refused their gift of immortality. I had refused it. Even faced with the cross!

I retched. The pain caught me as if I'd been kicked in the stomach. I turned. The basin was there, clean and polished, sitting on the floor. I dropped to my knees and heaved up more of their syrupy filth. Was there no water?

I looked around. There stood the pitcher and the cup. The cup was full and I spilt some of it as I put it to my lips, but it tasted thin and rancid and awful. I threw down the cup.

"You've poisoned me for natural things, you monsters. You will not win!"

My hands trembling, I picked up the cup, filled it once more and tried again to drink. But it tasted unnatural. To what can I compare it? It was not foul like urine; it was like water that is full of minerals and metal and will leave a chalk on you and choke you. It was bad!

I put it aside. Very well then. Time to study. Time to take up the candles, which I now did.

I went out of the cell. The hall was empty and glowing in the pale light that came from tiny windows over the low-ceilinged cells.

I turned to my right and approached the doors of the library. They were unlocked.

I entered with my candelabra. Once again, the tranquillity of Michelozzo's design brought a warmth to me, a faith in all things, a trust. Two rows of arches and Ionic columns moved down the center of the room to make a broad aisle to the far distant door, and on either side were the study tables, and all along the far walls were racks and racks of codices and scrolls.

Across the herringbone stones of the floor I walked barefoot, lifting the candle higher so that the light would fill up the vaulted ceiling, so happy to be here alone.

Windows on either side let in shafts of pale illumination through the overwhelming clutter of shelves, but how divine and restful were the high ceilings. How boldly he had done it, made a basilica of a library.

How could I have known, child that I was then, that this style would be imitated all over my beloved Italy? Oh, there were so many wondrous things then for the living and for all time.

And I? What am I? Do I live? Or am I walking always in death, forever in love with time?

I stood still with my candles. How my eyes loved the moonlighted splendor. How I craved to stand here forever, dreaming, near to things of the mind, and things of the soul, and far away in memory from the wretched enchained town on its cursed mountain and the castle nearby, which at this very moment probably gave forth its ghastly, ugly light.

Could I discern the order of this wealth of books?

The very cataloger of this library, the very monk who had done the work here, the very scholar, was now the Pope of all Christendom, Nicholas V.

I moved along the shelves to my right, holding high my candles. Would it be alphabetical? I thought of Aquinas, for I knew him more freely, but it was St. Augustine whom I found. And I had always loved Augustine, loved his colorful style and his eccentricities, and the dramatic manner in which he wrote.

"Oh, you wrote more about demons, you are better!" I said.

The City of God! I saw it, copy after copy. There were a score of codices of this very masterpiece, not to mention all of the other work of this great saint, his *Confessions*, which had gripped me as much as a Roman drama, and so much more. Some of these books were ancient, made of big sloppy parchment, others were extravagantly bound, some almost simple and very new.

In charity and consideration, I must take the most sturdy of these, even though there might be errors, and God only knew how hard monks worked to avoid errors. I knew which volume I wanted. I knew the volume on demons, because I had thought it so very fascinating and funny and so much poppycock. Oh, what a fool I'd been.

I took down the hefty fat volume, number nine of the text, slipping it into the crook of my arm, moved to the first desk and then carefully placed the candelabra in front of me, where it would light me but throw no shadows under my fingers, and I opened the book.

"It's all here!" I whispered. "Tell me, St. Augustine, what were they so that I may convince Ramiel and Setheus that they must help me, or give me the means to convince these modern Florentines, who care about nothing right now but making war with paid soldiers on the Serene Republic of Venice up north. Help me, Saint. I'm telling you."

Ah, Chapter Ten, of Volume Nine, I knew this . . .

Augustine was quoting Plotinus, or explaining him:

> . . . that the very fact of man's corporal mortality is due to the compassion of God, who would not have us kept for ever in the misery of this life. The wickedness of demons was not judged worthy of this compassion, and in the misery of their condition, with a soul subject to passions, they have not been granted the mortal body, which man had received, but an eternal body.

"Ah, yes!" I said. "And this is what Florian offered me, bragging that they did not age or decay and were not subject to disease, that I could have lived there with them forever. Evil, evil. Well, this is proof, and I have it here, and I can show it to the monks!"

I read on, skimming to find the kernels that would make my case grow. Down to Chapter Eleven:

> *Apuleius says also that the souls of men are demons. On leaving human bodies they become lares if they have shown themselves good, if evil, lemures or larvae.*

"Yes, lemures. I know this word. Lemures or larvae, and Ursula, she said to me that she had been young, young as me; they were all human and now they are lemures."

> *According to Apuleius, larvae are malignant demons created out of men.*

I was overcome with excitement. I needed parchment and pens. I had to note the place. I had to mark down what I had discovered and go on. For the next point was obviously to convince Ramiel and Setheus that they had gotten into the biggest—.

My thoughts were brought to an abrupt halt.

Behind me, a personage had come into the library. I heard a heavy footfall, but there was a muffled quality to it, and a great darkening occurred behind me, as though all the slim, sly beams of the moon that fell through the passage beyond had been cut off.

I turned slowly and looked over my shoulder.

"And why do you choose the left?" asked this personage.

He rose up before me, immense and winged, peering down at me, his face luminous in the flicker of the candles, his eyebrows gently raised but straight so that there was no arch to them to make them anything but severe. He had the riotous golden hair of Fra Filippo's brush, curling beneath a huge red battle helmet, and behind him his wings were heavily sheathed in gold.

He wore a suit of armor, with the breastplates decorated and the shoulders covered with immense buckles, and around his waist was a blue sash of silk. His sword was sheathed, and on one lax arm he wore his shield, with its red cross.

I had never seen his like.

"I need you!" I declared. I stood up, knocking the bench back. I reached out so that it would not clatter to the floor. I faced him.

"You need me!" he said in muted outrage. "You do! You who would lead off Ramiel and Setheus from Fra Filippo Lippi. You need me? Do you know who I am?"

It was a gorgeous voice, rich, silken, violent and piercing though deep.

"You have a sword," I said.

"Oh, and for what?"

"Killing them, all of them!" I said. "Going there with me by day to their castle. Do you know what I am speaking of?"

He nodded. "I know what you dreamt and what you babbled and what Ramiel and Setheus have gleaned from your feverish mind. Of course I know. You need me, you say, and Fra Filippo Lippi lies in bed with a whore who licks his aching joints, and one in particular that aches for her!"

"Such talk from an angel," I said.

"Don't mock me, I'll slap you," he said. His wings rose and fell as if he were sighing with them, or gasping rather, at me in umbrage.

"So do it!" I said. My eyes were feasting fiendishly on his glistering beauty, on the red silk cloak that was clasped just below the bit of tunic that showed above his armor, at the solemn smoothness of his cheeks. "But come with me to the mountains and kill them," I implored him.

"Why don't you go yourself and do it?"

"Do you think I can?" I demanded.

His face went serene. His lower lip gave the smallest most thoughtful pout. His jaw and neck were powerful, more powerful by far than the anatomy of Ramiel or Setheus, who seemed more youths, and this their splendid elder brother.

"You are not the Fallen One, are you?" I asked.

"How dare you!" he whispered, waking from his slumber. A terrible frown broke over him.

"Mastema, then, that's who you are. They said your name. Mastema."

He nodded and sneered. "They would, of course, say my name."

"Which means what, great angel? That I can call on you, that I have the power to command you?" I turned and reached for the book of St. Augustine.

"Put down that book!" he said impatiently yet coolly. "There is an angel standing before you, boy; look at me when I speak to you!"

"Ah, you speak like Florian, the demon in that far castle. You have the same control, the same modulation. What do you want of me, angel? Why did you come?"

He was silent, as if he couldn't produce an answer. Then, quietly, he put a question to me. "Why do you think?"

"Because I prayed?"

"Yes," he said coldly. "Yes! And because they have come to me on your account."

My eyes widened. I felt light fill them up. But the light didn't hurt them. A soft cluster of sweet noises filled my ears.

On either side of him there appeared Ramiel and Setheus, their milder, gentler faces focused on me.

Mastema raised his eyebrows again as he looked down at me.

"Fra Filippo Lippi is drunk," he said. "When he wakes up, he'll get drunk again until the pain stops."

"Fools to rack a great painter," I said, "but then you know my thoughts on that."

"Ah, and the thoughts of all the women in Florence," said Mastema. "And the thoughts of the great ones who pay for his paintings, if their minds were not on war."

"Yes," said Ramiel, glancing imploringly to Mastema. They were of the same height, but Mastema didn't turn, and Ramiel came forward some, as if to catch his eye. "If they weren't all so carried away with war."

"War is the world," said Mastema. "I asked you before, Vittorio di Raniari, do you know who I am?"

I was shaken, not by the question, but that the three had now come together, and that I stood before them, the only mortal being, and all the mortal world around us seemed to sleep.

Why had no monk come down the passage to see who whispered in the library? Why had no Watchman of the night come to see why the candles floated along the passage? Why the boy murmured and raved?

Was I mad?

It seemed to me quite suddenly and ludicrously that if I answered Mastema correctly, I would not be mad.

This thought brought from him a small laugh, neither harsh nor sweet.

Setheus stared at me with his obvious sympathy. Ramiel said nothing but looked again to Mastema.

"You are the angel," I said, "whom the Lord gives permission to wield that sword." There came no response from him. I went on. "You are the angel who slew the firstborn of Egypt," I said. No response. "You are the angel, the angel who can avenge."

He nodded, but only really with his eyes. They closed and then opened.

Setheus drew close to him, lips to his ears.

"Help him, Mastema, let us all go help him. Filippo cannot use our counsel now."

"And why?" demanded Mastema of the angel beside him. He looked at me.

"God has given me no leave to punish these demons of yours. Never has God said to me, 'Mastema, slay the vampires, the lemures, the larvae, the blood drinkers.' Never has God spoken to me and said, 'Lift your mighty sword to cleanse the world of these.' "

"I beg you," I said. "I, a mortal boy, beg you. Kill these, wipe out this nest with your sword."

"I can't do it."

"Mastema, you can!" declared Setheus.

Ramiel spoke up. "If he says he cannot, he cannot! Why do you never listen to him?"

"Because I know that he can be moved," said Setheus without hesitation to his compatriot. "I know that he can, as God can be moved."

Setheus stepped boldly in front of Mastema.

"Pick up the book, Vittorio," he said. He stepped forward. At once the large vellum pages, heavy as they were, began to flutter. He put it in my hand, and marked the place with his pale finger, barely touching the thick black crowded writing.

I read aloud:

And therefore God who made the visible marvels of Heaven and Earth does not disdain to work visible miracles in Heaven and Earth, by which

He arouses the soul, hitherto preoccupied with visible things, to the worship of Himself.

His finger moved, and my eyes moved with it. I read of God:

To Him, there is no difference between seeing us about to pray and listening to our prayers, for even when His angels listen, it is He Himself who listens in them.

I stopped, my eyes full of tears. He took the book from me to guard it from my tears.

A noise had penetrated our small circle. Monks had come. I heard them whispering in the corridor, and then the door swung open. Into the library they came.

I cried, and when I looked up I saw them staring at me, two monks whom I didn't know or didn't remember, had never known.

"What is it, young man? Why are you here alone crying?" the first spoke.

"Here, let us take you back to bed. We'll bring you something to eat."

"No, I can't eat it," I said.

"No, he can't eat it," said the first monk to the other. "It still makes him sick. But he can rest." He looked at me.

I turned. The three radiant angels stood silently staring at the monks who could not see them, who had no clue that the angels were there!

"Dear God in Heaven, please tell me," I said.

"Have I gone mad? Have the demons won out, have they so polluted me with their blood and their potions that I see things which are delusions, or am I come like Mary to the tomb to see an angel there?"

"Come to bed," said the monks.

"No," said Mastema, quietly addressing the monk who didn't even see him or hear him. "Let him stay. Let him read to quiet his mind. He is a boy of education."

"No, no," said the monk, shaking his head. He glanced to the other. "We should let him stay. He's a boy of education. He can read quietly. Cosimo said that he must have anything he desired."

"Go on, leave him now," said Setheus softly.

"Hush," said Ramiel. "Let Mastema tell them."

I was too flooded with sorrow and happiness to respond. I covered my face, and when I did so I thought of my poor Ursula, forever with her demon Court, and how she had wept for me. "How could that be?" I whispered into my own fingers.

"Because she was human once, and has a human heart," said Mastema to me in the silence.

The two monks were hurrying out. For one moment the collection of angels was as sheer as light, and I saw through them to the two retreating figures of the monks who closed up the doors as they left.

Mastema looked at me with his still, powerful gaze.

"One could read anything into your face," I said.

"So it is with almost all angels all of the time," he answered.

"I beg you," I said. "Come with me. Help me. Guide me. Do what you just did with those monks! That you can do, can't you?"

He nodded.

"But we can't do more than that, you see," said Setheus.

"Let Mastema say," said Ramiel.

"Go back to Heaven!" said Setheus.

"Please, the both of you, be quiet," said Mastema. "Vittorio, I cannot slay them. I have no leave. That you can do, and with your own sword."

"But you'll come."

"I'll take you," he said. "When the sun rises, when they sleep under their stones. But you must slay them, you must open them to the light, and you must set free those awful wretched prisoners, and you must stand before the townsmen, or let loose that crippled flock and flee."

"I understand."

"We can move the stones away from their sleeping places, can't we?" asked Setheus. He put up his hand to hush Ramiel before Ramiel could protest. "We'll have to do it."

"We can do that," said Mastema. "As we can stop a beam from falling on Filippo's head. We can do that. But we cannot slay them. And you, Vittorio, we cannot make you go through with it, either, if your nerve or your will fails."

"You don't think the miracle of my having seen you will uphold me?"

"Will it?" Mastema asked.

"You speak of her, don't you?"

"Do I?" he asked.

"I will go through with it, but you must tell me . . ."

"What must I tell you?" Mastema asked.

"Her soul, will it go to Hell?"

"That I cannot tell you," said Mastema.

"You have to."

"No, I have to do nothing but what the Lord God has created me to do, and that I do, but to solve the mysteries over which Augustine pondered for a lifetime, no, that is not what I have to do or should do or will do."

Mastema picked up the book.

Once again the pages moved with his will. I felt the breeze rising from them.

He read:

There is something to be gained from the inspired discourses of Scripture.

"Don't read those words to me; they don't help me!" I said. "Can she be saved? Can she save her soul? Does she possess it still? Is she as powerful as you are? Can you Fall? Can the Devil come back to God?"

He put down the book with a swift, airy movement that I could scarcely follow.

"Are you ready for this battle?" he asked.

"They'll lie helpless in the light of day," said Setheus to me. "Including her. She too will lie helpless. You must open the stones that cover them, and you know what you must do."

Mastema shook his head. He turned and gestured for them to get out of his way.

"No, please, I beg you!" said Ramiel. "Do it for him. Do it, please. Filippo is beyond our help for days."

"You know no such thing," said Mastema.

"Can my angels go to him?" I asked. "Have I none that can be sent?"

I had no sooner spoken these words than I realized that two more entities had taken form directly beside me, one on either side, and when I looked from left to right I saw them, only they were pale and remote from me, and they hadn't the flame of Filippo's guardians, only a quiet and quasi-visible and undeniable presence and will.

I looked at one for a long time and then the other, and could draw no descriptive words from my mind from them. Their faces seemed blank and patient and quiet. They were winged beings, tall, yes, I can say that much, but what more could I say, because I couldn't endow them with color or splendor or individuality, and they had no garments or motion to them or anything that I could love.

"What is it? Why won't they speak to me? Why do they look at me that way?"

"They know you," said Ramiel.

"You're full of vengeance, and desire," said Setheus. "They know it; they have been at your side. They have measured your pain and your anger."

"Good God, these demons killed my family!" I declared. "Do you know the future of my soul, any of you?"

"Of course not," said Mastema. "Why would we be here if we did? Why would any of us be here if it were ordained?"

"Don't they know that I faced death rather than take the demon blood? Would not a vendetta have required of me that I drink it and then destroy my enemies when I had powers such as theirs?"

My angels drew closer to me.

"Oh, where were you when I was about to die!" I declared.

"Don't taunt them. You have never really believed in them." It was Ramiel's voice. "You loved us when you saw our images, and when the demon blood was full inside you, you saw what you could love. That is the danger now. Can you kill what you love?"

"I will destroy all of them," I said. "One way or another, I swear it on my soul." I looked at my pale unyielding yet unjudging guardians, and then to the others who burnt so brightly against the shadows of the vast library, against the dark colors of the shelves and the crowded books.

"I will destroy them all," I vowed. I closed my eyes. I imagined her, lying helpless by day, and I saw myself bend and kiss her cold white forehead. My sobs were muffled and my body shook. I nodded again and again that I would do it, yes, I would do it, I would do it.

"At dawn," said Mastema, "the monks will have fresh clothes laid out for you, a suit of red velvet, and your weapons freshly polished, and your boots cleaned. All will be finished by then. Don't try to eat. It's too soon, and the demon blood is still churning in you. Prepare yourself, and we will take you north to do what has to be done in the light of day."

II

And the light shineth in darkness, and the darkness did not comprehend it.

— THE GOSPEL ACCORDING TO ST. JOHN 1.5

ONASTERIES wake early, if they ever sleep at all.

My eyes opened quite suddenly, and only then, as I saw the morning light cover the fresco, as if the veil of darkness had been drawn from it, only then did I know how deeply I had slept.

Monks moved in my cell. They had brought in the red velvet tunic, the clothes as Mastema described, and were just laying them out. I had fine red wool hose to wear with them, and a shirt of gold silk, and to go over that, another of white silk, and then a thick new belt for the tunic. My weapons were polished, as I had been told they would be—my heavy jeweled sword gleaming as though my father himself had been toying with it all of a peaceful evening long by the fire. My daggers were ready.

I climbed out of the bed and dropped down to my knees in prayer. I made the Sign of the Cross.

"God, give me the strength to send in your hands those who feed on death."

It was a whisper in Latin.

One of the monks touched me on the shoulder and smiled. Had the Great Silence not yet ended? I had no idea. He pointed to a table where there was food laid out for me—bread and milk. The milk had foam on the top of it.

I nodded and smiled at him, and then he and his companion made me a little bow and went out.

I turned around and around.

"All of you are here, I know it," I said, but I gave no more time to it. If they didn't come, then I had recovered my wits, but no such thing was true, any more than it was true that my father was alive.

On the table, not far from the food, and held in place beneath the weight of the candelabra, was a series of documents, freshly written and signed in ornate script.

I read them hastily.

They were receipts for all my money and jewels, those things which had been with me in my saddlebags when I came in. All these documents bore the seal of the Medici.

There was a purse of money there, to be tied to my belt. All my rings were there, cleaned and polished, so that the cabochon rubies were brilliant and the emeralds had a flawless depth. The gold gleamed as it had not in months perhaps, for my own negligence.

I brushed out my hair, annoyed at its thickness

and length, but having no time to ask for a barber to cut it shorter than my shoulders. At least it was long enough, and had been for a while, to stay back over my shoulders and off my forehead. It was luxurious to have it so clean.

I dressed quickly. My boots were a little snug because they had been dried by a fire after the rain. But they felt good over the thin hose. I made right all my fastenings and positioned my sword.

The red velvet tunic was plaited along the edges with gold and silver thread, and the front of it was richly decorated with the silver fleurs-de-lys, which is the most ancient symbol of Florence. Once my belt was tightly fastened, the tunic didn't come to halfway down my thigh. That was for handsome legs.

The whole raiment was more than fancy for battle, but what battle was this? It was a massacre. I put on the short flaring cloak they had given me, fastening its gold buckles, though it would be warm for the city. It was lined in soft thin dark-brown squirrel fur.

I ignored the hat. I tied on the purse. I put on my rings one by one until my hands were weapons on account of their weight. I put on the soft fur-lined gloves. I found a dark-amber-beaded rosary that I had not noticed before. It had a gold crucifix, which I kissed, and this I put in my pocket under my tunic.

I realized that I was staring at the floor, and that I was surrounded by pairs of bare feet. Slowly I lifted my gaze.

My angels stood before me, my very own guardians, in long flowing robes of dark blue, which appeared to be made of something lighter yet more opaque than silk. Their faces were ivory white and shimmering faintly, and their eyes were large and like opals. They had dark hair, or hair that seemed to shift as if it were made of shadows.

They stood facing me, their heads together, so that their heads touched. It was as though they were communing silently with one another.

They overwhelmed me. It seemed a terrifying intimacy that I should see them so vividly and so close to me, and know them as the two who had been with me always, or so I was to believe. They were slightly larger than human beings, as were the other angels I had seen, and they were not tempered by the sweet faces I had seen on the others, but had altogether smoother and broader countenances and larger though exquisitely shaped mouths.

"And you don't believe in us now?" one of them asked in a whisper.

"Will you tell me your names?" I asked.

Both shook their heads in a simple negation at once.

"Do you love me?" I asked.

"Where is it written that we should?" answered the one who had not yet spoken. His voice was as toneless and soft as a whisper, but more distinct. It might have been the same voice as the other angel.

"Do you love us?" asked the other.

"Why do you guard me?" I asked.

"Because we are sent to do it, and will be with you until you die."

"Lovelessly?" I asked.

They shook their heads again in negation.

Gradually the light brightened in the room. I turned sharply to look up at the window. I thought it was the sun. The sun couldn't hurt me, I thought.

But it wasn't. It was Mastema, who had risen up behind me as if he were a cloud of gold, and on either side of him were my arguers, my advancers of the cause, my champions, Ramiel and Setheus.

The room shimmered and seemed to vibrate without a sound. My angels appeared to glisten, and to grow brilliantly white and deep blue in their robes.

All looked to the helmeted figure of Mastema.

An immense and musical rustling filled the air, a singing sound, as if a great flock of tiny golden-throated birds had awakened and rushed upwards from the branches of their sun-filled trees.

I must have closed my eyes. I lost my balance, and the air became cooler, and it seemed my vision was clouded with dust.

I shook my head. I looked around me.

We stood within the castle itself.

The place was damp and very dark. Light crept in around the seams of the immense drawbridge, which was of course pulled up and locked into place. On either side were rustic stone walls, hung here and there with great rusted hooks and chains that had not been used in many a year.

I turned and entered a dim courtyard, my breath suddenly taken from me by the height of the walls that surrounded me, climbing to the distinct cube of the bright blue sky.

Surely this was only one courtyard, the one at the entrance, for before us there loomed another immense pair of gates, quite large enough to admit the greatest haywagons imaginable or some new-fangled engine of war.

The ground was soiled. High above on all sides were windows, rows upon rows of the double-arched windows, and all were covered over with bars.

"I need you now, Mastema," I said. I made the Sign of the Cross again. I took out the rosary and kissed the crucifix, looking down for a moment at the tiny twisted body of Our Tortured Christ.

The huge doors before me broke open. There was a loud creaking sound, then the crumpling of metal bolts, and the gates groaned back on their hinges, revealing a distant and sun-filled inner court of far greater size.

The walls through which we walked were some thirty to forty feet in depth. There were doors on either side of us, heavily arched in worked stone and showing the first signs of care that I had glimpsed since we entered.

"These creatures do not go and come as others do," I said. I hurried my pace so as to reach the full sun of the courtyard. The mountain air was too cool and too damp in the foul thickness of the passage.

Here, as I stood up, I saw windows such as I remembered, hung with rich banners and strung with lanterns that would be lighted by night. Here I saw tapestries carelessly thrown over window ledges as if rain were nothing. And very high up I saw the jagged battlements and finer white marble copings.

But even this was not the great courtyard that lay beyond. These walls too were rustic. The stones were soiled and untrodden in many a year. Water was pooled here and there. Rank weeds sprang from crevices, but, ah, there were sweet wildflowers, and I looked at them tenderly and reached out to touch them, and marveled at them, existing here.

More gates awaited us, these two—huge, wooden, banded in iron and severely pointed at the top in their deep marble archway—gave way and sprang back to let us pass through yet another wall.

Oh, such a garden greeted us!

As we made our way through another forty feet of darkness, I saw the great groves of orange trees ahead of us, and heard the cry of the birds. I wondered if they were not caught down here, prisoners, or could they soar all the way up to the top and escape?

Yes, they could. It was a great enough space. And here was the fine white marble facing I remembered, all the way to the summit, so high above.

As I made my way into the garden, as I walked on the first marble path that traversed the beds of violets and roses, I saw the birds coming and going, circling broadly in this wide place, so that they could clear the towers that rose so distantly and majestically against the sky.

Everywhere the scent of flowers overcame me. Lilies and irises were mingled in patches, and the oranges were ripe and almost red as they hung from the trees. The lemons were hard still and touched with green.

Shrubbery and vines hugged the walls.

The angels gathered around me. I realized that all along it was I who had led the way, I who had initiated any movement, and it was I who held us all still now, within the garden, and that they waited as I bowed my head.

"I am listening for the prisoners," I said. "But I can't hear them."

I looked up at more of the luxuriously decorated balconies and windows, the twin arches, and here and there a long loggia, but made of their style of filigree, not ours.

I saw flags fluttering, and all were in that dark blood-red color, stained with death. I looked down for the first time at my own brilliant crimson clothes.

"Like fresh blood?" I whispered.

"Tend to what you must do first," Mastema said. "Twilight can cover you when you go to the prisoners, but you must take your quarry now."

"Where are they? Will you tell me?"

"In deliberate sacrilege, and in old-fashioned rigor, they lie beneath the stones of the church."

There was a loud, searing noise. He had pulled out his sword. He pointed with it, his head turned, his red helmet on fire with the glint of the sun reflected off the marble-faced walls.

"The door there, and the stairs beyond it. The church lies on the third floor, up to our left."

I made for the door without further delay. I rushed up the steps, taking turn after turn, my boots clattering on the stone, not even looking to see if they followed me, not wondering how they did it, knowing only that they were with me, feeling their presence as if I could feel their breath on me when no breath came.

At last we entered the corridor, broad and open on our right to the courtyard below. There was an endless strip of rich carpet before us, full of Persian flowers deeply embedded within a field of midnight blue. Unfaded, untrammeled. On and on it went until it turned, ahead of us. And at the end of the corridor was the perfectly framed sky and the jagged speck of green mountain beyond.

"Why have you stopped?" Mastema asked.

They had materialized around me, in their settling garments and their never-still wings.

"This is the door to the church here, you know it."

"Only looking at the sky, Mastema," I said. "Only looking at the blue sky."

"And thinking of what?" asked one of my guardians in his toneless, clear whisper. He clung to me suddenly, and I saw his parchment-colored fingers, weightless, settled on my shoulder. "Thinking of a meadow that never existed and a young woman who is dead?"

"Are you merciless?" I asked him. I pressed close to him, so my forehead touched him, and I marveled to feel it against me and see his opalescent eyes so distinct.

"No, not merciless. Only one who reminds, and reminds, and reminds."

I turned to the doors of the chapel. I pulled on both giant hooks until I heard the clasp give, and then I opened wide one side and then the other, though why I made such a vast and broad escape for myself I do not know. Maybe it was a passage for my mighty band of helpers.

The great empty nave lay before me, which last night no doubt had been crowded with the gaudy blood-drenched Court, and above my head was their choir loft from which the most ethereal dirge had come.

Sun violently pierced the demonic windows.

I gasped in shock to see the webbed spirits emblazoned so immensely in the fractured and welded fragments of glittering glass. How thick was this glass, how heavily faceted, and how ominous the expressions of those webbed-winged monsters who leered at us as if they would come alive in the blazing light of day and stop our progress.

There was nothing to be done but to rip my eyes off them, to look down and away and along the great sprawling marble floor. I saw the hook, I saw it as it had been in the floor of my father's chapel, lying flat in a circle cut in the stone, a hook of gold, polished and smoothed so it did not rise above the floor and would not catch a toe or a heel. It had no cover.

It merely marked decisively the position of the one long main entrance to the crypt. One narrow marble rectangle cut into the center of the church floor.

I strode forward, heels echoing throughout the whole empty church, and went to pull the hook.

What stopped me? I saw the altar. At that very instant the sun had struck the figure of Lucifer, the giant red angel above his masses and masses of red flowers, which were fresh as they had been the night when I had been brought to this place.

I saw him and saw his fierce burning yellow eyes, fine gems set into the red marble, and saw the white ivory fangs that hung from his snarling upper lip. I saw all the fanged demons who lined the walls to the right and the left of him, and all their jeweled eyes seemed greedy and glorying in the light.

"The crypt," said Mastema.

I pulled with all my might. I couldn't budge the marble slab. No human could have done it. It would have taken teams of horses to do it. I locked both hands more tightly around the hook, yanking it harder, and still I couldn't budge it. It was like trying to move the walls themselves.

"Do it for him!" Ramiel pleaded. "Let us do it."

"It's nothing, Mastema; it's only like opening the gates."

Mastema reached out and pushed me gently

aside, so that I was caught on my own feet for a moment and then righted myself. The long narrow trapdoor of marble was raised slowly.

I was astonished at its weight. It was more than two feet in thickness. Only its facing was marble, the rest being a heavier darker, denser stone. No, no human could have lifted it.

And now, from the mouth below, there came a spear as if from a hidden spring.

I leapt back, though I had never been near enough to be in danger.

Mastema let the trapdoor fall on its back. The hinges were broken at once by its own weight. The light filled the space below. More spears awaited me, glinting in the sun, pointed at an angle, as if affixed in parallel to the angle of the stairs.

Mastema moved to the top of the stairs.

"Try to move them, Vittorio," he said.

"He can't. And if he trips and falls, he falls down into a pit of them," said Ramiel. "Mastema, move them."

"Let me move them," said Setheus.

I drew my sword. I hacked at the first of the spears and knocked off its metal point, but the jagged wooden shaft remained.

I stepped down into the crypt, at once feeling a coldness rise and touch my legs. I hacked again at the wood, and broke off more of it. Then I stepped beside it, only to find with my left hand that I felt a pair of spears awaiting me in the uneven light. Again I lifted my sword, the weight of it making my arm ache.

But I broke these two with swift blows until their metal heads had gone clattering from their wooden stems as well.

I stepped down, holding tight with my right hand so as not to slip on the steps, and suddenly, with a loud cry, I swung out and off the edge of nothing, for the stairway broke there and was no more.

With my right hand I grabbed at the shaft of the broken spear, which I already held in my left. My sword went clattering down below me.

"Enough, Mastema," said Setheus. "No human can do it."

I was hanging, both hands locked around this splintery wood, staring up at them as they rimmed the mouth of the crypt. If I fell, I would no doubt die, for the fall was that far. If I did not die, I would never get out to live.

I waited, and I said nothing, though my arms ached excruciatingly.

Suddenly, they descended, as soundlessly as they did all things, in a rush of silk and wings, slipping into the crypt at once, all of them, and surrounding me, embracing me and carrying me down in a soft plummet to the floor of the chamber.

I was at once let go. And I scrambled around in the dimness until I found my sword. I had it now.

I stood up, panting, holding it firmly, and then I looked up at the sharp distinct rectangle of brightness above. I shut my eyes, and bowed my head, and opened my eyes slowly so as to become accustomed to this deep damp dusk.

Here the castle had no doubt let the mountain rise up under it, for the chamber, though vast, seemed made of only the earth. At least this is what I saw before me, in the rude wall, and then turning around I saw my quarry, as Mastema had called them.

The vampires, the larvae—they lay sleeping, coffinless, cryptless, open in long rows, each exquisitely dressed body covered in a thin shroud of spun gold. They ringed three walls of the crypt. At the far end hung the broken stairs over nothingness.

I blinked and narrowed my eyes, and the light seemed to filter more fully upon them. I drew near to the first figure until I could see the dark-burgundy slippers, and the deep-russet hose and all of this beneath the webbing as if each night fine silkworms wove this shroud for the being, so thick and perfect and fine was it. Alas, it was no such magic; it was only the finest of what God's creatures can make. And it had been spun of the looms of men and women, and it had a fine-stitched hem.

I ripped off the veil.

I drew near the creature's folded arms, and then saw to my sudden horror that his sleeping face was quickened. His eyes opened, and one arm moved violently towards me.

I was yanked back out of the clutch of his fingers only just in time. I turned to see Ramiel holding me, and then he closed his eyes and bowed his forehead into my shoulder.

"Now you know their tricks. Watch it. You see.

It folds its arm back now. It thinks it's safe. It closes its eyes."

"What do I do! Ah, I'll kill it!" I said.

Snatching up the veil in my left hand, I raised my sword in my right. I advanced on the sleeping monster, and this time, when the hand rose, I snared it with the veil, swirling the fabric around it, while, with my sword, I came down like the executioner on the block.

At once the head rolled off onto the floor. A wretched sound came, more from the neck perhaps than from the throat. The arm flopped. By light of day, it could not struggle as it might have in the dark of night in my early battle, when I had decapitated my first assailant. Ah, I had won.

I snatched up the head, watching the blood spill out of the mouth. The eyes, if they had ever opened, were now shut. I hurled the head into the middle of the floor beneath the light. At once the light began to burn the flesh.

"Look at it, the head's burning!" I said. But I myself didn't stop.

I went to the next, snatching the transparent silken shroud from a woman with great long braids, taken to this eerie death in the prime of her life, and snaring her rising arm, severed her head with the same fury and caught it up by one braid and hurled it to land by its mate.

The other head was shriveling and turning black in the light that poured down from the high opening above.

"Lucifer, you see that?" I called out. The echo

came back to taunt me, "See that? See that? See that?"

I rushed to the next. "Florian!" I cried out, as I grabbed the veil.

Terrible error.

When he heard his name, his eyes snapped open even before I had drawn abreast of him, and like a puppet yanked on a chain he would have risen if I had not struck him hard with my sword and gashed open his chest. Expressionless, he fell back. I brought the sword down on his tender gentlemanly neck. His blond hair was caked with blood, and his eyes went half-mast and empty and died before my sight.

I snatched him up by his long hair, this bodiless one, this leader of them all, this silver-tongued fiend, and I hurled his head into the smoking, stinking pile.

On and on I went, down the line to the left, why to the left I do not know, except it was my path, and each time I pulled back the veil, I leapt forward with ferocious speed, snaring the arm if it should rise, but sometimes gaining such momentum on it that it had no time to rise, and chopping off the head so fast that I became sloppy and my blows ugly, and I smashed the jawbones of my foes, and even their shoulder bones, but I killed them.

I killed them.

I ripped off their heads and fed them to the mountain, which had gained such smoke now that it seemed a simmering fire of autumn leaves. Ashes rose from it, tiny thin ashes, but in the main, the heads languished, greasy and blackening, and the mass thickened and the ashes were only a few.

Did they suffer? Did they know? Where had their souls fled on invisible feet in this harsh and terrible moment when their Court was dissolved, when I roared in my work and stomped my feet and threw back my head and cried and cried until I couldn't see through my tears.

I had done with some twenty of them, twenty, and my sword was so thick with blood and gore that I had to wipe it clean. On their bodies, making my way back to go down the other side of the crypt, I wiped it, on one doublet after another, marveling at how their white hands had shriveled and dried up on their chests, at how the black blood flowed so sluggishly by day from their torn necks.

"Dead, you are all dead, and yet where did you go, where did the living soul in you go!"

The light was dimming. I stood breathing heavily. I looked up at Mastema.

"The sun is high overhead," he said gently. He was untouched, though he stood so near to them, the charred and reeking heads.

It seemed the smoke issued more truly from their eyes than anywhere else, as if the jelly melted into smoke more surely.

"The church is dim now, but it is only midday. Be quick. You have twenty more this side, and you know it. Work."

The other angels stood stock-still, clustered together, the magnificent Ramiel and Setheus in their rich robes, and the two simpler, plainer, more somber souls—all of them looking at me in utter suspense. I saw Setheus look at the pile of smoldering heads, and then again at me.

"Go on, poor Vittorio," he whispered. "Hurry on."

"Could you do it?" I asked.

"I cannot."

"No, I know that you are not permitted," I said, my chest aching from the exertion and now the talk I forced from myself. "I mean could you do it? Could you bring yourself to do it!"

"I am not a creature of flesh and blood, Vittorio," Setheus answered helplessly. "But I could do what God told me to do."

I went on past them. I looked back at them in their glorious radiance, the cluster of them, and the masterly one, Mastema, his armor gleaming in the falling light, and his sword so brilliant against his flank.

He said nothing.

I turned. I ripped off the first veil. It was Ursula.

"No." I stood back.

I let the veil drop. I was far enough away from her that she didn't appear to wake; she didn't move. Her lovely arms lay folded still in the same pose of graceful death which all of them had borne, only with her it was sweet, as if in her most innocent girlhood a gentle bane had taken her, not mussing so much as a single hair of long rippling unbraided locks. They made a nest of gold for her head and her shoulders, her swan neck.

I could hear my heaving breaths. I let the edge of my sword drag, singing on the stones. I licked at my parched lips. I didn't dare to look at them, though I knew they were collected only a few yards from me, staring at me. And in the thick stillness, I heard the crisping and sizzling of the burning heads of the damned.

I thrust my hand inside my pocket, and I drew out the rosary of amber beads. My hand shook shamefully as I held it, and then I lifted it, letting the crucifix dangle, and I hurled it at her, so that it struck her, just above her small hands, right on the white swell of her half-bared breasts. It lay there, the crucifix nestled in the curve of her pale skin, and she didn't so much as stir.

The light clung to her eyelashes as if it were dust.

Without excuse or explanation, I turned to the next one, ripping off the veil and assaulting him or her, I knew not which, with a loud raucous cry. I grabbed up the severed head by its thick brown locks and threw it crashing past the angels into the mass of slop that lay at their feet.

Then to the next. Godric. Oh, God, this will be sweet.

I saw his bald head before I ever touched the veil, and now, tearing the veil loose, hearing it rip on account of my carelessness, I waited for him to open his eyes, waited for him to rise up halfway from the slab and glare at me.

"Know me, monster? Know me?" I roared. The sword sliced through his neck. The white head hit the floor, and with my sword I speared it through its dripping stump of a neck. "Know me, monster?" I cried again to the fluttering eyes, the gaping, drooling red mouth. "Know me?"

I walked with him to the pile of the other heads and laid him like a trophy on top of it. "Know me?" I wailed again.

And then in a fury I went back to my work.

Two more, then three, then five, then seven and then nine, and then some six more, and the Court was finished, and all its dancers and Lords and Ladies were dead.

And then, reeling to the other side, I made swift work of those poor peasant servants, who had no veils to cover their simple bodies, and whose feeble half-starved white limbs could scarce rise in defense.

"The huntsmen, where are they?"

"At the far end. It is almost dark in here. Take great care."

"I see them," I said. I drew myself up and caught my breath. They lay in a row of six, heads to the wall like all the others, but they were perilously close together. It would be a hard approach.

I laughed suddenly at the simplicity of it. I laughed. I snatched off the first veil and chopped at the feet. The corpse rose and then my blade could easily see the place to strike, while the blood had already begun to gush.

The second, I cut to stumps at once and then sliced across the middle, and only descended on the head before his hand had caught my blade. I ripped back my sword and chopped the hand off him. "Die, bastard, you who stole me with your fellow; I remember you."

And at last I came to the final one and had his bearded head hanging from my hand.

Slowly I walked back with this one, kicking others before me, others I had not had the strength to hurl very far, and I kicked them like so much refuse until the light fell on all of them.

It was bright now. The afternoon sun was coming in the west side of the church. And the opening above gave forth a terrific and fatal heat.

Slowly I wiped my face with the back of my left hand. I laid down my sword, and I felt for the napkins the monks had put in my pockets, and I took these and cleaned my face and cleaned my hands.

Then I picked up my sword, and I went to the foot of her bier again. She lay as before. The light was nowhere near her. It could not have touched any of them where they lay.

She was safe on her bed of stone, her hands as still as before, fingers beautifully folded, the right hand over the left, and on her mound of white breast there rested the Crucified Christ in gold. Her hair was stirring in a faint draft that seemed to come from the narrow opening above. But this was a mere halo of tendrils about her otherwise lifeless face.

Her hair, in its loose ripples, without its ribbons or pearls, had fallen a little over the edges of the bier, so narrow was it, and so had the folds of her long gold-embroidered dress. It was not the same that she'd worn when I'd seen her. Only the deep rich blood red was the same, but all the rest was splendid and ornate and new, as if she were a regal princess, always prepared for the kiss of her prince.

"Could Hell receive this?" I whispered. I drew as close as I dared. I could not bear the thought of her arm rising in that mechanical fashion, the sudden clutch of her fingers on the empty air or her eyes opening. I couldn't bear it.

The points of her slippers were small beneath her hem. How daintily she must have lain down to her rest at sunrise. Who had pulled closed the trapdoor, whose chains had fallen? Who had set the trap of the spears, whose engines I had never inspected or compassed with my thoughts?

For the first time in the dimness, I saw a tiny golden circlet on her head, lying just around the crown and fixed by the tiniest pins into the waves so that its single pearl rested on her forehead. Such a small thing.

Was her soul so small? Would Hell take it, like the fire would take any tender part of her anatomy, like the sun would burn to horror her immaculate face?

In some mother's womb she had once slept and dreamt, and into some father's arms been placed.

What had been her tragedy to bring her to this foul and reeking grave, where the heads of her slain companions lay burning slowly in the sun's ever patient, ever indifferent light?

I turned on them. I held my sword down at my side.

"One, let one only live. One!" I declared.

Ramiel covered his face and turned his back on me. Setheus continued to stare but shook his head. My guardians only gazed at me with their level coldness, as they always had. Mastema stared at me, soundlessly, concealing whatever thought he possessed behind his serene mask of a face.

"No, Vittorio," he said. "Do you think a bevy of God's angels has helped you past these barriers to leave one such as these to live?"

"Mastema, she loved me. And I love her. Mastema, she gave me my life. Mastema, I ask in the name of love. I beg in the name of love. All else here has been justice. But what can I say to God if I slay this one, who has loved and whom I love?"

Nothing in his countenance changed. He only regarded me with his eternal calm. I heard a terrible sound. It was the weeping of Ramiel and Setheus. My guardians turned to look at them, as though surprised, but only mildly so, and then their dreamy soft eyes fixed again, unchanging, on me.

"Merciless angels," I said. "Oh, but such is not fair, and I know it. I lie. I lie. Forgive me."

"We forgive you," said Mastema. "But you must do what you have promised me you would do."

"Mastema, can she be saved? If she herself renounces . . . can she . . . is her soul still human?"

No answer came from him. No answer.

"Mastema, please, tell me. Don't you see? If she can be saved, I can stay here with her, I can wring it out of her, I know I can because her heart is good.

It's young and good. Mastema, tell me. Can such a creature as she is be saved?"

No answer. Ramiel had lain his head against Setheus's shoulder.

"Oh, please, Setheus," I said. "Tell me. Can she be saved? Must she die by my hand? What if I stay here with her, and wring it out of her, her confession, her final disavowal of all that she has ever done? Is there no priest who can give her absolution? Oh, God . . ."

"Vittorio," came the whisper from Ramiel. "Are your ears stopped with wax? Can you hear those prisoners starving, crying? You have not even set them free yet. Will you do it by night?"

"I can do it. I can yet do it. But can I not stay here with her, and when she finds she is all alone, that all the others have perished, that all the promises of Godric and Florian were tyranny, is there no way that she can render her soul to God?"

Mastema, without ever a change in his soft cold eyes, slowly turned his back.

"No! Don't do it, don't turn away!" I shouted. I caught hold of his powerful silk-clad arm. I felt his unsurmountable strength beneath the fabric, the strange, unnatural fabric. He gazed down at me.

"Why can't you tell me!"

"For the love of God, Vittorio!" he roared suddenly, his voice filling the entire crypt. "Don't you realize? We don't know!"

He shook me loose, the better to glare down at me, his brows furrowed, his hand closing on the hilt of his sword.

"We don't come from a species that has ever known forgiveness!" he shouted. "We are not flesh and blood, and in our realm things are Light or they are the Darkness, and that is all we know!"

In a fury, he turned and marched towards her. I rushed after him, pulling at him, but unable to deter him a fraction from his purpose.

He plunged his hand down, past her groping hands, and clutched her tiny neck. Her eyes stared up at him in that terrible, terrible blindness.

"She has a human soul in her," he said in a whisper. And then he drew back as if he did not want to touch her, couldn't bear to touch her, and he backed away from her, shoving me away, forcing me back as he did.

I broke into weeping. The sun shifted, and the shadows began to thicken in the crypt. I turned finally. The patch of light above was now pale. It was a rich radiant gold, but it was pale.

My angels stood there, all gathered, watching me and waiting.

"I'm staying with her here," I said. "She'll wake soon. And I'll put it to her, that she pray for God's grace."

I knew it only as I said it. I understood it only as I made it plain.

"I'll stay with her. If she renounces all her sins for the love of God, then she can remain with me, and death will come, and we will not lift a hand to hasten it, and God will accept us both."

"You think you have the strength to do that?" Mastema asked. "And you think it of her?"

"I owe her this," I said. "I am bound. I never lied to you, not to any of you. I never lied to myself. She slew my brother and sister. I saw her. No doubt she killed many of them, my own. But she saved me. She saved me twice. And to kill is simple, but to save is not!"

"Ah," said Mastema as though I'd struck him. "That's true."

"So I'll stay. I expect nothing from you now. I know I cannot get out of here. Perhaps even she cannot."

"Of course she can," said Mastema.

"Don't leave him," said Setheus. "Take him against his will."

"None of us can do that, and you know it," said Mastema.

"Only out of the crypt," pleaded Ramiel, "as if from a canyon into which he's fallen."

"But it is not such a thing, and I cannot."

"Then let us stay with him," said Ramiel.

"Yes, let us stay," said my two guardians, more or less at the same time and in similar muted expressions.

"Let her see us."

"How do we know that she can?" asked Mastema. "How do we know that she will? How many times does it happen that a human being can see us?"

For the first time I saw anger in him. He looked at me.

"God has played such a game with you, Vittorio!" he said. "Given you such enemies and such allies!"

"Yes, I know this, and I will beg Him with all my strength and the weight of all my suffering for her soul."

I didn't mean to close my eyes.

I know that I did not.

But the entire scene was altered utterly. The pile of heads lay as before, and some at random, shriveling, drying up, the acrid smoke still rising from them, and the light above had darkened, yet it was still golden, golden beyond the broken stair, and the jagged broken spears, golden with the last burnt dregs of the late afternoon.

And my angels had gone.

12

DELIVER ME NOT INTO
TEMPTATION

OR all my youth, my body could take no more. Yet how could I remain in this crypt, waiting for her to awake, without attempting some form of exit?

I gave no thought to the dismissal by my angels. I deserved it, but I was convinced of the rectitude of the chance I meant to give her, that she throw herself on the mercy of God, and that we leave this crypt and, if necessary, find the priest who could absolve her human soul of all her sins. For if she could not make a perfect confession for the love of God alone, well, then, the absolution would surely save her.

I poked around the crypt, stepping among the drying-up corpses. What light there was gleamed on dried founts of blood that ran down the sides of the stone biers.

At last I found what I had hoped to find, a great ladder that could be lifted and thrown up to the ceiling above. Only, how could I wield such a thing?

I dragged it towards the center of the crypt, kicking out of my path the heads which were now damaged beyond reprieve, and I laid down the ladder, and stepped at midpoint, between two of the rungs, and tried from there to lift it.

Impossible. I simply did not possess the leverage. It weighed too much, slight as it was, because it was so long. Three or four strong men might have hoisted it sufficiently to make its topmost rungs catch on the broken spears, but I alone could not do it.

Alas, there was another possibility. A chain, or a rope, that could be tossed to the spears above. In the gloam, I made a search for such but found none.

No chains anywhere here? No coil of rope?

Had even the young larvae been able to leap the gap between the floor and the broken stairway?

At last I moved along the walls, searching for any bump or hook or excrescence which might indicate a storeroom or, God forbid, another crypt of these fiends.

But I could find nothing.

Finally, I staggered towards the center of the room again. I gathered all the heads, even the loathsome bald head of Godric, which was now black like leather with its yellowed slits of eyes, and I piled these heads where the light could not fail to continue its work on them.

Then, stumbling over the ladder, I fell on my knees at the foot of Ursula's bier.

I sank down. I would sleep this little while. No, not sleep, rest.

Not willing it, indeed, fearing it and regretting it, I felt my limbs go limp and I lay on the stone floor, and my eyes closed in a blessed restorative sleep.

How curious it was.

I had thought her scream would awaken me, that like a frightened child she would have risen up in the darkness on the bier, finding herself alone with so many dead ones.

I had thought the sight of the heads in the pile would have terrified her.

But no such had happened.

Twilight filled the space above, violet-colored, like the flowers of the meadow, and she stood over me. She had put the rosary around her neck, which is not common, and she wore it as a beautiful ornament with the gold crucifix turning and twisting in the light, a glinting speck of gold that matched the specks of light in her eyes.

She was smiling.

"My brave one, my hero, come, let's escape this place of death. You've done it, you have avenged them."

"Did you move your lips?"

"Need I do that with you?"

I felt a thrill pass through me as she lifted me to my feet. She stood looking up into my face, her hands firmly on my shoulders.

"Blessed Vittorio," she said. Then clasping me about the waist, she rose upwards and we passed the broken spears, without so much as touching their splintered tips, and found ourselves in the chapel in the dusk, the windows darkened and the shadows playing gracefully but mercifully around the distant altar.

"Oh, my darling, my darling," I said. "Do you know what the angels did? Do you know what they said?"

"Come, let's free the prisoners as you wish," she told me.

I felt so refreshed, so full of vigor. It was as if I'd suffered no exhausting labor at all, as if war hadn't worn down my limbs and broken me, as though battle and struggle hadn't been my portion for days.

I rushed with her through the castle. We threw open the doors, one pair after another, on the miserable occupants of the coop. It was she who scurried on her light, feline feet through the pathways beneath the orange trees and the bird aviaries, overturning the kettles of soup, crying out to the poor and the lame and the hopeless that they were free, that no one imprisoned them now.

In a twinkling we stood on a high balcony. I saw far below their miserable procession in the half-light, the long winding line of them progressing down the mountain under the purple sky and the rising evening star. The weak helped the strong; the old carried the young.

"Where will they go, back to that evil town? Back to the monsters who gave them up in sacrifice?" I was in a fury suddenly. "Punished, that's what they must be."

"In time, Vittorio; there is time. Your poor sad

victims are free now. This is our time, yours and mine, come."

Her skirts went out in a great dark circle as down we flew, down and down, down past the windows, and down past the walls, until my feet were allowed to touch the soft ground.

"Oh, Lord God, it's the meadow, look, the meadow," I said. "I can see it as clearly under the rising moon as ever I saw it in my dreams."

A sudden softness filled me completely. I twined her in my arms, my fingers digging deep into her rippling hair. All the world seemed to sway about me, and yet I was anchored in dance with her, and the soft airy movement of the trees sang to us as we were bound together.

"Nothing can ever part us, Vittorio," she said. She tore loose. She ran ahead of me.

"No, wait, Ursula, wait!" I cried. I ran after her, but the grass and the irises were tall and thick. It wasn't so like the dream, but then again it was, because these things were alive and full of the verdant smell of the wild, and the sylvan woods were gently heaving their limbs on the scented wind.

I fell down exhausted and let the flowers climb up on either side of me. I let the red irises peer down upon my upturned face.

She knelt above me. "He will forgive me, Vittorio," she said. "He will forgive all in his infinite mercy."

"Oh, yes, my love, my blessed, beautiful love, my savior, He will."

The tiny crucifix dangled down against my neck.

"But you must do this for me, you who let me live below, you who spared me and fell asleep in my trust at the feet of my grave, you must do this . . ."

"What, blessed one?" I asked. "Tell me and I'll do it."

"Pray first for strength, and then into your human body, into your wholesome and baptized body, you must take all the demon blood out of me which you can, you must draw it from me, and thereby free my soul from its spell; it will be vomited forth out of you like the potions we gave you, which cannot hurt you. Will you do it for me? Will you take the poison out of me?"

I thought of the sickness, of the vomit that had streamed from my mouth in the monastery. I thought of it all, the terrible gibbering and madness.

"Do this for me," she said.

She lay against me and I felt her heart trapped in her chest, and I felt my own, and it seemed I had never known such dreamy languor. I could feel my fingers curl. For an instant it seemed they rested on hard rocks in this meadow, as if the backs of my hands had found harsh pebbles, but once again I felt the broken stems, the bed of purple and red and white irises.

She raised her head.

"In the Name of God," I said, "for your salvation, I will take whatever poison I must from you; I will draw off the blood as if from a cankerous wound, as if it were the corruption of a leper. Give it to me, give me the blood."

Her face was motionless above mine, so small, so dainty, so white.

"Be brave, my love, be brave, for I must make room for it first."

She nestled in against my neck, and into my flesh there came her teeth. "Be brave, only a little more to make room."

"A little more?" I whispered. "A little more. Ah, Ursula, look up, look up at Heaven and Hell in the sky, for the stars are balls of fire suspended there by the angels."

But the language was stretched and meaning-less and became an echo in my ears. A darkness shrouded me, and when I lifted my hand it seemed a golden net covered it and I could see far, far away, my fingers shrouded in the net.

The meadow was suddenly flooded with sun-light. I wanted to break away, to sit up, to tell her, Look, the sun has come, and you're not hurt, my precious girl. But on and on there came these waves of divine and luscious pleasure passing through me, pulled from me, pulled up from my loins, this coaxing and magnificent pleasure.

When her teeth slipped from my flesh, it was as if she had tightened the grip of her soul on my organs, on all parts of me that were man and babe once, and human now.

"Oh, my love, my darling, don't stop." The sun made a bewildering dance in the branches of the chestnut trees.

She opened her mouth, and from her came the stream of blood, the deep dark kiss of blood. "Take it from me, Vittorio."

"All your sins into me, my divine child," I said. "Oh, God help me. God have mercy on me. Mastema—."

But the word was broken. My mouth was filled with the blood, and it was no rank potion mixed of parts, but that searing thrilling sweetness that she had first given me in her most secretive and perplexing kisses. Only this time it came in an overwhelming gush.

Her arms were tucked beneath me. They lifted me. The blood seemed to know no veins within but to fill my limbs themselves, to fill my shoulders and my chest, to drown and invigorate my very heart. I stared up at the twinkling playing sun, I felt her blinding and soft hair across my eyes but peered through its golden strands. My breath came in gasps.

The blood flowed down into my legs and filled them to my very toes. My body surged with strength. My organ pumped against her, and once more I felt her subtle feline weight, her sinuous limbs hugging me, holding me, binding me, her arms crossed beneath me, her lips sealed to mine.

My eyes struggled, grew wide. The sunlight filled them, and then contracted. It contracted, and my sighs seemed to grow immense, and the beating of my heart to echo, as though we were not in a wild meadow, and the sounds that came from my empowered body, my transformed body, my body so full of her blood, echoed off stone walls!

The meadow was gone or never was. The twilight was a rectangle high above. I lay in the crypt.

I rose up, throwing her off, back away from me as she screamed in pain. I sprang to my feet and stared at my white hands outstretched before me.

A horrid hunger reared up in me, a fierce strength, a howl!

I stared up at the dark-purple light above and screamed.

"You've done it to me! You've made me one of you!"

She sobbed. I turned on her. She backed up, bent over, her hand over her mouth, crying and fleeing from me. I ran after her. Like a rat she ran, round and round the crypt, screaming.

"Vittorio, no, Vittorio, no, Vittorio, no, don't hurt me. Vittorio, I did this for us; Vittorio, we are free. Ah, God help me!"

And then upwards she flew, just missing my outstretched arms. She had fled to the chapel above.

"Witchlet, monster, larva, you tricked me with your illusions, with your visions, you made me one of you, you did it to me!" My roars echoed one upon the other as I scrambled about in the dark till I found my sword, and then dancing back to gain my momentum, I too made the leap and cleared the spears and found myself high up on the floor of the church, and she hovering with glittering tears before the altar.

She backed up into the bank of red flowers that barely showed in the starlight that passed through the darkened windows.

"No, Vittorio, don't kill me, don't do it. Don't," she sobbed and wailed. "I am a child, like you, please, don't."

I tore at her, and she scrambled to the end of the sanctuary. In a rage, I swung at the statue of Lucifer with my sword. It tottered and then crashed down, breaking on the marble floor of the cursed sanctuary.

She hovered at the far end. She dropped down on her knees and threw out her hands. She shook her head, her hair flying wildly from side to side.

"Don't kill me, don't kill me, don't kill me. You send me to Hell if you do; don't do it."

"Wretch!" I moaned. "Wretch!" My tears fell as freely as hers. "I thirst, you wretch. I thirst, and I can smell them, the slaves in the coop. I can smell them, their blood, damn you!"

I too had gone down on my knees. I lay down on the marble, and kicked aside the broken fragments of the hideous statue. With my sword I snagged the lace of the altar cloth and brought it down with all its many red flowers tumbling on me, so that I could roll over into them and crush my face into their softness.

A silence fell, a terrible silence full of my own wailing. I could feel my strength, feel it even in the timbre of my voice, and the arm that held the sword without exhaustion or restraint, and feel it in the painless calm with which I lay on what should have been cold and was not cold, or only goodly cold.

Oh, she had made me mighty.

A scent overcame me. I looked up. She stood just above me, tender, loving thing that she was, with her eyes so full of the starlight now, so glinting and quiet and unjudging. In her arms she held a young human, a feeble-minded one, who did not know his danger.

How pink and succulent he was, how like the roasted pig ready for my lips, how full of naturally cooking and bubbling mortal blood and ready for me. She set him down before me.

He was naked, thin buttocks on his heels, his trembling chest very pink and his hair black and long and soft around his guileless face. He appeared to be dreaming or searching the darkness, perhaps for angels?

"Drink, my darling, drink from him," she said, "and then you'll have the strength to take us both to the Good Father for Confession."

I smiled. The desire for the feeble-minded boy before me was almost more than I could endure. But it was a whole new book now, was it not, what I might endure, and I took my time, rising up on my elbow as I looked at her.

"To the Good Father? You think that's where we'll go? Right away, just like that, the two of us?"

She began to cry again. "Not right away, no, not right away," she cried. She shook her head. Beaten.

I took him. I broke his neck when I drained him dry. He made not a sound. There was no time for fear or pain or crying.

Do we ever forget the first kill? Do we ever?

Through the coop I went all that night, devouring, feasting, gorging on their throats, taking what I wanted from each, sending each to God or to Hell, how could I ever know, bound now to this earth with her, and she feasting with me in her dainty way, ever watching for my howls and wails, and ever catching hold of me to kiss me and ply me with her sobs when I shook with rage.

"Come out of here," I said.

It was just before sunrise. I told her I would spend no day beneath these pointed towers, in this house of horrors, in this place of evil and filthy birth.

"I know of a cave," she said. "Far down the mountains, past the farmlands."

"Yes, somewhere on the edge of a true meadow?"

"There are meadows in this fair land without count, my love," she said. "And under the moon their flowers shine as prettily for our magical eyes as ever they do for humans by the light of God's sun. Remember His moon is ours.

"And tomorrow night . . . before you think of the priest . . . you must take your time to think of the priest—."

"Don't make me laugh again. Show me how to fly. Wrap your arm around my waist and show me how to drop from the high walls to safety in a descent that would shatter a man's limbs. Don't talk of priests anymore. Don't mock me!"

". . . before you think of the priest, of Confession," she went on, undeterred in her dainty sweet small voice, her eyes brimming with tears of love, "we'll go back to the town of Santa Maddalana while it's fast asleep, and we'll burn it all down around them."

13

CHILD BRIDE

E didn't put the torch to Santa Maddalana. It was too much of a pleasure to hunt the town.

By the third night, I had stopped weeping at sunrise, when we retired together, locked in each other's arms inside our concealed and unreachable cave.

And by the third night, the townspeople knew what had befallen them—how their clever bargain with the Devil had rebounded upon them— and they were in a panic, and it was a great game to outsmart them, to hide in the multitude of shadows that made up their twisted streets, and to tear open their most extravagant and clever locks.

In the early hours, when no one dared to stir, and the good Franciscan priest knelt awake in his cell, saying his rosary, and begging God for understanding of what was happening—this priest, you remember, who had befriended me at the inn, who had dined with me and warned me, not in anger like his Dominican brother, but in kindness—while this priest prayed, I crept into the Franciscan church and I too prayed.

But each night I told myself what a man says to himself under his breath when he couches with his adulterous whore: "One more night, God, and then I'll go to Confession. One more night of bliss, Lord, and then I'll go home to my wife."

The townspeople had no chance against us.

What skills I did not acquire naturally and through experimentation, my beloved Ursula taught to me with patience and grace. I could scan a mind, find a sin and eat it with a flick of my tongue as I sucked the blood from a lazy, lying merchant who had put out his own tender children once for the mysterious Lord Florian, who had kept the peace.

One night we found that the townsmen had been by day to the abandoned castle. There was evidence of hasty entry, with little stolen or disturbed. How it must have frightened them, the horrid saints still flanking the pedestal of the Fallen Lucifer in the church. They had not taken the golden candlesticks or the old tabernacle in which I discovered, with my groping hand, a shriveled human heart.

On our last visit to the Court of the Ruby Grail, I took the burned leathery heads of the vampires from the deep cellar and I hurled them like so many stones through the stained-glass windows. The last of the brilliant art of the castle was gone.

Together, Ursula and I roamed the bedchambers of the castle, which I had never glimpsed or even imagined, and she showed me those rooms in which the members of the Court had gathered for dice or chess or to listen to small ensembles of music. Here and there we saw evidence of something stolen—a coverlet ripped from a bed and a pillow fallen to the floor.

But obviously the townspeople were more afraid than greedy. They took little from the castle.

And as we continued to prey upon them, artfully defeating them, they began to desert Santa Maddalana. Shops lay open when we came into the empty streets at midnight; windows were unbolted, cradles empty. The Dominican church had been deconsecrated and abandoned, its altar stone removed. The cowardly priests, whom I had not granted the mercy of a quick death, had abandoned their flock.

The game became ever more invigorating to me. For now, those who remained were quarrelsome and avaricious and refusing to give up without a fight. It was simple to sort the innocent, who believed in the faith of the vigil light or the saints to protect them, from those who had played with the Devil and now kept an uneasy watch in the dark with sword in hand.

I liked to talk to them, spar with them verbally, as I killed them. "Did you think your game would go on forever? Did you think the thing you fed would never feed on you?"

As for my Ursula, she had no stomach for such sport. She could not endure the spectacle of suffering. The old Communion of Blood in the castle had for her been tolerable only because of the music, the incense and the supreme authority of Florian and Godric, who had led her in it with every step.

Night after night, as the town was slowly emptied, as the farms were deserted, as Santa Maddalana, my school town, became ever more ruined, Ursula took to playing with orphaned children. She sat sometimes on the church steps cradling a human infant and cooing to it, and telling it stories in French.

She sang old songs in Latin from the courts of her time, which had been two hundred years ago, she told me, and she talked of battles in France and in Germany whose names meant nothing to me.

"Don't play with the children," I said. "They'll remember it. They'll remember us."

A fortnight went by before the community was irreparably destroyed. Only the orphans remained and a few of the very old, and the Franciscan father, and his father, the elfin little man who sat in his lighted room at night, playing a game of cards with himself, as if he did not even now guess what was going on.

On the fifteenth night, it must have been, when we arrived in the town, we knew at once that only two persons were left. We could hear the little old man singing to himself in the empty Inn with the doors open. He was very drunk, and his wet pink head gleamed in the light of the candle. He slapped the cards down on the table in a circle, playing a game of solitaire called "clock."

The Franciscan priest sat beside him. He looked

up at us, fearlessly and calmly, as we came into the Inn.

I was overcome with hunger, ravening hunger, for the blood in them both.

"I never told you my name, did I?" he asked me.

"No, you never did, Father," I said.

"Joshua," he said. "That's my name, Fra Joshua. All the rest of the community has gone back to Assisi, and they took with them the last of the children. It's a long journey south."

"I know, Father," I said. "I've been to Assisi, I've prayed at the shrine of St. Francis. Tell me, Father, when you look at me, do you see angels around me?"

"Why would I see angels?" he asked quietly. He looked from me to Ursula. "I see beauty, I see youth fixed in polished ivory. But I don't see angels. I never have."

"I saw them once," I said. "May I sit down?"

"Do as you like," he said to me. He watched us, drawing himself up in his hard simple wooden chair, as I seated myself opposite him, much as I had been on that day in the village, only now we were not in the fragrant arbor under the sun but inside, in the Inn itself, where the candlelight gave more volume and more warmth.

Ursula looked at me in confusion. She didn't know what was in my mind. I had never witnessed her speaking to any human being except for me myself and for the children with whom she'd played—in other words, only with those for whom her heart had quickened and whom she did not mean to destroy.

What she thought of the little man and his son, the Franciscan priest, I couldn't guess.

The old man was winning the card game. "There, you see, I told you. Our luck!" he said. He gathered up his greasy loose cards to shuffle them and to play again.

The priest looked at him with glazed eyes, as though he could not gather his own wits even to fool or reassure his old father, and then he looked at me.

"I saw these angels in Florence," I said, "and I disappointed them, broke my vow to them, lost my soul."

He turned from his father to me sharply.

"Why do you prolong this?" he asked.

"I will not hurt you. Neither will my companion," I said. I sighed. It would have been that moment in a conversation when I would have reached for the cup or the tankard and taken a drink. My hunger hurt me. I wondered if the thirst hurt Ursula. I stared at the priest's wine, which was nothing to me now, nothing, and I looked at his face, sweating in the light of the candle, and I went on:

"I want you to know that I saw them, that I talked to them, these angels. They tried to help me to destroy those monsters who held sway over this town, and over the souls of those here. I want you to know, Father."

"Why, son, why tell me?"

"Because they were beautiful, and they were as real as we are, and you have seen us. You have seen hellish things; you have seen sloth and treachery, cowardice and deceit. You see devils now, vampires. Well, I want you to know that with my own eyes I saw angels, true angels, magnificent angels, and that they were more glorious than I can ever tell you in words."

He regarded me thoughtfully for a long time, and then he looked at Ursula, who sat troubled and looking up at me, rather afraid that I would unduly suffer, and then he said:

"Why did you fail them? Why did they come with you in the first place, and if you had the aid of angels, why did you fail?"

I shrugged my shoulders. I smiled. "For love."

He didn't answer.

Ursula leaned her head against my arm. I felt her free hair brushing my back as she let me feel her weight.

"For love!" the priest repeated.

"Yes, and for honor as well."

"Honor."

"No one will ever understand it. God will not accept it, but it's true, and now, what is there, Father, that divides us, you and I, and the woman who sits with me? What is between us—the two parties—the honest priest and the two demons?"

The little man chuckled suddenly. He had slapped down a marvelous run of cards. "Look at that!" he said. He looked up at me with his clever little eyes. "Oh, your question, forgive me. I know the answer."

"You do?" asked the priest, turning to the little old man. "You know the answer?"

"Of course, I do," said his father. He dealt out

another card. "What separates them now from a good Confession is weakness and the fear of Hell if they must give up their lives."

The priest stared at his father in amazement.

So did I.

Ursula said nothing. Then she kissed me on the cheek. "Let's leave them now," she whispered. "There is no more Santa Maddalana. Let's go."

I looked up, around the darkened room of the Inn. I looked at the old barrels. I looked in haunted perplexity and appalling sorrow at all things that humans used and touched. I looked at the heavy hands of the priest, folded on the table before me. I looked at the hair on his hands, and then up at his thick lips and his large watering and sorrowful eyes.

"Will you accept this from me?" I whispered. "This secret, of angels? That I saw them! I! And you, you see what I am, and you know therefore that I know whereof I speak. I saw their wings, I saw their halos, I saw their white faces, and I saw the sword of Mastema the powerful, and it was they who helped me sack the castle and lay waste to all the demons save for this one, this child bride, who is mine."

"Child bride," she whispered. It filled her with delight. She looked at me, musingly, and hummed a soft, old-fashioned air, one of those threads of songs from her times.

She spoke to me in an urgent persuasive whisper, squeezing my arm as she did:

"Come, Vittorio, leave these men in peace, and come with me, and I'll tell you how indeed I was a

266

child bride." She looked at the priest with renewed animation. "I was, you know. They came to my father's castle and purchased me as such, they said that I must be a virgin, and the midwives came and brought their basin of warm water, and they examined me and they said I was a virgin, and only then did Florian take me. I was his bride."

The priest stared fixedly at her, as if he could not move if he wanted to move, and the old man merely glanced up again and again, cheerfully, nodding as he listened to her, and went on playing with his cards.

"Can you imagine my horror?" she asked them. She looked at me, tossing her hair back over her shoulder. It was in its ripples again from the plaits in which she'd had it bound earlier. "Can you imagine when I climbed onto the couch and I saw who was my bridegroom, this white thing, this dead thing, such as we look to you?"

The priest made no answer. His eyes filled slowly with tears. Tears!

It seemed a lovely human spectacle, bloodless, crystalline, and such an adornment for his old soft face, with its jowls and fleshy mouth.

"And then to be taken to a ruined chapel," she said, "a ruined place, full of spiders and vermin, and there before a desecrated altar, to be stripped and laid down and taken by him and made his bride."

She let go of my arm, her arms forming a loose embracing gesture. "Oh, I had a veil, a great long beautiful veil, and a dress of such fine flowered silk, and all this he tore from me, and took me first with his lifeless, seedless stone-hard organ and then with his fang teeth, like these very teeth which I have now. Oh, such a wedding, and my father had given me over for this."

The tears coursed down the priest's cheeks.

I stared at her, transfixed with sorrow and rage, rage against a demon I had already slaughtered, a rage that I hoped could reach down through the smoldering coals of Hell and find him with fingers like hot tongs.

I said nothing.

She raised her eyebrow; she cocked her head.

"He tired of me," she said. "But he never stopped loving me. He was new to the Court of the Ruby Grail, a young Lord and seeking at every turn to increase his might and his romance! And later, when I asked for Vittorio's life, he couldn't refuse me on account of our vows exchanged on that stone altar so long ago. After he let Vittorio leave us, after he had him cast down in Florence, certain of Vittorio's madness and ruin, Florian sang songs to me, songs for a bride. He sang the old poems as though our love could be revived."

I covered my brow with my right hand. I couldn't bear to weep the blood tears that flow from us. I couldn't bear to see before me, as if painted by Fra Filippo, the very romance she described.

It was the priest who spoke.

"You are children," he said. His lip trembled. "Mere children."

"Yes," she said in her exquisite voice, with certainty and a small accepting smile. She clasped my left hand in hers and rubbed it hard and tenderly. "Children forever. But he was only a young man, Florian, just a young man himself."

"I saw him once," said the priest, his voice thick with his crying but soft. "Only once."

"And you knew?" I asked.

"I knew I was powerless and my faith was desperate, and that around me were bonds that I could not loose or break."

"Let's go now, Vittorio, don't make him cry anymore," said Ursula. "Come on, Vittorio. Let's leave here. We need no blood tonight and cannot think of harming them, cannot even . . ."

"No, beloved, never," I said to her. "But take my gift, Father, please, the only clean thing which I can give, my testimony that I saw the angels, and that they upheld me when I was weak."

"And won't you take absolution from me, Vittorio!" he said. His voice rose, and his chest seemed to increase in size. "Vittorio and Ursula, take my absolution."

"No, Father," I said. "We cannot take it. We don't want it."

"But why?"

"Because, Father," said Ursula kindly, "we plan to sin again as soon as we possibly can."

14

THROUGH A GLASS DARKLY

SHE didn't lie.

We journeyed that night to my father's house. It was nothing for us to make that journey, but it was many miles for a mortal, and word had not reached that forlorn farmland that the threat of the night demons, the vampires of Florian, was gone. Indeed, it is most likely that my farms were still deserted because ghastly tales were given out by those who had fled Santa Maddalana, traveling over hill and valley, mouth to mouth.

It didn't take me long to realize, however, that the great castle of my family was occupied. A horde of soldiers and clerks had been hard at work.

As we crept over the giant wall after midnight, we found that all the dead of my family had been properly buried, or placed in their proper stone coffins beneath the chapel, and that the goods of the household, all of its abundant wealth, had been taken away. Only a few wagons remained of those which must have already started their progress south.

The few who slept in the offices of my father's

steward were keepers of the accounts of the Medici bank, and on tiptoe, in the dim light of a star-studded sky, I inspected the few papers they had left out to dry.

All of the inheritance of Vittorio di Raniari had been collected and catalogued, and was being taken on to Florence for him, to be placed in safety with Cosimo until such time as Vittorio di Raniari was twenty-four years of age and could thereby assume responsibility for himself as a man.

Only a few soldiers slept in the barracks. Only a few horses were quartered in the stables. Only a few squires and attendants slept in proximity to their Lords.

Obviously the great castle, being of no strategic use to Milanese or German or French or Papal authority, or to Florence, was not being restored or repaired, merely shut down.

Well before dawn, we left my home, but before going, I took leave of my father's grave.

I knew that I would come back. I knew that soon the trees would climb the mountain to the walls. I knew that the grass would grow high through the crevices and cracks of the cobblestones. I knew that things human would lose all love of this place, as they had lost their love of so many ruins in the country round.

I would return then. I would come back.

That night, Ursula and I hunted the vicinity for the few brigands we could find in the woods, laughing gaily when we caught them and dragged them from their horses. It was a riotous old feast.

"And where now, my Lord?" my bride asked me

271

towards morning. We had again found a cave for shelter, a deep and hidden place, full of thorny vines that barely scratched our resilient skin, behind a veil of wild blueberries that would hide us from all eyes, including that of the great rising sun.

"To Florence, my love. I have to go there. And in its streets, we'll never suffer hunger, or discovery, and there are things which I must see with my own eyes."

"But what are those things, Vittorio?" she asked.

"Paintings, my love, paintings. I have to see the angels in the paintings. I have to . . . face them, as it were."

She was content. She had never seen the great city of Florence. She had, all her wretched eternity of ritual and courtly discipline, been contained in the mountains, and she lay down beside me to dream of freedom, of brilliant colors of blue and green and gold, so contrary to the dark red that she still wore. She lay down beside me, trusting me, and, as for me, I trusted nothing.

I only licked the human blood on my lips and wondered how long I might have on this earth before someone struck off my head with a swift and certain sword.

15

THE IMMACULATE CONCEPTION

HE city of Florence was in an uproar.

"Why?" I asked.

It was well past curfew, to which no one was paying much attention, and there was a huge crowd of students congregated in Santa Maria Maggiori—the Duomo—listening to a lecture by a humanist who pleaded that Fra Filippo Lippi was not such a pig.

No one took much note of us. We had fed early, in the countryside, and wore heavy mantles, and what could they see of us but a little pale flesh?

I went into the church. The crowd came out almost to the doors.

"What's the matter? What's happened to the great painter?"

"Oh, he's done it now," said the man who answered me, not even bothering to look at me or at the slender figure of Ursula clinging to me.

The man was too intent on looking at the lecturer, who stood up ahead, his voice echoing sharply in the overwhelming large nave.

"Done what?"

Getting no answer, I pushed my way a little deeper into the thick, odiferous human crowd, pulling Ursula with me. She was still shy of such an immense city, and she had not seen a Cathedral on this scale in the more than two hundred years of her life.

Once again I put my question to two young students, who turned at once to answer me, fashionable boys both, about eighteen, or what they called then in Florence *giovani*, being the most difficult of youths, too old to be a child, such as I was, and too young to be a man.

"Well, he asked for the fairest of the nuns to pose for the altarpiece that he was painting of the blessed Virgin, that's what he did," said the first student, black-haired and deep-eyed, staring at me with a cunning smile. "He asked for her as a model, asked that the convent choose her for him, so that the Virgin he painted would be most perfect, and then . . ."

The other student took it up.

". . . he ran off with her! Stole the nun right out of the convent, ran off with her and her sister, mind you, her blood-kindred sister, and has set up his household right over his shop, he and his nun and her sister, the three of them, the monk and the two nuns . . . and lives in sin with her, Lucrezia Buti, and paints the Virgin on the altarpiece and does not give a damn what anyone thinks."

There was jostling and pushing in the crowd about us. Men told us to be quiet. The students were choking on their laughter.

"If he didn't have Cosimo," said the first student, lowering his voice in an obedient but mischievous whisper, "they'd string him up, I mean her family, the Buti, would at least, if not the priests of the Carmelite Order, if not the whole damned town."

The other student shook his head and covered his mouth not to laugh out loud.

The speaker, far ahead, advised all to remain calm and let this scandal and outrage be handled by the proper authorities, for everyone knew that nowhere in all of Florence was there a painter any greater than Fra Filippo, and that Cosimo would tend to this in his own time.

"He's always been tormented," said the student beside me.

"Tormented," I whispered. "Tormented." His face came back to me, the monk glimpsed years ago in Cosimo's house in the Via Larga, the man arguing so fiercely to be free, only to be with a woman for a little while. I felt the strangest conflict within, the strangest darkest fear. "Oh, that they don't hurt him again."

"One might wonder," came a soft voice in my ear. I turned, but I saw no one who could have spoken to me. Ursula looked about.

"What is it, Vittorio?"

But I knew the whisper, and it came again, bodiless and intimate, "One might wonder, where were his guardian angels on the day that Fra Filippo did such a mad thing?"

I turned in a mad frantic circle, searching for

the origin of the voice. Men backed away from me and made little gestures of annoyance. I snatched up Ursula's hand and made for the doors.

Only when I was outside in the piazza did my heart stop pounding. I had not known that with this new blood I could feel such anxiety and misery and fear.

"Oh, run off with a nun to paint the Virgin!" I cried out under my breath.

"Don't cry, Vittorio," she said.

"Don't speak to me as if I were your little brother!" I said to her, and then was full of shame. She was stricken by my words, as if I'd slapped her. I took her fingers and kissed them. "I'm sorry, Ursula, I am sorry."

I pulled her along beside me.

"But where are we going?"

"To the house of Fra Filippo, to his workshop. Don't question me now."

Within moments we had found our way, echoing and clattering down the narrow street, and we stood before the doors that were shut up and I could see no light, save in the third-story windows, as though he had had to flee to that height with his bride.

No mob was gathered here.

But out of the darkness there came suddenly a handful of filth heaved at the bolted doors, and then another and then a volley of stones. I stepped back, shielding Ursula, and watched as one passerby after another slunk forward and hurled his insults at the shop.

Finally, I lay against the wall opposite, staring

dully in the darkness, and I heard the deep-throated bell of the church ring the hour of eleven, which meant surely that all men must vacate the streets.

Ursula only waited on me and said nothing, and she noted it quietly when I looked up and saw the last of Fra Filippo's lights go out.

"It's my doing," I said. "I took his angels from him, and he fell into this folly, and for what did I do it, for what, that I might possess you as surely now as he possesses his nun?"

"I don't know your meaning, Vittorio," she said. "What are nuns and priests to me? I have never said a word to wound you, never, but I say such words now. Don't stand here weeping over these mortals you loved. We are wedded now, and no convent vow or priestly anointment divides us. Let's go away from here, and when by light of lamps you want to show me the wonders of this painter, then bring me, bring me to see the angels of which you spoke rendered in pigment and oil."

I was chastened by her firmness. I kissed her hand again. I told her I was sorry. I held her to my heart.

How long I might have stood with her there, I don't know. Moments passed. I heard the sound of running water and distant footsteps, but nothing of consequence, nothing which mattered in the thick night of crowded Florence, with its four- and five-story palaces, with its old half-broken towers, and its churches, and its thousands upon thousands of sleeping souls.

A light startled me. It fell down upon me in

bright yellow seams. I saw the first, a thin line of brilliance. It cut across her figure, and then there came another, illuminating the alley-like street beyond us, and I realized that the lamps had been lighted within Fra Filippo's shop.

I turned just as the bolts inside were made to slide back with a low, grating noise. The noise echoed up the dark walls. No light shone above, behind the barred windows.

Suddenly the doors were opened and slapped back softly, soundlessly almost, against the wall, and I saw the deep rectangle of the interior, a wide shallow room filled with brilliant canvases all blazing above candles enough to light a Bishop's Mass.

My breath left me. I clutched her tightly, my hand on the back of her head as I pointed.

"There they are, both of them, the *Annunciations!*" I whispered. "Do you see the angels, the angels who kneel, there, and there, the angels who kneel before the Virgins!"

"I see them," she said reverently. "Ah, they are more lovely even than I supposed." She shook my arm. "Don't cry, Vittorio, unless it's for beauty's sake, only for that."

"Is that a command, Ursula?" I asked. My eyes were so clouded I could scarce see the poised flat kneeling figures of Ramiel and Setheus.

But as I tried to clear my vision, as I tried to gather my wits and swallow the ache in my throat, the miracle I feared more than anything in this world, yet craved, yet hungered for—that miracle commenced.

Out of the very fabric of the canvas, they

appeared simultaneously, my silk-clad blond-haired angels, my haloed angels, to unravel from the tight weave itself. They turned, gazing at me first and then moving so that they were no longer flat profiles but full robust figures, and then they stepped out and onto the stones of the shop.

I knew by Ursula's gasp that she had seen the same vivid series of miraculous gestures. Her hand went to her lips.

Their faces bore no wrath, no sadness. They merely looked at me, and in their sweet soft looks was all the condemnation I have ever understood.

"Punish me," I whispered. "Punish me by taking away my eyes that I can never see your beauty again."

Very slowly, Ramiel shook his head to answer no. And Setheus followed with the same negation. They stood side by side in their bare feet, as always, their abundant garments too light for movement on the heavy air, as they merely continued to gaze.

"What then?" I said. "What do I deserve from you? How is it that I can see you and see your glory even still?" I was a wreck of childish tears again, no matter how Ursula stared at me, no matter how she tried with her silent reproach to make the man of me.

I couldn't stop myself.

"What then? How can I see you still?"

"You'll always see us," Ramiel said softly, tonelessly.

"Every time you ever look at one of his paintings, you will see us," said Setheus, "or you will see our like."

There was no judgment in it. There was merely the same lovely serenity and kindness that they had always bestowed on me.

But it was not finished. I saw behind them, taking dark shape, my own guardians, that solemn ivory pair, draped in their robes of shadowy blue.

How hard were their eyes, how knowing, how disdainful yet without the edge which men lend to such passions. How glacial and remote.

My lips parted. A cry was there. A terrible cry. But I dared not rouse the night around me, the infinite night that moved out over the thousands of slanted red-tile rooftops, out over the hills and the country, out under the numberless stars.

Suddenly the entire building began to move. It trembled, and the canvases, brilliant and shimmering in their bath of burning light, were glittering as if shaken by a tremor of the very earth itself.

Mastema appeared suddenly before me, and the room was swept backward, broadened, deepened, and all those lesser angels were swept back from him as if by a soundless wind that cannot be defied.

The flood of light ignited his immense gold wings as they spread out, crowding the very corners of the vastness and pushing it even to greater breadth, and the red of his helmet glared as if it were molten, and out of his sheath, he drew his sword.

I backed up. I forced Ursula behind me. I pushed her back against the damp cold wall and imprisoned her there, behind me, as safe as I could make her on the face of the earth, with my arms stretched back to hold her so that she could not, must not, be taken away.

"Ah," said Mastema, nodding, smiling. The sword was uplifted. "So even now you would go into Hell rather than see her die!"

"I would!" I cried. "I have no choice."

"Oh, yes, you have a choice."

"No, not her, don't kill her. Kill me, and send me there, yes, but give her one more chance . . ."

Ursula cried against my shoulders, her hands clinging to my hair, catching hold of it, as if by means of it she'd be safe.

"Send me now," I said. "Go ahead, strike off my head and send me to my judgment before the Lord that I may beg for her! Please, Mastema, do it, but do not strike her. She does not know how to ask to be forgiven. Not yet!"

Holding the sword aloft, he reached out and grabbed my collar and jerked me towards him. I felt her fly against me. He held me beneath his face, and glowered down at me with his beaming eyes.

"And when will she learn, and when will you?"

What could I say? What could I do?

"I will teach you, Vittorio," said Mastema in a low, seething whisper. "I will teach you so that you know how to beg forgiveness every night of your life. I will teach you."

I felt myself lifted, I felt my garments blown by the wind, I felt her tiny hands clinging to me, and the weight of her head on my back.

Through the streets we were being dragged, and suddenly there appeared before us a great crowd of idle mortals issuing from a wine shop, drunken and laughing, a great jumble of swollen, natural faces and dark breeze-tossed clothes.

"Do you see them, Vittorio? Do you see those upon whom you feed?" Mastema demanded.

"I see them, Mastema!" I said. I groped for her hand, trying to find her, hold her, shield her. "I do see them, I do."

"In each and every one of them, Vittorio, there is what I see in you, and in her—a human soul. Do you know what that is, Vittorio? Can you imagine?"

I didn't dare to answer.

The crowd spread out over the moonlighted piazza, and drew closer to us, even as it loosened.

"A spark of the power that made all of us is within each of them," cried Mastema, "a spark of the invisible, of the subtle, of the sacred, of the mystery—a spark of that which created all things."

"Ah, God!" I cried out. "Look at them, Ursula, look!"

For each and every one of them, man, woman, it did not matter old or young, had taken on a powerful hazy golden glow. A light emanated from and surrounded and embraced each figure, a subtle body of light shaped to the very form of the human being who walked in it, unheeding of it, and the entire square was full of such golden light.

I looked down at my own hands, and they too were surrounded by this subtle, etheric body, this

lovely gleaming and numinous presence, this precious and unquenchable fire.

I pivoted, my garments snagging around me,
and I saw this flame envelop Ursula. I saw her living and breathing within it, and, turning back to
the crowd, I saw again that each and every one of
them lived and breathed in it, and I knew suddenly,
understood perfectly—I would always see it. I
would never see living human beings, be they
monstrous or righteous, without this expanding,
blinding, fire of the soul.

"Yes," Mastema whispered in my ear. "Yes. Forever, and every time you feed, every time you raise
one of their tender throats to your cursed fangs,
every time you drink from them the lurid blood
you would have, like the worst of God's beasts,
you will see that light flicker and struggle, and
when the heart stops at the will of your hunger,
you will see that light go out!"

I broke away from him. He let me go.

With her hand only, I ran. I ran and ran towards
the Arno, towards the bridge, towards the taverns
that might still be open, but long before I saw the
blazing flames of the souls there, I saw the glow of
the souls from hundreds of windows, I saw the
glow of souls from beneath the bottoms of bolted
doors.

I saw it, and I knew that he spoke the truth. I
would always see it. I would see the spark of the
Creator in every human life I ever encountered,
and in every human life I took.

Reaching the river, I leant over the stone railing.

I cried out and cried out and let my cries echo over the water and up the walls on either side. I was mad with grief, and then through the darkness there came a toddling child towards me, a beggar, already versed in words to speak for bread or coins or any bit of charity that any man would vouchsafe him, and he glowed and sputtered and glittered and danced with brilliant and priceless light.

16

AND THE DARKNESS
GRASPED IT NOT

VER the years, every time I saw one of Fra Filippo's magnificent creations, the angels came alive for me. It was only for an instant, only enough to prick the heart and draw the blood, as if with a needle, to the core.

Mastema himself did not appear in Fra Filippo's work until some years later, when Fra Filippo, struggling and arguing as always, was working for Piero, the son of Cosimo, who had gone to his grave.

Fra Filippo never did give up his precious nun, Lucrezia Buti, and it was said of Filippo that every Virgin he ever painted—and there were many— bore Lucrezia's beautiful face. Lucrezia gave Fra Filippo a son, and that painter took the name Filippino, and his work too was rich in magnificence and rich in angels, and those angels too have always for one instant met my eyes when I came to worship before those canvases, sad and brokenhearted and full of love and afraid.

In 1469, Filippo died in the town of Spoleto, and there ended the life of one of the greatest painters the world has ever known. This was the man who was put on the rack for fraud, and who had debauched a convent; this was a man who painted Mary as the frightened Virgin, as the Madonna of Christmas Night, as the Queen of Heaven, as the Queen of All Saints.

And I, five hundred years after, have never strayed too far from that city which gave birth to Filippo and to that time we call the Age of Gold.

Gold. That is what I see when I look at you.

That is what I see when I look at any man, woman, child.

I see the flaming celestial gold that Mastema revealed to me. I see it surrounding you, and holding you, encasing you and dancing with you, though you yourself may not behold it, or even care.

From this tower tonight in Tuscany, I look out over the land, and far away, deep in the valleys, I see the gold of human beings, I see the glowing vitality of beating souls.

So you have my story.

What do you think?

Do you not see a strange conflict here? Do you see a dilemma?

Let me put it to you this way.

Think back to when I told you about how my father and I rode through the woods together and we spoke of Fra Filippo, and my father asked me what it was that drew me to this monk. I said that it

286

was struggle and a divided nature in Filippo which so attracted me to him, and that from this divided nature, this conflict, there came a torment to the faces which Filippo rendered in paint.

Filippo was a storm unto himself. So am I.

My father, a man of calm spirits and simpler thoughts, smiled at this.

But what does it mean in relationship to this tale?

Yes, I am a vampire, as I told you; I am a thing that feeds on mortal life. I exist quietly, contentedly in my homeland, in the dark shadows of my home castle, and Ursula is with me as always, and five hundred years is not so long for a love as strong as ours.

We are demons. We are damned. But have we not seen and understood things, have I not written things here that are of value to you? Have I not rendered a conflict so full of torment that something looms here which is full of brilliance and color, not unlike Filippo's work? Have I not embroidered, interwoven and gilded, have I not bled?

Look at my story and tell me that it gives you nothing. I don't believe you if you say that.

And when I think back on Filippo, and his rape of Lucrezia, and all his other tempestuous sins, how can I separate them from the magnificence of his paintings? How can I separate the violation of his vows, and his deceits and his quarrels, from the splendor which Filippo gave to the world?

I am not saying I am a great painter. I am not such a fool. But I say that out of my pain, out of

my folly, out of my passion there comes a vision—
a vision which I carry with me eternally and which
I offer to you.

It is a vision of every human being, bursting
with fire and with mystery, a vision I cannot deny,
nor blot out, nor ever turn away from, nor ever
belittle nor ever escape.

Others write of doubt and darkness.

Others write of meaninglessness and quiet.

I write of indefinable and celestial gold that will
forever burn bright.

I write of blood thirst that is never satisfied. I
write of knowledge and its price.

Behold, I tell you, the light is there in you. I see
it. I see it in each and every one of us, and will
always. I see it when I hunger, when I struggle,
when I slaughter. I see it sputter and die in my
arms when I drink.

Can you imagine what it would be like for me
to kill you?

Pray it never takes a slaughter or a rape for you
to see this light in those around you. God forbid it
that it should demand such a price. Let me pay the
price for you instead.

THE END

SELECTED AND ANNOTATED
BIBLIOGRAPHY

I went to Florence to receive this manuscript directly from Vittorio di Raniari. It was my fourth visit to the city, and it was with Vittorio that I decided to list here a few books for those of you who might want to know more about the Age of Gold in Florence and about Florence itself.

Let me recommend first and foremost, and above all others, the brilliant *Public Life in Renaissance Florence* by Richard C. Trexler, published today by Cornell University Press.

Professor Trexler has also written other wonderful books on Italy, but this book is a particularly rich and inspiring one, especially for me, because Professor Trexler's analyses and insights regarding Florence have helped me to understand my own city of New Orleans, Louisiana, better than anything directly written by anyone about New Orleans itself.

New Orleans, like Florence, is a city of public spectacles, rituals and feast days, of demonstrations of communal celebration and belief. It is almost impossible to realistically explain New Orleans, and its Mardi Gras, its St. Patrick's Day and its annual Jazz Fest, to those who have not been here. Professor Trexler's brilliant scholarship gave me tools to gather thoughts about and observations pertaining to those things I most love.

Other works by Professor Trexler include his *Journey of*

the Magi: Meanings in History of a Christian Story, a work only recently discovered by me. Readers familiar with my previous novels might remember the intense and blasphemously fervent relationship between my character the vampire Armand and the Florentine painting *The Procession of the Magi*, created for Piero de' Medici by Benozzo Gozzoli, which can be seen in all its glory in Florence today.

On the subject of the great painter Fra Filippo Lippi, let me first recommend his biography by the painter Vasari for its rich though unauthenticated details.

Also, there is the bright and shiny book *Filippo Lippi*, published by Scala, text by Gloria Fossi, which is for sale in numerous translations in Florence and other places in Italy as well. The only other book of which I know that is exclusively devoted to Filippo is the immense *Fra Filippo Lippi* by Jeffrey Ruda, subtitled *Life and Work, with a Complete Catalogue*. It is published by Phaidon Press in England and distributed in America by Harry N. Abrams.

The most enjoyable books for the general reader that I have read on Florence and on the Medici have been by Christopher Hibbert, including his *Florence: The Biography of a City*, published by Norton, and *The House of Medici: Its Rise and Fall*, published by Morrow.

There is also *The Medici of Florence: A Family Portrait*, by Emma Micheletti, published by Becocci Editore. *The Medici* by James Cleugh, published originally in 1975, is available now through Barnes & Noble.

Popular books on Florence and Tuscany—travelers' observations, loving memoirs and tributes—abound. Primary sources in translation—that is, letters and diaries and histories written during the Renaissance in Florence—are everywhere on library and bookstore shelves.

In trying to render correctly Vittorio's quotations from Aquinas, I used the translation of the *Summa Theologica* by Fathers of the English Dominican Province. In dealing with St. Augustine, I have used Henry Bettenson's translation of *The City of God*, published by Penguin Books.

I caution readers to avoid abridged versions of Augustine's works. Augustine lived in a pagan world where the most theologically scrupulous Christians still believed in the demonic existence of fallen pagan gods. To understand Florence and her fifteenth-century romance with the joys and freedoms of a classical heritage, one must read Augustine and Aquinas in their full context.

For those who would read more about the marvelous museum of San Marco, there are countless works on Fra Angelico, the monastery's most famous painter, which include descriptions and details regarding the building, and there are many books available on the architecture of Florence entire. I owe a debt of gratitude not only to the museum of San Marco for having so beautifully preserved the architectural work of Michelozzo, so praised in this novel, but for the publications readily available in the shop there on monastery's architecture and art.

In closing, let me add this: if Vittorio were asked to name a recording of Renaissance music which best captures the mood of the High Mass and Communion which he witnessed at the Court of the Ruby Grail, it would inevitably be the *All Souls' Vespers*, requiem music from Córdoba Cathedral, performed by the Orchestra of the Renaissance led by Richard Cheetham—though I must confess, this music is described as circa 1570—some years after Vittorio's fearful ordeal. The recording is available on the Veritas label, through Virgin Classics London and New York.

In closing these notes, allow me one final quote from St. Augustine's *The City of God*.

> *For God would never have created a man, let alone an angel, in the foreknowledge of his future evil state, if he had not known at the same time how he would put such*

creatures to good use, and thus enrich the course of the world history by the kind of antithesis which gives beauty to a poem.

I personally do not know whether or not Augustine is right.

But I do believe this: it is worthwhile to try to make a painting, or a novel . . . or a poem.

Anne

Anne Rice

A NOTE ON THE TYPE

This book was set in Monotype Dante, a typeface designed by Giovanni Mardersteig (1892–1977). Conceived as a private type for the Officina Bodoni in Verona, Italy, Dante was originally cut only for hand composition by Charles Malin, the famous Parisian punch cutter, between 1946 and 1952. Its first use was in an edition of Boccaccio's *Trattatello in laude di Dante* that appeared in 1954. The Monotype Corporation's version of Dante followed in 1957. Though modeled on the Aldine type used for Pietro Cardinal Bembo's treatise *De Aetna* in 1495, Dante is a thoroughly modern interpretation of that venerable face.

Composed by Creative Graphics,
Allentown, Pennsylvania

Printed and bound by Quebecor Printing,
Fairfield, Pennsylvania

Designed by Virginia Tan